FORSAKING ALL OTHERS

FORSAKING ALL OTHERS

EMILIE LORING

LITTLE, BROWN AND COMPANY
BOSTON · TORONTO

FIRST EDITION

T 07/71

Published simultaneously in Canada
by Little, Brown & Company (Canada) Limited

PRINTED IN THE UNITED STATES OF AMERICA

FORSAKING ALL OTHERS

I

IN spite of the STANDING ROOM ONLY sign under the words MATINÉE TODAY, a patient line, made up for the most part of women, stretched from the box office, through the lobby, and out into West Forty-fourth Street, where they stood huddled against the blustering December wind. Snow blew in their faces with such force that it felt like points of steel. Those in the lobby were more fortunate. They were sheltered from the wind and they could look at the pictures showing scenes from the smash comedy hit, *Heat Wave,* and the big portrait of the star, Jennifer Haydon.

Any number of people had attempted to explain the phenomenon of Jennifer Haydon who, three years after her first walk-on part on Broadway, was starring in a play written for her and tailored to fit, and which seemed headed for as long a run as *My Fair Lady* and *Hello, Dolly* combined.

Jennifer Haydon, the critics admitted, was not a great actress or a great beauty, but she was irresistible. The smile that crinkled around her eyes before it reached her lips, the voice with its warmth and its overtones of lurking laughter, the quality of vitality that crossed the footlights like a charge of electricity, all these were the qualities that drew standing-room-only audiences week after week, willing to brave the brutal cold and then stand for two hours to watch the play.

The line outside the theater moved slowly toward the lobby. A black Lincoln drew up at the stage entrance and the chauffeur opened the door. A girl got out lightly and someone exclaimed, "There she is!" She flashed a brilliant smile and waved her hand. Then she pulled the collar of her sable coat closer around her throat and ran across the sidewalk to the stage door, looking back to wave her hand again before the door closed behind her, and leaving the people in line with the curious impression that the air had grown warmer.

"They say she's not a bit spoiled by all her success . . . They say she gets dozens of proposals . . . They say Arthur Miller and Tennessee Williams and Thornton Wilder are all writing plays for her . . . They say . . . They say . . . I wonder what it is like to have everything you want."

Jennifer said hello to the doorkeeper. "Beastly day, isn't it, Hal?"

"A little stinker. But it don't keep people away from your show. Oh, there's a guy waiting to see you."

"But I never see people before a performance. You know that, Hal."

"He brought a card from Mr. Beaver so I figured it would be all right to let him in."

"Well, in that case —" Jennifer went with her quick, light step to the dressing room with a star painted on the door, wondering why the man who had written *Heat Wave* for her was sending someone to see her, and roused herself to apologize to a scene shifter whom she had bumped into.

"That's okay, Miss Haydon." He beamed at her. "Say, my wife was wondering — could you maybe give me an autograph for her?"

"Of course. Would she like a picture of me?"

"Gee, Miss Haydon, that would be swell. She'd be crazy about it." He chuckled. "I guess she'd feel I have special pull with you, and that would sure build up my stock at home."

Jennifer laughed. "Remind my dresser and she'll put out a picture for me to sign while I'm changing." As usual she paused outside her dressing room to trace with a slim finger the star painted on the door. Then, half amused and half embarrassed at her childishness, she went in to be assailed by the familiar mingled scents of flowers, perfume, and greasepaint. Her dresser, who was pressing her second-act costume, forestalled any comment by saying, "I told him you didn't see anyone before a performance, Miss Haydon, but he just wouldn't listen."

"My name is Prince. Mayley Prince." The man was shaped like an egg, with a pointed head, a thick body, short legs, and small feet. He was almost absurdly unattractive but he was completely self-possessed. Because he had launched more successful television programs than any other individual in the business, he could afford to be indifferent to such trivial matters as his personal appearance. "I'm flying back to Hollywood at six tonight. That's why I have to talk to you now."

"Let me get ready for the first act and you can talk then. I'll be dressed in twenty minutes."

As soon as he had gone Jennifer tossed her coat to her dresser and unzipped her smart red wool dress. The dresser hung them up for her, wrapped a towel around her shoulders and another around her hair. Jennifer applied cold cream and worked at her makeup without wasted motion. Then the maid slipped over her head the first-act costume — a thin summer cotton that made her look about fourteen — and shook out the thick, wavy, golden-brown hair — which, along with her big gray eyes, was the actress's greatest beauty — brushed it, and tied it at the nape of her neck with a white ribbon.

"I'll see Mr. Prince now." While she waited, Jennifer looked at the cards that had accompanied gifts of fresh flowers and set them aside to acknowledge. When the maid came back with the ovoid man the actress said, "See that the flowers are sent to the children's ward this time, Mary. Sit down, Mr. Prince. I have twelve minutes before I'm on."

He chuckled. "You look like a schoolgirl and you're as businesslike as a bank."

"I have to be, especially on matinée days when I try to allow extra time for rest between performances. What can I do for you?"

"It's a question of what I can do for you. You've come a long way, Miss Haydon, in a mighty short time, but so far your reputation has been restricted to New York. I want you known to the whole country. I've checked and found out that you don't have a 'run of the show' contract for *Heat Wave*. You are legally free to move out whenever you want to."

"But I don't want to," Jennifer pointed out. "I love the play and I love working in it. I can't imagine anything I'd like better."

Prince ignored this interruption. "To make it short and sweet I want you to have your own television program." He repeated, "Your own television program. I have a sponsor lined up. I can guarantee you twice the salary you are earning now just as a starter and I can get you practically any working budget you need. Beaver is itching to break into TV and he'd jump at the chance to be your writer. Well, that's the story. Double money for thirteen weeks and after that you can probably write your own ticket. I'm not going to try to sell you on the idea. You know as well as I do that it would put you right at the top of the heap. There's only one hitch. With the motion picture studios going on the auction block there's a terrific rush for television jobs and there are only a few hours of prime time, so this is a now-or-never deal."

There was a tap on the door. "First call, Miss Haydon."

Prince stood up. "Think it over. Call me at my Hollywood office when you've made up your mind. But don't wait too long." Actors were leaving their dressing rooms, moving toward the stage. Prince held out a fat hand. "I won't say good-by because I hope we'll be working together from now on. See you in Hollywood." He let himself out and the hovering dresser rushed in, studied Jennifer's makeup, and applied powder.

For a minute Jennifer stood in the wings, sensing the mood of the audience. It was going to be a good one. There was no coughing, no restless stirring. There was a spontaneous burst of laughter. It was going to be fine. Matinée audiences are always different from evening audiences.

On the stage a man's voice rose irritably and he banged his fist on a table. That was Jennifer's cue. She flung open the double doors upstage center and poised for a moment at the top of a flight of stairs. There was a stir and then a wave of applause.

At this moment, Jennifer thought, I am on top of the world. Anything is possible, anything at all. Then she flashed her brilliant, much-photographed smile, ran down the stairs, and spoke her first line.

ii

The actors, hands linked, bowed to the storm of applause, bowed again, and then stepped back, leaving Jennifer alone. She bowed and smiled and waved, and at last the curtains swirled together and she went to her dressing room. On matinée days she did not go home until after the night performance. It was simpler to have a small salad or a chicken sandwich in her dressing room and her real meal at midnight. She had trained herself to sleep for an hour after the matinée but she knew that it would be useless to try today; she had too much to think of.

Half a dozen times during the performance she had nearly forgotten her lines. In fact, she had gone through a whole scene almost unconscious that she was doing it. The great Mayley Prince had offered her her own television show! There were few actors who had not had that dream, now that movies were fading, but for how many had the dream come true?

I'll think it over carefully, she assured herself, but in her heart she knew that her decision had been made the instant Prince had spoken. Once in a lifetime! Perhaps every human being reached at some moment the peak of his life and his ambitions, but how many recognized the moment when it came?

Hilda Harris, her understudy, who had been reading the script of a play, looked up as Jennifer went toward her dressing room. "You were better than ever this afternoon, Miss Haydon. Even if I do get the chance I won't be able to hold an audience the way you do. Not that it looks as though I'd have the chance. You're so darned healthy!"

Jennifer laughed mischievously. "You never know. Your opportunity may be right around the corner."

Before she opened the door of her dressing room she heard the cough and the whimper and her laughter died. As she expected, Margaret was waiting with Richard on her lap, Richard with his cheeks flushed scarlet with fever and so dulled that he was willing to be held instead of trying to run around.

"I keep saying *not* on matinée days," the maid said frantically. "I keep telling her you have to rest before you give another performance."

Jennifer looked at Margaret, saw the tension that deepened the lines around her lips, saw the way she clutched the two-year-old boy as though shielding him from some danger.

"It's all right, Mary. I shan't need you for a while." When the dresser had gone, after a final reproachful look at Jennifer's housekeeper, Jennifer picked up the baby, soothing him, rocking him gently. "Heavens, he has a terribly high fever, Margaret! He's burning up."

"That medicine for fever just makes him sick and I don't want to give it to him anymore. I just don't dare."

"Why on earth did you bring him out on such a raw, windy day?"

"I didn't know what else to do," the housekeeper defended herself. "*He* came this afternoon with his lawyer and he tried to take Richard away, then and there. He said he had a right to his dead brother's child and you were unfit to take care of him; in fact, that you don't take care of him."

"That's not true! You know it's not true."

"It isn't so much what Joseph said. It's that lawyer of his who has me worried. He's a crook if I ever saw one, acts more like a man who needed a lawyer than one who was a lawyer. Between them they are going to make trouble for you, Jenny."

"But how can they? Louise was my sister. The last thing she said before she lost consciousness was, 'You'll look after Richard, won't you?' She gave him to me. There's nothing Joseph can do; and, anyhow, he was only Richard's half-brother. I have the best claim."

"Here, let me take the poor lamb while you get off that makeup. You're smearing grease all over him," Margaret said with the tone of authority that Jennifer frequently resented but never complained about. Margaret had been the housekeeper all Jennifer's life, first for her parents and, when they died, for Jennifer's older sister Louise, who had married Richard Colfax. Three months earlier her husband had been reported missing in action in Vietnam. In a state of shock Louise had run her car into a telephone pole and died two days later of multiple injuries. So Margaret had joined Jennifer's staff to look after the small boy who was so accustomed to her that he made the transition without any difficulty.

Jennifer wrapped her hair in a towel and scooped cold cream out of a big jar. She could hardly wait to tell Margaret about the tremendous thing that had happened to her, but she thought she had better let Margaret talk first. The housekeeper was the kind of person who could follow only one line of thought at a time and Jennifer wanted all her attention when she told her about Mayley Prince's offer.

"What frightened you so much?" she asked.

"Joseph isn't a bit like his brother. Richard was just plain good and Joseph is bad all the way through. His father knew what he was doing when he drew up that will, leaving everything to Richard except for a small monthly allowance for Joseph. Then he spoiled it by adding the clause saying that if Richard died and left no issue the whole estate was to go to Joseph. It was just asking for trouble."

"But Ricky is very much alive," Jennifer pointed out, "and the estate can't be settled for — what is it? — seven years, I think, before Richard's death can be presumed under law."

"And how long would Ricky be alive if Joseph got custody of him?" the older woman asked grimly.

Jennifer dropped the soiled towel on the floor and stared at her. "Margaret! You don't know what you are suggesting. Anyhow, Joseph can't have Ricky. I have him. Louise left him to me."

"And the boy stands between Joseph and several million dollars. Believe me, Jenny, Joseph and his lawyer could make out a real convincing case for taking Ricky away from you. If you put up a fight they are going to ask for a court order."

"I'd like to see them try!" Jennifer's eyes blazed with fury.

"No, you wouldn't like it at all, Jenny. You don't know how to deal with men like that."

"But what kind of case could be made against me?" Jennifer had to raise her voice as the scene shifters moved a heavy piece of furniture with a screaming sound.

"Well, for one thing, you are unmarried, and, at least according to Joseph, that means you cannot provide the boy with a normal home life, while he and his wife have that little farm upstate where Ricky could have — at least that's what Joseph claims — healthy home surroundings and the love of a mother as well as the guidance of a father. Then, for another thing, you are an actress and everyone, Joseph said, knows the kind of life an actress leads."

"But that is absolute rot! I never heard anything so idiotic. Anyone would think I was acting in one of those naked plays or in burlesque instead of a really brilliant comedy. And I lead a far more disciplined life than most girls my age. Why, it seems to me there's no time for anything but work."

"I know, I know," the housekeeper hastened to agree with the overwrought girl. "But it isn't what is true that counts; it's what your job can be made to look like to outsiders."

"Well, I can't help that. I am *not* married and I *am* an actress. What else do they have against me?"

For the first time Margaret hesitated, studying rather fearfully the stormy face of the girl to whom she was devoted. Little Richard, who had been dozing restlessly in her arms, wheezed as he tried to catch his breath.

"It was just bad luck, Joseph and that crooked lawyer of his coming when Ricky was having one of his attacks. Joseph insisted on taking his temperature and it was 103. He said the child was being neglected. He wanted to know who Ricky's doctor was and how long it had been since you consulted him. And he said he was going to get a baby specialist to examine the boy. That's why I brought him here. I just didn't know what else to do."

Jennifer's clear gray eyes met those of the housekeeper levelly. "Do you think I've neglected him, Margaret? Tell me the truth."

"You support him and you've given him everything you could under the circumstances: a lovely room and the best of food and fabulous toys, and you hired me to take care of him. After all, you can't carry on a demanding profession and succeed the way you have if you scatter your energy in too many directions, and Ricky would probably have these attacks anyhow. He's just like his father that way."

"What you are really saying is that I don't give him enough personal attention, that I've put my job first. Perhaps that is true, but I had to!"

"I know my dear. I'm not criticizing you."

Jennifer sat looking with unseeing eyes at the clutter on her dressing table; the costumes hanging against the wall in the order in which they were worn during the play, with matching shoes under them; the vases of flowers on dressing table and stands; the signed photographs on the walls. Her finger tapped on the edge of the table, over and over. Then she reached for the telephone and dialed a familiar number, one that represented her chief support and her most trusted adviser.

"Dr. Ferguson? This is Jenny. I know it is outrageous to call you at home but . . . No, not for me, for my nephew . . . At eight-thirty? But I have a performance tonight." She saw Margaret's expression and added quickly, "Of course I will come then; my understudy will take over here. Bless you."

She put down the telephone, opened the door, and beckoned to her waiting dresser. "I'll change for the street. I've got to see a doctor tonight and it's an emergency. My understudy is in the Green Room. Inform her and the stage manager, and you had better have her try on the costumes. She is taller than I am and you may have to make some alterations. But first call my apartment. I'll need the car at once, and tell them I'll be home for dinner but I must finish by eight o'clock."

As often in the past the housekeeper was struck by Jenny's crisp efficiency where her job was concerned in contrast with her total incompetence in managing an apartment or handling domestic chores.

Jennifer let the dresser drop her street dress over her head and hold the sable coat. Then she scrawled a note that read, "Hie to high fortune!" and selected a vase of long-stemmed roses whose fragrance scented the air. "Take these to Miss Harris, please."

"Do you think she can manage?" Margaret asked.

"Oh, yes," Jennifer said glumly, "she's good. She'll be very good indeed once she gets more confidence, especially if she tries to play herself and not me. The audience will love her."

iii

The doctor leaned back in his chair and looked thoughtfully at the anxious girl who sat beside his desk. He had known her all her life and had watched her grow from an enchanting small girl with willful ways to a poised woman of twenty-one, successful, hard-working, ambitious.

For several years he had virtually retired from active practice, not reluctant to surrender most of his responsibilities to younger men with younger ideas and more up-to-date training. But his wife declared that he had merely substituted one form of practice for another, because he had become a kind of father confessor, available day and night for consultation with people in trouble. The only difference was that he was not paid for his advice.

"Well?" he asked at length. "What really brought you to me in such a panic, young woman? From what you've told me of young Richard's medical history, he has had this problem before. It's nothing new."

"I wanted you to examine him and judge for yourself about his condition. Joseph Colfax went to my apartment this afternoon while I was at the theater. He had his lawyer with him and he wanted to take Ricky away. He discovered that Ricky was running a temperature of 103 and he said I wasn't fit to have him because I am unmarried and an actress and I neglect the boy. He threatened to bring a child specialist of his own and he is going to fight to get legal custody of him."

Jennifer's hands gripped the arms of her chair. "I don't know what to do. If Joseph gets Ricky he — it's horrible to say but you know how the Colfax will stands . . . . Without him Joe could have everything when the estate is finally settled. I'm frightened, Dr. Ferguson."

"I thought at the time it was a foolish will. Queer how a hardheaded, clear-thinking man like Colfax can come such a cropper when it's a question of disposing of the money he had intelligence enough to earn in the first place. Joseph never was any good. His father should have been satisfied to leave him that small income; he couldn't do much harm with that. But I suppose he hated to have his money go out of the family entirely. A great pity. He left quite a lot, didn't he?"

"About three million, and probably more by now, of course. It will be a great deal more at the end of seven years, when Richard can be presumed dead."

"So Joseph wants to get control of the boy. He's not the paternal type and he was always jealous of Rick. Never pretended to like him though I always thought Rick did his best. I can see why you are worried. I wouldn't like to see the boy in Joseph's hands."

"I promised Louise I would look after her son the very best I could."

"I remember," the doctor said gently.

"And it isn't true that I neglect him."

"No." After a moment the doctor repeated, "No."

Jennifer drew a long breath. "All right, I can see that you don't really believe that. Neither does Margaret, though she tried hard to be kind and spare my feelings. Just what is wrong with Ricky, doctor?"

"Nothing that can't be dealt with." He looked at the clear gray eyes with their dark fringe of lashes, at the stubborn chin and the soft mouth. Character there and intelligence and driving energy. She had made a brilliant success as an actress but she had worked hard and single-mindedly to achieve it. And yet past knowledge of her made him aware that, in the long run, ambition would always yield to generosity.

"There is nothing wrong with the boy that can't be dealt with," he repeated. "Richard has inherited his father's tendency to bronchial asthma. This is his third attack this winter. It should not be allowed to recur, you know."

"Then what ought I do, doctor? Margaret can't stay with me much longer. Her mother's not well and she naturally has the stronger claim. And there is always a risk with hiring a stranger. Ricky might not like her or she might be bribed by Joseph to harm him. What am I to do?"

It was some time before Dr. Ferguson answered her despairing question. "How much are you willing to give up for the boy?"

Her reply came promptly, without hesitation. "Anything. He is all I have left of Louise and I did love her so much."

"Richard needs a warm and dry climate like Arizona or New Mexico or the Mojave Desert."

"Desert?" Jennifer stared at him blankly.

"It's a good thing that you aren't married. It would be asking a lot to expect a man to give up his work and start all over in the desert."

"I have work too," Jennifer said hotly. "The theater isn't going to move out to the desert for my convenience, and today I was offered my own television show, the most tremendous thing that ever happened to me."

There was another long pause and then Dr. Ferguson said, "Sometimes I have wondered why you don't marry, Jenny. There is nothing wrong with your looks that I can see." A smile lurked on his lips.

"Men don't usually want part-time wives."

"Children don't usually want part-time mothers." Abruptly the doctor stood up, terminating the interview.

"I was unreasonable to expect so much of you. I'll try to help you find some other solution. Good night, my dear."

"Good night, doctor." Jennifer groped blindly for the door and went into the bitter night. Margaret was waiting in the car, holding Ricky against her shoulder to help him breathe.

Jennifer was silent on the ride to her Park Avenue apartment.

II

"IT'S a pity," Dr. Ferguson said. "A great pity. You are fascinated by the problems involved in respiratory ailments. You have all the qualifications to combine research with specialized practice. You have, besides, a lively curiosity, infinite patience, and an inquiring mind. After a few years you would be ready to become a consultant, continue your research, and perhaps do some teaching."

"I'm grateful for your good opinion and your faith in me," the young man said.

"But the program I've outlined doesn't suit you. Is that it?"

"It suits me right down to the ground but the truth is that I can't afford the time to specialize. I went through college and medical school on scholarships. These past two years as intern have been great but I've just about scraped the bottom of the barrel. I've got to start practice right away."

Dr. Ferguson looked at the tall young man who sat beside his desk. Bradley Maxwell had attracted his attention first as a brilliant student in medical school. Then he had helped him get the prize plum of an internship at Bellevue Hospital, where he could acquire more varied experience than at any other institution in the country.

"We can't afford to waste a man of your promise. Let's

see what we can work out. Suppose I put up the equivalent of a living wage for a couple of years while you continue to work in the field of respiratory ailments. I'd like to help you get an appointment at some first-rate teaching hospital." He put up a hand to halt Brad's protest. "Not as a gift, you understand; just a damned sound investment in the future."

"No, sir," Brad said firmly. "I'm deeply grateful but—no debts! My father was a nice guy but he was like the man Flammonde in the Edwin Arlington Robinson poem: 'And what he needed for his fee/ To live he borrowed graciously.' "

"You aren't leaving much scope," the older man warned him. "You'll have to settle for being a general practitioner. It's a dog's life, Brad. A dog's life. Not the same stimulation. Not the kind of money you could earn as a specialist. It is as foolish to underrate the advantages of money as it is to overrate them. A lot of people who pretend not to care about earning a good income are either too lazy or too incompetent to do so. And money can be a power for good as well as for evil. I see no reason why a man should not arrange his life for his own best advantage if he doesn't infringe on the rights of others."

Bradley Maxwell was fully aware of the price he would have to pay for his refusal to accept help. "But general practice has its compensations," he said cheerfully. "Variety, for one thing. And then you treat a whole person and not just a symptom."

"The trouble, one of the troubles, with being a family doctor of the old school is that patients have more confidence in an older and more experienced man. It takes time in a big city to build a sound practice."

"I realize that. What I'll have to do is try to find a country practice where I'll be accepted in the beginning because of the shortage of doctors. If it's a choice between a young doctor or no doctor the people will have to accept me."

"But then," Dr. Ferguson pointed out, "you would have to depend entirely on your own resources. No hospital within many miles perhaps. You'd have to do your own laboratory work and be your own technician." He broke off, pinching his lower lip between his fingers, frowning thoughtfully.

"What is it, doctor?"

"I was thinking of a letter I got this morning from a former colleague of mine, telling me of a small western town that hasn't a single doctor. He went there to look over the situation but he didn't like the town, the climate, or the isolation from hospitals and specialists. He said some local bigwig offered to endow a hospital if they can get a satisfactory man to practice there. Apparently the last incumbent had to leave under a cloud."

"Do you think I could take over his practice?"

"I'm afraid not, Brad." The older man was regretful.

"Why not?"

"Because for one thing you are so young."

"I know, but I'll grow out of that. Anyhow, I'm twenty-six."

"And you look like a schoolboy."

Brad brushed this objection aside impatiently. "But when people find that I know my job — and you say there isn't another doctor available —"

"But they will be wary. Their much-trusted doctor was a widower who stirred up a witch's brew of gossip with a woman patient. So if a young, unattached, and attractive man tries to establish a practice there, the people are bound to be suspicious of him. What a pity you aren't married, Brad! Your youthful appearance wouldn't be such a strike against you if you were a family man as well as a family doctor."

"Well, I'm not and it's too late to do anything about that now."

Dr. Ferguson's eyes twinkled. "Hardly too late at twenty-six. No girl of your own?"

"If you will tell me, sir, when an intern has time for any personal life or the cash to take a girl out to dinner and a show, I'd be glad to know it. Do you realize what it costs for a good meal and theater tickets and taxis and God knows what else in New York? At least forty bucks."

"Theater tickets," Dr Ferguson said, struck by an association of ideas. "Now that is definitely a thought." He added quite untruthfully, "I was wondering what to do with myself tonight. Let's plan to go out to dinner and take in a show."

"Thanks very much, sir. I'd enjoy that. I suppose you are sure I couldn't build a practice out in that little western town?"

"I'm afraid they will hold out for Benedick the Married Man. Once bitten twice shy, you know."

"Well, I'll just have to find something else. Of course I'd rather set up for myself but I can't afford to wait. There must be an older guy who needs someone to make house calls or to take over his practice while he is on vacation or something. See you tonight."

Dr. Ferguson watched the tall young man, his dark head held proudly, shoulders back, walk out of his consulting room. Bradley Maxwell had all the makings of a fine physician. He should have an opportunity to specialize, to get on the staff of a first-rate teaching hospital, and to do research. Well, he didn't want to be helped; he preferred to carry his own weight; and, though Dr. Ferguson regretted his decision, he respected him for it. In a day when young people demand that they be given all sorts of privileges it was pleasant to find one who preferred to carry his own weight.

Now what was that idea I had, he wondered. Oh, yes. He opened his address book and looked up Jennifer Haydon's unlisted number. He dialed.

"Of course," she agreed when he had made his request. "There are always a few house seats available. I'll call the box office and have the tickets left in your name."

"May I make another appeal to your generosity and bring my young friend around after the play? I'm rather old to become a stage-door Johnny but I'm curious about backstage life."

"Of course," she said again, but without her usual warm friendliness, and Dr. Ferguson knew that she still resented his implied criticism of her treatment of Ricky.

"Have you come to any decision about the boy?"

"Joseph Colfax just left. He has been here half the afternoon and he threatened that he would keep coming back until he gets Ricky. And I've just got notice that there is going to be a custody hearing. What with that television offer — and I'll never again have a chance like that! — and Ricky coughing terribly, and Joseph threatening, I'm just about frantic."

"I've got a kind of a sort of an idea," the doctor said.

"Oh, doctor!"

"It wouldn't save your career, I'm afraid, but it would save Ricky."

"I—see," she said blankly. "I'll arrange about the tickets, doctor." She broke the connection.

ii

After the biting wind in the street the theater seemed hot. The audience was restless and there was a lot of coughing. Latecomers squeezed in front of the two doctors, causing them to miss several lines of dialogue. Then the leading man's fist crashed on a table, the double doors at the top of the stairs were flung open, and the girl appeared. There was a moment of caught breath and then a storm of applause. The actress seemed to be surprised by that ovation and then a brilliant smile transformed her face. She ran down the stairs and spoke her first line. With a little sigh the expectant audience settled back.

The coughing and restless movements had stopped. Dr. Ferguson took a sidelong look at his companion. Bradley Maxwell was leaning forward, a delighted smile on his lips as he watched the girl. Then as his own attention was gripped by her performance, the older man's amusement faded. He had not fully realized before how talented Jenny was; he had not grasped the extent of her impact on an audience; he had not foreseen the magic illusion she created. He knew how hard she had worked to get where she was, and apparently the television offer she had mentioned was a brilliant one and not to be repeated. He had no right to ask her to sacrifice fame and fortune in her chosen field for the sake of a little boy who was not even her own son. And yet the child could not live in this climate and

Joseph Colfax was quite capable of obtaining a court order that would give him possession of his half-nephew. In that case, Dr. Ferguson thought grimly, Richard's future might be problematical indeed.

There was nothing to be gained by anticipating the worst. After all, the young people were free agents. He could suggest a plan that would solve the dilemma for them both, but the decision would have to lie in their hands, not in his. The doctor dismissed his worries, as he had learned to do many years before, and leaned back to devote his attention entirely to the play.

Not being a frequent playgoer he was not particularly knowledgeable about technique but he did notice that while Jenny was the undisputed star who held the audience in the hollow of her hand, she never stole attention from other players; in fact, their performances seemed better when she was on the stage than when she was off, as though she sparked some quality in them.

The audience applauded wildly as the actors took their curtain calls, the sound rising in volume when Jenny stood alone at last, young and lovely and glowing.

"Well," Bradley said on a long breath when the final curtain had fallen and the house lights come up. The audience, cumbersome in winter coats and furs, began its slow exodus along the aisles. "That was really something, doctor. Isn't she marvelous?"

"Would you like to meet her?"

"Meet her?"

"Why not? She's an old friend of mine. I've known her all her life. In fact, these are house seats she got for me tonight and she is expecting us backstage."

As though in confirmation, an usher leaned over to say,

"Dr. Ferguson? Miss Haydon asked me to bring you back to her dressing room. No, not that way. Down front and through the door at the right of the stage. Up three steps here. That's it."

The boy opened the door and the two doctors stepped into an alien world of what appeared to be complete confusion. The bemused younger man recognized a bookcase painted on canvas, which had been part of the library set in the second act.

The leading man, who a few minutes earlier had been pledging eternal devotion to the star, was wiping greasepaint from his face with a towel, his collar open and turned back, grinning at a twelve-year-old girl who bore a striking resemblance to him.

"Hey, kid, how did you get here tonight?"

"I got straight A and Mom promised I could come to a night show as a treat. Mom said maybe we could stop for some ice cream on the way home."

"Getting into bad habits," he grumbled with mock disapproval. "Well, wait until I get out of these clothes and your mother and I will introduce you to some dizzy night life — ice cream at Schrafft's. Now keep out of the way so you won't be mowed down by the scene shifters."

A harassed young man, promptbook in hand, asked, "You looking for someone?"

"Miss Haydon. We seem to have mislaid the usher who was sent to show us the way."

"Straight ahead. Door behind the stairs. Marked with a star."

Dr. Ferguson tapped on the door and a middle-aged woman with iron-gray hair fastened in a tight knot and a trim apron over a black dress looked them over.

"Dr. Ferguson and a friend," the older man told her. "Miss Haydon is expecting us."

"Come in, doctor," called the voice which during the play had already become hauntingly familiar to Brad Maxwell. He swallowed, ran a finger inside his collar, and straightened his tie.

She was standing against a framework of flowers — roses, carnations, orchids, many-tinted arrangements — and she was still wearing the backless black-velvet evening gown of the last act. There were diamonds in her ears and a double strand of pearls around her neck. Brad was aware of the heavy makeup. Then she was smiling at Dr. Ferguson and acknowledging the introduction of his young friend, who mumbled something unintelligible.

"You have given two hard-working men a great evening, Jenny."

"I'm so glad. It's a gay play, isn't it?"

He peered more closely at her. "You aren't getting enough sleep."

She tried to laugh. "Heavens, does it show? That will never do."

The laugh sounded rather brittle. She wasn't, Brad thought, the simple, enchanting girl she had appeared when she had made her entrance in the first act. This was a successful actress, a bit hard, self-consciously gracious to her public.

"I have brought you two together for a purpose," Dr. Ferguson said. "Can we talk here?"

There was a tap at the door and the dresser stuck in her head to say, "There are quite a few people who would like to speak to you. I have the names."

Jenny smiled at the doctor. "I guess that's the answer.

We'll go up to my apartment where we can talk. My private life never starts until after midnight. If you'll wait in the Green Room." And to the dresser she said crisply, "Just three minutes for each one and then help me get out of this dress."

When Jenny joined the two men she was wrapped in the sable coat. Sleek, polished, prosperous. For some reason which he did not care to define to himself Bradley Maxwell resented the evidences of prosperity.

"I'll get a taxi," Dr. Ferguson offered.

"My car will be here, and there is supper at home. There is always plenty because I often bring people back with me. I can't talk at Sardi's or any place where I am recognized. People keep breaking in."

She led the way to the stage door, smilingly signed some autograph albums, and waved to admirers who had waited in the cold for her to appear.

The long, sleek car was warm and luxuriously comfortable in contrast to the penetrating wind that was blowing snow in the faces of defenseless pedestrians and adding to the high snowbanks along Forty-fourth Street. By the flashing neon lights over the theater marquees and shops Dr. Ferguson studied Jenny's profile. Too much tension there.

"Aren't you overdoing it?" he asked.

She laughed with an edge of irritation. "You shouldn't say things like that to me, doctor. Not enough sleep. Overdoing. I must look like a hag."

"Nothing of the sort, as you well know."

"Actually, I live on as strict a regimen as a ballet dancer. A rigid diet. So much time allotted for sleep and rest. Time for massage and exercise. Time to have my hair done and get fitted for clothes and have my picture taken. Time for press and radio interviews and television appearances. These aren't fun things; they are just part of the job."

The lobby of the apartment building on Park Avenue struck Bradley as being as big as Grand Central Station, with carpets so deep the feet sank into them, comfortable chairs, subdued lamps, paneled walls on which were hung well-lighted oil paintings that imitated the Dutch School.

The elevator door slid open noiselessly on a narrow hallway and a single door, which was standing open. A uniformed maid was waiting to admit them.

The living room was immense, the windows covered by floor-length lemon satin draperies. There were a couple of modern paintings on the walls, whose rich color added gaiety and warmth to the room. Brad had plenty of time to examine it because nearly a quarter of an hour passed before his hostess returned. She had changed to lemon-velvet house pajamas, which matched the draperies.

"Supper's ready," she said, and led the way to a small room with a table set for three. The conversation remained impersonal during the meal until Jennifer heroically refused the dessert and had an apple and a glass of milk.

"You're too slender to worry about weight," Dr. Ferguson told her.

"Now is when the trouble starts. An actress can't afford to be self-indulgent about food."

"How is Ricky?"

"He is still finding it difficult to breathe. And he's so little. I can't explain to him why I can't make him more comfortable."

"Shall I take a look at him?"

"I didn't ask you here for that."

"How touchy you are tonight, Jenny!"

Rather to his surprise she blushed deeply as though the comment had really hurt her. "I'm sorry. Of course I'd like you to see him; I'd be grateful."

"How about letting Dr. Maxwell come along? I'd like to have his opinion."

"A doctor! I hadn't realized that. You seem so young to be a doctor." She had to look a long way up to see his face, an engaging face with a good nose and chin and steady, deep-set dark eyes and thick dark hair whose curl was rigorously controlled.

He grinned. "That's a cross I have to bear. Nothing that another ten years won't cure."

The little boy's room was papered with fairy-tale characters. There was a bin filled with toys, and a tricycle stood against one wall. Ricky lay propped up on pillows, his breath wheezing.

"What medication is he getting?" Dr. Ferguson asked in a low tone.

"Nothing but what you prescribed last night. The stuff he was taking before that made him sick."

"No fever. That's good." He turned to his young companion. "What do you think, Brad?"

The boy began to cough and Brad lifted him in his arms, holding him gently. "Any history of asthma?"

"His father."

Brad turned to Jenny. "Is your husband's condition acute or chronic?"

"My — oh, I'm not married. Ricky isn't my son. He is my nephew."

When the three returned to the living room Dr. Ferguson said, "I told you I had an idea, Jenny, that might solve the problem of the boy's health and your right to keep him. It would also solve a problem of Dr. Maxwell's. Here it is in a nutshell. You want to protect Ricky from his father's half-brother, who would like to get his hands on the Colfax money and doesn't mean well by the boy, who is an obstacle to his getting it. Joseph might succeed in obtaining legal custody on three counts: You are unmarried; you are an actress; and, he claims, you are neglecting the health of the child, who must have a warm, dry climate to live in.

"Now we come to Brad's dilemma. He has to start practicing medicine without delay because the coffer is nearly empty. Building a sound practice in a big city is slow work. There is a small town on the edge of the Mojave Desert where a doctor is desperately needed, but people there would be wary of a physician who is young, attractive, and unattached because the last incumbent stirred up a scandal with a woman patient.

"What I had in mind was this: If you two were to get married, Brad as a family man would be all set. Joseph Colfax would be left without any valid complaint against Jenny. Ricky would be able to lead a normal, healthy life. And there's another factor. The people of Desert Winds must have a doctor. A wealthy man has promised to endow a hospital as soon as there is a reliable practitioner in the place. Many lives might be saved. At present, as I understand it, they have to depend on a hospital twenty miles away. It occurred to me that, as neither of you has any — uh — emotional attachments, this would be an ideal solution for you both."

"That," said Jenny, "is the most preposterous suggestion I ever heard."

"You are nuts, doctor," Brad said bluntly. "It wouldn't work. Not for twenty-four hours."

Dr. Ferguson was bland. "Why not?"

"Because we are young; we are normal people; we are flesh and blood. Why, the propinquity alone would make that kind of situation impossible."

Anger smoldered in Jenny. "If you think for one single minute, Dr. Maxwell, that your charms are going to sweep me off my feet you'll find you are mistaken."

"I didn't say anything about my charms," he retorted, "but common sense would tell you, if you have any common sense —"

Dr. Ferguson looked from one stormy young face to the other. His brows shot up. Well, well, he thought in amusement. The magnet and the steel. The needle and the north. Well, well.

"If you had any common sense," Jenny snapped, "you would know I don't have to have anyone pick out a husband for me. I've had dozens of proposals. Dozens."

"Even after the poor guys got a load of your temper? You amaze me."

"Why, you —" Jenny choked in her rage.

The older man pulled out a handkerchief and pressed it to his lips to conceal his broad smile.

The maid came into the room. "Mr. Joseph Colfax is calling from the lobby."

"Tell him I can't see him."

A few minutes later the maid returned. She was obviously flustered. "I'm sorry, Miss Haydon; he's at the door and I can't make him go away."

She was shoved unceremoniously aside by a man who might have been good looking if it had not been for the weakness of his mouth and his eyes. He looked from one man to the other and then turned to Jenny.

"So you can't see me! Are you trying to cut me off from my dead brother's only child? Well, you can't do it, Jenny. I figured you'd be seeing men up here at this time of night. When I tell them in court how you entertain men at one o'clock in the morning it will sound fine, won't it? I expect Richard to be ready to leave as soon as the custody hearing is over. Is that clear? Letting the poor baby lie around with a fever, neglected, while you are —"

Bradley Maxwell stood up, six-foot-two of angry young man. "Where do you want me to throw this thing?"

Joseph took a rapid step backward. "You have no right to touch me."

There was fear in Jenny's face. "Don't get him angry; you mustn't get him angry. It would only make him worse."

"Let him get as angry as he likes, but not here." Brad caught Joseph's arm and twisted it behind his back. "Get out and stay out until you know how to conduct yourself in the presence of ladies. Is that clear?"

"What business is that of yours? I'm not leaving that helpless child in the hands of a cheap actress who —" Joseph yelped as Brad jerked his arm farther behind him.

"Apologize to Miss Haydon."

"What's it to you?"

"Because she is my future wife. Now get out before I really hurt you."

III

"IT wouldn't save your career but it would save Ricky."
Jenny lay sleepless while the words sounded over and over in her ears. It wasn't fair! She had worked like a dog to get where she was, bent all her energy toward one objective, and it had paid off. Few actresses of her age had leading playwrights vying with each other to produce a vehicle for them. She loved all of it: the lights, the greasepaint, the audience response. Above all, the moment when the lights went up and her real life began. And now she had a chance to play not only for a single audience but for a nation. Mayley Prince had tossed her the golden apple for which almost every actress was striving.

Once in a lifetime. No second chance. Jenny buried her face in the pillow. It isn't fair! It isn't fair!

"It wouldn't save your career but it would save Ricky."

There must be some other way of saving Ricky. But there was no other way. He had to live in a warm, dry climate if he was to live at all, and he must live under such conditions that Joseph could not find a pretext for taking him away.

But perhaps she could salvage something. Suppose she gave up Broadway and its excitement and achievement for southern California, where Ricky could thrive on the desert. Suppose she could build a television program there, flying back and forth from Hollywood to the desert.

"Children don't usually want part-time mothers."

It isn't fair to sacrifice everything for Richard. He isn't even my own child. No one else would do as much. It isn't fair. Louise never meant to do this to me.

For a moment Louise's face was clear before her. Louise had been four years older and the family beauty. When their parents died, it had been Louise who looked after Jenny. Even after she married Richard Colfax she wanted to keep Jenny with her, but Jenny had gone out alone to make a place for herself in the theater. She had stuck doggedly to the path she had determined on, in spite of Louise's protests.

"It's such a hard life, Jenny. And so uncertain. You don't ever know whether a play will have a long run or fold up after the opening night, and you might be out of work weeks or months between jobs."

But Jenny had moved into a theatrical boardinghouse not far from Columbus Circle, where in the beginning the lights and the sounds of traffic kept her awake most of the night. She had told herself and Louise that the dingy life was glamorous. Louise's happiness had been a glow that warmed everything around her and, with the birth of young Richard, she had been ecstatically happy. The happiness had dimmed when her husband went to Vietnam and was snuffed out by a telegram: MISSING IN ACTION.

Jenny had forged ahead, attracted the attention of critics from the outset, moved from walk-ons to small parts to second lead and finally achieved stardom in a play that had been written for her. And Louise, stunned by her husband's disappearance, had had a car smashup.

Happily her face had not been marred but it was as white as the pillow on the hospital bed. Her hand had clutched desperately at Jenny's. "You'll look after Richard, won't you?"

Jenny's eyes stung with tears. She trusted me to do my best for Richard and I have failed her.

There is no choice. I can't let Louise's son fall into Joe Colfax's hands. She remembered his ignominious departure from her apartment, marched out by Bradley Maxwell. Who would have believed that the young doctor was such a man of action? A puzzling character. Anyone would think, by the way he talked, that he hated her, and yet there was a look in his eyes that belied the words. And he had had the insolence to intimate that she was bound to fall in love with him. Propinquity, he had said. He needn't worry. A guy still struggling just to get on his feet. He'd show up badly beside most of the men she had known, the men who had wanted to marry her. Jenny was puzzled to realize how extremely annoyed she was with Bradley Maxwell.

After all, he had handled Joe without any difficulty and he had silenced him by saying that Jenny was going to marry him. At least that would cut the ground out from under Joe's objections. She would be married, she would no longer be an actress, and Ricky would have not only a father's but a doctor's care.

Of course, it was one thing to put Joe out of her apartment; after all, Bradley Maxwell was a far bigger, stronger, and younger man. It would be another to face him at the custody hearing. True, Dr. Ferguson had promised to be there to support her, when the time came.

He had also promised to consult his own lawyer and have him act for Jenny. At least she would not have to face the unknown terrors of the court by herself. Vaguely she imagined something like the fireworks in a Perry Mason courtroom scene.

She lay sleepless, her thinking confused, her worries ranging from Richard's safety to Mayley Prince's magnificent offer to the incredibly strange possibility of marriage with Bradley Maxwell.

As a rule Jenny had experienced no difficulty in coping with the young men who surrounded her, but Bradley Maxwell was an unknown quantity. She felt uneasily that he might be difficult to manage. At least she had a few weeks of respite. After a great deal of long-distance telephoning Bradley had flown out to California to obtain his license to practice in that state, and Dr. Ferguson was in touch with staff members of the hospital nearest Desert Winds in an attempt to expedite his appointment there.

Meanwhile, Jenny had set herself the Herculean task of soothing an irate management and the people who had invested in *Heat Wave,* and persuading them not only to accept her resignation from the cast of a sellout but to give her understudy a chance to replace her instead of looking elsewhere for an actress of proven star quality. Hour after hour she rehearsed Hilda Harris patiently, urging her to be herself and not simply play an imitation of Jenny.

ii

Jenny arrived one morning for the custody hearing, a black morning with bitter winds screaming through the streets, blowing dirty snow and bits of paper through the air. She found Joe Colfax attended not only by his obedient and frightened wife but by a sharp-faced lawyer. She also found Dr. Ferguson with his lawyer.

The latter smiled down at her as he shook hands. "This is very kind of you," she told him.

"I'm delighted to be of service, Miss Haydon, not only because of the great pleasure you have given me in the theater but because of what Dr. Ferguson has told me about you and the fine thing you are doing."

"Do you think it will come out all right?"

"Why, of course," he said in surprise.

The whole proceeding was unexpectedly informal. Joe's lawyer made the first move. Miss Haydon, he said, was an unmarried actress whose environment was not a suitable one in which to bring up a child. The little fellow had had a fever of 103 but had not had a doctor's care. Mr. Colfax, the boy's uncle, wanted to give his nephew a better chance in life. On the Colfax farm he would be properly cared for and have the devotion of a father as well as a mother. In the New York apartment of Miss Haydon, he managed to imply, there were nightly orgies. Mr. Colfax felt that $15,000 a year from the estate would enable him to take complete care of the boy. A restraining order should be issued so that little Richard could not be taken out of the state, and Mr. Colfax asked to be awarded legal custody of his nephew.

Dr. Ferguson's lawyer got up in a leisurely manner, his voice relaxed and assured in contrast to the angry, waspish voice of Joe's lawyer. If his Honor would permit him, there were a few points to straighten out. One, in regard to the restraining order. Dr. Ferguson, whose record as a physician was available, would testify that the boy must live in a warm, dry climate as he was subject to frequent attacks of bronchial asthma.

Two, Miss Haydon, as had been pointed out by his honorable colleague, was an actress, a brilliant and successful actress. That fact made all the more remarkable her voluntary sacrifice of her profession, giving up the theater and her spectacular career for the sake of the child who had been entrusted to her by her beloved sister on her deathbed. Miss Haydon planned to remove the child from New York at once and take him to the desert where he could live a normal, healthy life.

Three, Miss Haydon waived any possible claim to any part of the Colfax estate, now or in the future, and asked for no remuneration for supporting her nephew.

Four, Miss Haydon was shortly to become the wife of a physician, so the child was assured a normal home life with a father's care as well as that of a doctor.

Five, it was important to study the will of the late Herbert Colfax. Because of a clause giving the entire estate to Joseph Colfax in case his half-brother died without issue, it would be awkward for Joseph to assume responsibility for the child's welfare. The death of the boy while in his custody could give rise to unpleasant speculations. No doubt, Mr. Colfax had not considered this possibility and he would be happy to relinquish any claim to the boy or to the boy's inheritance.

The judge decided in Jenny's favor. Then he leaned forward to smile into the wide, dark-lashed gray eyes. "This is a fine thing you are doing, Miss Haydon. A noble thing, if I may say so. I must be speaking for many New Yorkers when I say that you will be greatly missed here in Manhattan where you have brought so much delight to so many."

As Jenny left the room, Joe gripped her arm and forced her to look at him. "This isn't the end, you know. Far from it. You are just asking for trouble, lady, and I'm the one to provide it. That Tarzan of yours can't always be around."

"What now?" Dr. Ferguson asked her at the court-house entrance.

"I've got to arrange about closing my apartment."

"You're keeping it?"

"I own it. I doubt if I could find anything I liked as well. Anyhow, I'll need something to come back to. And I still have to buy clothes for Richard and me that will be suitable for the heat of the desert instead of Manhattan in March. And I have three more performances to give."

"When are you going to be married?"

"Next Thursday. That's the earliest day. Dr. Maxwell called me last night when he returned from the coast. He has some arrangements of his own to make, I understand." She had no interest at all in Dr. Maxwell's arrangements.

"This morning," Dr. Ferguson told her, "I checked on the situation at Desert Winds. The former doctor's house is available and furnished. His office is attached to the house and is well equipped, so there will be no problem."

"No problem at all," Jenny said bitterly.

For once she was not aware of the interested eyes, the nudges, the whispered, "That's Jennifer Haydon," as she crossed the sidewalk to her waiting car, and she was unresponsive to the greeting of the doorman at her apartment building.

As her maid removed her coat Jenny asked, "Any calls?"

As usual there were a number of calls, the messages carefully recorded. Jenny looked through them. Brad? Who was this Brad who said he'd be there at four? Oh, of course, Bradley Maxwell, the man she was going, so improbably, to marry. What right had he to tell her at what time he would come to see her? He had a lot to learn and the sooner he did it the better for all concerned.

When the maid announced Dr. Maxwell promptly at four Jenny was on the telephone. For five minutes she had been trying to convince a stunned Mayley Prince that his offer was being rejected.

"Look here, dear," he explained for the third time, "you don't turn down an offer like this."

"But I am turning it down."

"If you are looking for a better deal, you won't get it."

"I'm not looking for a better deal. I understand that this is a now-or-never offer. But I have no choice. I'm leaving the stage permanently after tomorrow night's performance."

"Good God! Do you have leprosy or something?"

"I'm going out to the desert."

"You'd better see a doctor, sweetheart." Prince sounded genuinely alarmed.

"I have seen a doctor. I am marrying one."

"You are *what?*"

"Getting married!" Jenny shouted in exasperation and slammed down the telephone.

Her first impression when she turned away from the telephone and saw Bradley Maxwell was that she had forgotten how tall he was. Her second impression was that she had forgotten how good-looking he was. Her third impression was that he was looking at her in an odd sort of way and that he seemed to be irritatingly at home in her apartment.

"Dr. Ferguson tells me that it's all right about the boy," he said, "and the former doctor's house and office are available in Desert Winds, so we can move right in. The doctor left his equipment there as well as his furniture, and there is some sort of laboratory. That's a break for me. Now," he opened a notebook and pulled out a pen as if, she thought resentfully, he were about to take down her case history, "there are some things to settle. We'll get our blood tests on Monday, arrange about the license, and get married on Thursday, as I suggested over the telephone last night. We might as well have that done by the clerk or whoever handles these things, don't you think?"

He made the wedding ceremony sound like a minor operation or having a tooth extracted.

"Unless," he went on, unaware of her mounting indignation, "you know anyone who would be interested in your wedding."

"Look here, Dr. Maxwell," Jenny said, sitting up very straight in her chair, her chin jutting out belligerently, "there are thousands of people in New York who would be interested in my wedding." As he looked alarmed she went on, "Oh, you don't need to worry. I wouldn't dream of asking them to come to a shabby little affair like that."

"Well, I thought," he began as though dealing with an unreasonable patient who must be humored, "that would cause the least trouble and be simpler all around."

"Listen, you oaf!" she stormed, "let's have a few things

clear. I'm getting married strictly on Ricky's account.
You can take care of your patients — and God help them
— and I make my own decisions. Is that clear?"

"That depends on circumstances. My practice comes
first. That's the reason I am marrying you and it's the
only reason. No man wants a prima donna in the house."
He broke off as the telephone rang. When Jenny had
finished talking he went on heatedly, "You can make your
own decisions up to the point where they cause trouble,
and then you stop. The woman who marries a doctor has
to be Caesar's wife." Again there was time off for the
telephone. Again Brad picked up the conversation. "Keep
your dramatics for the stage and we'll get along all right."

"Oh, we will, will we! Well, let me tell you —" Again
the telephone rang and Jenny refused an invitation. She
was as aware as he was of the contrast between her sweet
telephone voice and the angry one in which she spoke to
him. By the time she had put down the telephone she had
somehow got over her annoyance. Anyhow, the doctor's
eyes were dancing as he watched her struggle with her
temper. It was the first time any man had dared to laugh
at her.

He stretched out his hand. "Come on, Jenny," he said
cajolingly, "it's going to be all right. No reason why we
couldn't get along fine. Anyhow, I won't be underfoot
much of the time. If I'm the only physician in the place
I'll be busy, run off my feet most likely. Have you ever
thought of what it's like?"

"What?"

"Having a doctor in the house."

"It's the last thing I'd have thought of."

He gave her a lazy smile. "Well, there will be plenty

of time for that." Seeing that she was about to explode again he went on hastily, "Now about getting out there. We'll have to fly. I'll see about plane tickets tomorrow."

"Why not drive? You'll need a car anyhow. Whoever heard of a country doctor without a car?"

"I don't own a car and I can't afford a down payment on one. There may be some lean months ahead."

"Look here, doctor. Let's be sensible. This isn't a regular marriage. There's no reason on earth why you should feel obliged to support me. I intend to pay my own way — and Ricky's, of course. I have a car. Why can't we take that?"

"That Lincoln! Lady, it's as big as a Pullman. Country doctors don't drive cars like that. Anyhow, I'm not going to have my wife supporting me."

"When I'm your wife and not just your partner in a sort of business arrangement you can start yelling and laying down the law. Not until then."

The two angry and determined young people glared at each other. Then Jenny began to laugh. This time she was the one to hold out her hand as a token of peace and friendship. With some satisfaction she saw his response to her smile. That was more like it. She would have him tamed within a week.

She looked at her watch. "You'll have to go, doctor. I've no more time now."

"Formality is fine in its place but my name is Bradley and you might as well get used to it. My friends call me Brad."

"All right, Bradley." Seeing his grin she felt like slapping him. "I always sleep for an hour before I go to the theater. You had better pick up a map somewhere so we can work out the best route west for this time of year."

"Okay. I'll come along sometime tomorrow."

"Heavens, no! Saturday is matinée day and there's an evening performance too. My last performance." For a moment her face was somber and then she said crisply, "You had better come on Sunday but not before eleven-thirty. We'll have breakfast and make plans then."

He stood looking down at her and took her hand, his long fingers closing around it gently. "I heard you telling that man Prince over the telephone that you had no choice. I'll be getting a very gallant companion, Jennifer Haydon. Some day, if there is any justice, you'll be able to take up your career again. Now you rest. I'll just have a look at Ricky and then I'll let myself out." He left her staring after him, while he went to Ricky's room. As he opened the door Jenny heard the little boy's rasping cough.

iii

The Saturday matinée had been difficult enough. It had seemed to Jenny that the applause would never stop. Her dressing room was almost choked with flowers; telegrams fluttered like autumn leaves in a brisk wind. On top of that, the whole cast, with the understandable exception of her understudy, was in a highly emotional state. There was genuine regret at losing Jenny; there was also genuine anxiety about the understudy, who might not be able to carry the play. What had seemed destined for a record-breaking run might fade out in a matter of weeks. There were all kinds of rumors about Jenny's reasons for leaving the stage and the smash hit of the season.

Sleep or even rest was out of the question before the

evening performance. It's the last time, Jenny told herself, the very last time in all my life. She looked around the dressing room at the massed flowers, the autographed pictures, the greasepaint, the costumes hanging against the wall. This couldn't be happening to her. It couldn't be.

She tried to console her weeping dresser. "You aren't losing your job, you know, Mary. Miss Harris is delighted to keep you on because you know the ropes and what is needed and how to handle it."

"But it won't be the same," the maid wailed.

There was a tap at the door. "First call, Miss Haydon."

She checked her makeup, straightened the seams in her stockings, tucked a stray lock of hair into place, and went out into the half world that exists behind the scenes. She heard the familiar words coming from the stage, the tempo increasing and excitement building for her entrance, heard a fist bang on the table. And flung open the double doors.

The applause rose and fell like waves. People were standing, shouting her name. The cast remained motionless. This tribute was for Jennifer Haydon. For a long moment she stood looking out at the audience but tonight her famous smile was absent. She lifted her hands a little and let them drop helplessly. The tears spilled down her cheeks.

IV

FOR several days the road had led south, away from
March winds and snow and sleet. They were not, Brad
had pointed out, trying to make a record. No sense in ar-
riving all tired out because there were bound to be confusion and problems at the other end and they might as
well be in good shape to meet whatever came. Three
hundred to four hundred miles a day would be plenty.
Stop before dark and get a good rest.

Now the road led west. Already Jenny had replaced
her sable coat with one of cloth. The southern route might
provide milder weather, clearer roads, and avoid the
danger of snowbound mountain passes but it was dull
and, for the most part, not scenic. Brad had said that they
could cross in seven days, allowing time for unforeseen
delays, now that all big cities had beltways to bypass them
so travelers would not be caught in a network of busy
city traffic.

Holding the car at a steady seventy Jenny watched the
miles fall away. Having been born in New England and
having lived for the past five years in Manhattan, she
knew little about her own country beyond the area of a
few hundred miles. The very concept of size was new to
her, as it must be, indeed, to anyone who has not ex-

perienced it. The road stretched on into the horizon, state after state falling away behind them, each with its own identity in spite of the superficial sameness of super-markets, filling stations, and shopping areas.

There was the difference between plain and hill and mountain, between village and modern city, between wasteland and fruitful land, between wealth and poverty, between ugliness and heart-stopping beauty.

Jenny was surprised by her own excitement. She found herself crying out, "Look!" and sharing her delight and wonder with Brad.

In the beginning she had found it impossible to go to sleep before two or three in the morning. When Brad hammered on the door of her motel room at six she stumbled out of bed, half asleep, and dressed Ricky awkwardly. It had always been Margaret who took care of him. Jenny had provided for his support and played with him when she had a spare half hour. Now she was plunged into the demands of motherhood, which could not wait for her to learn. Ricky's needs had to be met as they arose. She wasn't making a good job of it and she knew it.

Brad supervised the boy's meals, kept him entertained during the long days in the car when the small boy grew fretful and restless because of his enforced inactivity. Brad's patience seemed to be inexhaustible. It was to him that young Richard turned instinctively for love and security, having been thrust into this strange life on wheels where there was no chance for a small boy to run except when they stopped for gas or meals or for the night and Brad took him for a walk, rain or shine.

"You walk him as though he were a puppy," Jenny said. "All you need is a leash."

"He's got to have some regular exercise," Brad said mildly. In dark slacks and a heavy turtleneck sweater he seemed even younger than he had in street clothes; less remote but, oddly enough, less easy to approach. Jenny had found Dr. Maxwell easier to understand than this good-looking and casual Brad to whom, as she had to keep reminding herself, she was married.

Marriage had not made any difference in their relationship. There had been an unexpected moment when he had slipped the wedding ring on her finger and she had looked up to see the searching question in his eyes. And there had been the kiss he had given her under the approving eyes of the clerk and the two witnesses whom he had called from a neighboring office. No token kiss, that, but one with his mouth firm and warm on hers. On the whole their relationship was relaxed and unselfconscious but with intervals of fleeting irritation. At no time did he refer to their married status. If the motel clerks were surprised when they rented two rooms at night they made no comment.

Most mornings Brad drove while she dozed uneasily, and after she was thoroughly awake they took turns at the wheel. By the fourth day the unaccustomed early morning awakenings made it easier for Jenny to get to sleep before midnight, and the days were so varied that there was no time in which to miss the theater and the familiar world she had left behind her.

"So that's the Mississippi River," she said in disappointment, looking down from a high, narrow bridge on an uninspiring body of water, its banks flat and low. "No wonder it overflows. And how ugly it is!"

"You can't expect everything to be beautiful."

"Well, the Hudson River is beautiful every foot of the way from the Battery to Albany. You have to admit that," she said as though he disputed the fact. She constantly found herself arguing with Brad.

"You know what, Jenny? The trouble with you is that you are provincial. The fact that you've been living in New York among sophisticated people doesn't mean you belong to the hub of the universe. There's hardly a mile of the thirty-five hundred miles we are traveling that isn't the hub of the universe for someone. There are a whole lot of good things outside of New York."

Aware that he was carrying the war into enemy country she adroitly shifted its focus. "Where were you born, Brad?"

"North Dakota. A town of thirteen families. Quite a metropolis."

"What was it like?"

"Desert. Ugly. Sagebush and rattlesnakes and barren ground. Bitter blinding blizzards in winter so a man could get lost and freeze to death between his house and his barn. Scorching summers when the temperature didn't drop at night. A primitive section that the modern world had passed by. Outhouses and no running water. No electricity. Coal ranges for cooking and wood stoves for heating the house if you were careful not to let them go out. Water hauled from the nearest well. Ice cut from the river in winter and laid down underground in straw for the summer. Once a week we got in the car and drove to the next biggest town, five hundred inhabitants. There was a baseball game on Saturday afternoon and a movie at night. We really lived it up on Saturdays. But that was in the summer, of course. In the winter we mostly stayed home."

"What could force anyone to live there?" Jenny wondered.

"My father inherited a ranch but he went broke. Then he ran the village general store, but not very successfully; in fact, not successfully at all."

"How did your mother feel about living that way? What sort of person was she, Brad?"

Brad was silent for a while. "She was a young schoolteacher who went out to a dude ranch for her summer vacation. That's when she met and married Father. Very pretty. Very romantic. She had been seeing western movies and she thought life was made up of excitement and glamour and heroics. Actually she had to live in a shack with no modern conveniences. And Dad went broke on the ranch, as I said, ran a little store, and failed at that. When he died he must have owed money to everyone in town and half the county. But Mother had fallen in love with him. He was not a good husband and certainly not a good provider, and yet, to some extent, she stayed in love with him right up to the time she died. But she was never blinded by her love. She didn't want me to be like him."

"What made you decide to be a doctor?"

"I can't remember when I wanted to be anything else. Hey, there, young man, stop pulling my hair. Let's draw up at the next filling station and I'll take him for a run. Little guys his age need a lot of action."

Jenny watched the tall man and the very small one start across the filling station, saw Ricky kite ahead, his short legs working like pistons, and letting out squeals of delight in motion, while Brad followed slowly, knowing he could catch the boy with his longer stride.

There were other days when Brad asked about life in the theater. A lot of glamour, he supposed. It seemed odd to a hard-working and impoverished young intern, who saw sick people all day and all night, to think of acting as a real job or, in fact, as anything that could be taken seriously.

It wasn't like that, Jenny assured him. She described the long, heartbreaking job of getting a start, the weary trek to the agents' offices, dingy places, for the most part over theaters or Broadway shops; and the panic when she was given a part to read for fear she would muff it and there could be no second chance. There was the first walk-on part and the excitement when the lights went up and one felt the audience waiting to be entertained, sometimes challenging the actors to entertain them. There was the shabby theatrical apartment house with its small, hot rooms and its constantly changing people; the has-beens holding on desperately because they were unfit for any other work; the young who felt they could tackle Hamlet or Lady Macbeth and knew that opportunity was just around the corner. There were the weeks of rehearsal when the dry bones of the play began to take on flesh and life; the out-of-town tryouts, "sort of trying it out on the dog," and the strain and fear and excitement of the Broadway opening.

There was the first real part and a lucky evening when a critic noticed her and singled out her performance for enthusiastic comment. That play had only a short run but the next part came at once and provided a bigger and more important part. Jenny had had a lot of praise this time, which had not endeared her to the leading lady. And then Jacob Beaver, the gifted young playwright, caught her performance and he came around to talk to her and take her out to a late supper. On Sundays he began to drop by, not talking much but studying her, her personality, her speech patterns, her way of moving. And then he had written *Heat Wave* for her and both the play and the star had been smash hits. It had seemed to her that she had reached the peak: stardom and a chance at her own television program and nationwide fame. Every actor's dream. The once-in-a-lifetime opportunity.

"You hated to give that up, didn't you?"

"How would you feel, Brad, if you had to refuse the biggest opportunity of your whole life, knowing there could be no second chance?"

"I don't know," he admitted. "Why did you?"

She looked at him. "There was no choice. My sister trusted me to be responsible for Ricky's welfare."

Brad was silent for a long time. The maddening girl kept him off balance, showed him different faces. He had been rocked off his feet when he first saw her poised at the top of a flight of stairs, and by the end of that performance he had been completely dazzled. After that he had met her with the makeup thick on her face; he had seen her, sleek and prosperous, greeting her public; he had heard her brittle talk. He had begun to grasp her quality when he had heard her say "There is no choice" when it came to a choice between Richard's welfare and her own. He had encountered her generosity: helping her understudy acquire the lead, providing Brad himself with the use of her car, insisting that she pay all of her own expenses and Ricky's. Each morning she worked out meticulously the cost of motel rooms, food, and sundries, and paid her share.

On this trip her moods changed so constantly that he was bewildered. Just when he thought he had a key to her he encountered a stranger. When they seemed to be irreconcilable enemies she would dazzle him with her smile. And sometimes she might have been the girl next door. For the first time he understood how Cleopatra's inexhaustible fascination had rested in her infinite variety. You would never be bored with this girl, never take her for granted. If you did she was sure to upset the apple cart. From the moment when he had faced Joseph Colfax and thrown him out of her apartment, he had known pretty well what his own attitude toward Jenny was; but he had set out on a course of action and he was grimly determined to abide by it.

There were days when they laughed at nothing in particular and became dramatic over matters that did not really concern them, or argued violently about politics and war and student protest as opposed to student violence. Little by little, without intending it, they were revealing their minds and their backgrounds and their beliefs to each other.

Ricky's attack of asthma had cleared up. His cheeks were red, his eyes a deep blue, his fair hair as soft as silk, like Louise's. He was a beautiful child, and a resemblance to his mother became more evident every day. "What an adorable boy," a woman in the next car exclaimed while Jenny was waiting one day for Brad to bring Richard back from a walk. "And such a handsome husband! He reminds me of Mayor Lindsay. You're a lucky girl to have so attractive a family."

Jenny started to say they were not her family and bit back the words. In a few minutes Brad came back, said, "Move over and I'll drive for a while," and lifted Ricky in beside her. As he put the car in gear the woman waved to them.

"What was that all about?" Brad inquired.

"I have such an attractive little family," Jenny said glumly. A week ago all eyes would have been on her; now she was being relegated to the background as wife and mother.

Brad chuckled. "That's what she thinks. Cheer up, Kate."

"Kate?"

"Katherine the shrew."

Jenny glowered at him. A small hand touched her face and she saw Richard looking at her anxiously. She and Brad were all the security he had and she knew how she must seem to him at this moment. She made herself laugh until she had coaxed back his smile.

Brad switched off the heat in the car. "Tomorrow you won't need that coat. Have you noticed? Below zero when we left New York and it must be over fifty now. Tomorrow we'll be heading into summer: New Mexico, Arizona, and then California."

"Will it be beautiful on the desert?"

"Well, of course, it isn't going to be neat and pretty like New England, with every foot of the land manicured. They have a lot of land out there and practically no water, and nature isn't easy to tame. The country we'll be going through from now on will be rugged and rough and terrible and wonderful and lonely."

Ricky wriggled away from Jenny and onto Brad's lap. His hands clutched at the wheel. "Car," he said. "Drive."

"Brad! Did you hear that? His words were just as clear!"

"You know something, Jenny? We've got us a smart little guy."

ii

"I didn't know," Jenny said, "that it would be like this. I thought — a desert — well, that it would have sand dunes, like the pictures of the Sahara."

"Parts of it are like that."

"But this — rough and rocky and hilly and — empty. We haven't seen a house in nearly an hour and there's not a single car on the road. It's frightening. And all those roadside warnings about not leaving the car. Why?"

Brad had switched on the air conditioning. "Sunstroke for one thing. Poisonous snakes for another. Big cats occasionally, such as mountain lions or cougars. But the chief danger is that there are no landmarks. You could easily become lost if you wandered off the road and out of sight of the car, and that wouldn't be an easy death."

"And those huge tanks marked 'Water for cars only.' What are they for?"

"People see a straight, empty road ahead and no interesting scenery so they are inclined to drive as fast as they can — eighty, ninety, a hundred miles an hour, so they can click off the road in a hurry or, if they don't have their cars air-conditioned, in the faint hope of stirring up a breeze. They overheat their motors and build up pressure in their tires. We don't want a blowout here, so easy does it. You see, we aren't going over sixty and the motor is still cool."

Brad's hands rested lightly on the wheel. He was wearing shorts and a thin sport shirt. Ricky wore nothing but shorts, his body already turning brown. The last few days they had been able to enjoy the swimming pools at their motels and Brad had kept the boy in the sun as long as he dared without causing sunburn. Jenny wore darkblue linen slacks and a sleeveless linen blouse.

"A week ago it was winter," she said in a tone of wonder, "and now the temperature is — what?"

"About ninety, but with this air conditioning it doesn't matter."

"I didn't know the sky could be like this, so deep a blue. And look, Brad! What's that? It looks a bit like a chicken. No, on second thought, it looks like nothing on earth."

Brad laughed. "That's one of nature's comedians, a roadrunner."

"But how can it live here? Nothing seems to grow. What does it eat?"

"Snakes and Gila monsters."

"Ugh! How much farther is it?"

Brad stopped the car and opened a map, waiting patiently while Ricky wriggled until he got his head over the edge so that he could see too. "We're practically there, as I figure it. Just another ten miles. Say a ten-minute drive."

"Ten miles! You mean the town's in a place like this?" There was disbelief in Jenny's voice.

"You knew it was a desert town. What did you expect? Neon lights? New York? Hollywood? Even Las Vegas?"

"I don't know. But not this. Why, there's nothing at all, Brad."

He looked at her dismayed face, started to speak, and changed his mind. He folded the map and lifted Richard off his lap. The little boy raised his voice in a bellow of protest.

"Hey, you!" Brad said, sounding shocked, and the crying stopped.

"I wish I could handle him as well as you do," Jenny admitted.

"You'll learn. He's actually a happy child and he hasn't been raised with too much permissiveness. Once he learns what is allowed and what isn't you'll have no trouble because he'll understand what is expected and have a sense of security. The unhappy and mixed-up kids are the ones who get indulgence one day and discipline the next. They never know where they stand. Hey, look ahead, Jenny! I guess that is Desert Winds, our future home."

"Where?" she asked in bewilderment. "I can't see anything. Oh! Do you mean where the sun is reflected on windows? There? *That's* Desert Winds?"

"Must be. According to the map there isn't another town for thirty miles."

"Oh," she said blankly. Then she snapped, "Richard, stop hitting me!"

Another mile and they had turned off the highway, driving slowly along a two-lane road that seemed to lead from nowhere to nowhere, with the desert creeping to its very edge. There was a sign: WELCOME TO DESERT WINDS, Speed 30. There was a neat building with a sign, KELLY FOR DINNERS. There was a liquor store. There was a one-room bank and a movie theater with a sign, "Shows every Thursday evening at 7 and 9 P.M." There was a liquor store. There were two grocery stores and a pharmacy, all of which sold liquor as a sideline. There was a small, nondescript shop call the Emporium that displayed bathing suits and bright slacks and shorts. There was a lunch stand that advertised tacos, spaghetti, and hot dogs. There was a real estate office. There was a liquor store and a garage.

Brad drove up to a pump at the garage. When he rolled down the window a blast of air as hot as a furnace came in.

"Fill 'er up?"

"Please, and check the oil and water, will you? And can you tell me where the doctor's house is?"

"Well, now that's a shame. We don't have a doctor in town now. You'll have to go on to Four Corners, about thirty miles southwest of here."

"I don't need a doctor," Brad said. "I am a doctor. I've come here to practice medicine."

"You don't say!" The garage attendant thrust out a hand that was black with grease. "You sure look young," he said dubiously. "Have you got a regular license?"

Brad grinned. "All correct."

"What's your name, doc?"

"Maxwell. Meet my family."

The look of doubt vanished as the attendant looked at Jenny and Richard. "Glad to meet you folks and I sure hope you stay. My mother was saying just this morning I'd have to get her over to Four Corners somehow on account of her arthritis is so bad. I said I couldn't take the time off to drive her that far because there's no one to spell me. I suppose you'll be living in the doctor's house."

"That's right. I hope it is ready for us."

"You'll have to go up to the motel. The woman who runs it has the keys to the house."

"Where is the motel?"

"Turn west for five blocks and then right. It's at the end of the street."

"They really mean end, don't they?" Jenny said when Brad pulled up before the motel. End of the world, for the road stopped there and beyond were low rocky hills with little growth of any kind and not so much as a footpath.

At the motel the desert had not been allowed to have its own way. There were flower boxes and flowering bushes and palm trees.

Brad eased out from under the wheel and opened the door marked OFFICE. He tapped on a little bell on the desk and a woman came out from a room at the back. She was in her middle forties, tall and slim, with dark hair whose streaks of silver were belied by the unlined face and firm chin line. She wore a bright-colored slack suit, the standard apparel for this part of the world. She smiled at Brad and pushed a card and pen toward him so he could register.

"You're in luck. I just had a cancellation," she said.

"Oh, I'm not stopping here. I understand you have the keys to the doctor's house."

She did not hide her surprise. "Are you the new doctor?"

"That's right. I am Bradley Maxwell."

She opened a drawer and took out a keyring and a separate key. "The ring has all the house keys. The single one is for the office."

"My wife and boy are out in the car," Brad said casually.

"Oh, you're married! Good." She did not attempt to conceal her relief.

Brad was becoming increasingly aware of how right Dr.

Ferguson had been. His youthful appearance was a real stumbling block. Without the stability of his marriage he would have a difficult time making himself accepted, particularly in a community which had become disillusioned with its previous doctor.

"I hope the house is ready for us."

"The doctor left all his furniture and I had the electricity and gas and water turned on and the telephones in the house and office connected as soon as I heard you were coming. Dorothy, who cleans for me, gave the place a good going over. You'll like the house; it's well built and has air conditioning and a swimming pool. The kitchen and bathrooms are modern, all copper plumbing. Aside from the Penrose place, it's much the best house in town. You'll pass the school on your right. Then turn left past the church. Next block has only two houses as that section is just being opened up. This is a new town, you know. Your house is the big one with the two front doors."

"Thank you."

"It will be a great comfort for all of us, having a doctor again. Remember to be very careful of the sun at first if you aren't used to it. You can get a really bad burn before you're aware of what is happening. If there is any way I can be of use to Mrs. Maxwell, please tell her not to hesitate to ask. I am Helen Gates. Mrs. Gates."

"Thank you. Oh, there's one thing. Do you know who was the doctor's office nurse?"

"Jane Matthews, she got married and moved out to Beverly Hills just last week."

"Do you know of anyone who has the training to be an office nurse?"

"Sarah Caldwell, but you wouldn't have a chance of

getting her. She fell in love with the doctor she worked for in San Francisco and her mother brought her out here just to break off the affair. Of course, if Sarah had had any guts she would have stayed and married her doctor. Well, you can't turn a rabbit into a lioness, I suppose. I'll ask around but the chances are that you will have to get someone from another town, maybe even Pasadena or Los Angeles. It's hard to persuade the young ones to come to a little place where there's not much in the way of amusement and not many chances to marry. And an older woman might be too set in her ways to meet the requirements of a doctor with more up-to-date training."

Brad grinned. "Well, you can't win them all. Just the same, I'd appreciate it if you would inquire." He went back to the car. "Just a few blocks," he said as he handed Jenny the keyring. "She's Mrs. Gates, very pleasant, and said she'd be glad to do anything she could to help Mrs. Maxwell."

"Mrs. who? Oh!"

"She says it's about the best house in town: air conditioning, swimming pool, the works."

"It could be the best within a hundred miles," Jenny said bitterly, "and still not be worth having." She looked with a jaundiced eye at the nondescript houses they were passing. Some owners had made valiant efforts to hold back the desert by planting, some had compromised by making rock gardens, and some had surrendered and let the desert creep up to the door.

The doctor's house was considerably larger than the others, a long green stucco with wide windows and two front doors, one of them marked OFFICE. There was a carport at one side, wide enough for three cars, and an extra parking space beyond the house for patients' cars.

Across the street there was a small white frame house. Someone had pulled the curtains to one side and was watching them.

Brad drove the car up to the door. "Well," he said with false cheerfulness, "here we are. You go in with Ricky and I'll bring along the luggage."

The stale air that rushed out was at least cooler than the sun blazing down on her head. She had better get some kind of head covering, Jenny supposed. She looked around. The living room was carpeted in a shaggy material designed to save work rather than provide beauty. Neutral drapes covered the wide windows, shutting out the heat and the desert. The furniture was nondescript and without a scrap of individuality: a taupe couch and chairs, a dining table in a nook near the kitchen, which was separated from the living room by a wide counter. At the back there were three bedrooms and two baths. On one side of the living room a door led into the doctor's office. On the other side a door opened onto a patio enclosed in high walls which, she learned later, were some sort of protection against the high desert winds and the scourge of blowing sand. In the middle there was a swimming pool.

The beds had been stripped to the mattresses. Jenny went back to the kitchen. The refrigerator had been turned on, but like the cupboards it was barren of food. *I hate this place,* she thought despairingly. *I hate it. I hate it. I don't know what to do. I've never cooked a meal in my whole life and I don't know where the bedding is or — or anything.*

"Mama," Ricky said, reaching for her hand for comfort in this alien place. "Mama."

"It's all right, little chicken," she assured him, trying to keep her voice reassuring and gay. "We'll go out and shop for dinner. Won't that be fun?"

The front door opened and Brad dropped a couple of suitcases on the floor. He did not spare a glance for his new home. "We'd better get the air conditioning going." He did not notice her despairing look.

"Give me the car keys, Brad. There's no food in the house."

"All right. Better leave the boy with me. He's had all the driving he can take for one day."

"Don't let him go out. The sun is still terribly hot."

"I'll keep him inside. He needs to run around and then have a cool bath and a light supper."

"Yes, doctor." Jenny got in the car and slammed the door. Brad did not notice. He had a screwdriver and he was whistling cheerfully while he put up a shiny new sign that read: BRADLEY MAXWELL, M.D.

V

𝒜 first meal at their own table should have been a memorable occasion. Actually both Jenny and Brad made a pretense of eating the frozen dinners, each deep in thought, each concerned with his own problems.

"Where can I hire a housekeeper?" Jenny asked.

"What's that?" Brad looked up absently. "Oh, I doubt if it would be possible. Anyhow, there won't be much work in a house like this."

"But I don't know how!"

"I don't suppose anyone does to start with. Jenny, I've got a nice setup over there, some first-class equipment, an examination room, a little laboratory, an office and a reception room just big enough for a couple of chairs, a couch, and a desk. Later I'll have to make a lot of improvements in the laboratory or maybe build one on if I can get any financing. The only hitch is that I don't have an office nurse. I'll have to ask you to fill in until I can get one."

"Me!" Jenny stared at him in disbelief.

"Not so loud. You'll wake Ricky and I can tell you I had a time getting him to settle down and go to sleep."

"I don't know how to be an office nurse. Not the first thing."

"Well, you can learn."

"But —"

"Look, Jenny, there are rules about that. I have to have an office nurse. I'll get one as quickly as I can but you'll just have to lend a hand in the meantime."

The telephone rang and they both jumped at the unexpected sound.

"This is Dr. Maxwell . . . No, I just moved in this afternoon . . . Who? . . . Where? . . . In half an hour." He put down the telephone and looked at Jenny. "What do you know? My first private patient! A Mrs. Caldwell. Lives in Hot Springs Canyon, wherever that is. We're in business, girl!" He went into his room, whistling. In a few minutes he came out. He had changed from shorts to a lightweight suit and he was carrying his bag. "Be seeing you." He went out and Jenny heard the car door slam. Across the street a curtain in the living room dropped into place.

There was no sound in the house but the faint whirring of the air-conditioner. No sound outside. *No sound!* No sirens, no traffic, no footsteps, no voices. Nothing at all. Eight-thirty. In New York she would be looking at her flowers, making up her face, while her dresser waited with her first-act costume, hearing the subdued bustle from backstage and the muted noises of taxi horns on Forty-fourth Street with its flashing lights over the marquees of theaters. The night would just be beginning. Jenny pushed aside her almost untouched dinner, dropped her head on her arms, and cried.

The two-tone door chime startled her. She wiped her eyes, blew her nose, and went to open the door. For a moment she hesitated, afraid of the unknown. Then she eased the door wide enough open to see out and was re-assured by the sight of the woman who was standing there, a gray-haired woman whose angular body was not improved by a shapeless housedress. She carried a flashlight in her hand.

"Mrs. Maxwell?" She had a nasal twang.

"Yes." Jenny did not move.

"I live across the street. I'm Mrs. Fulmer. I saw you move in today."

"Oh." Jenny hesitated but as the woman remained planted she stood back reluctantly. "Won't you come in?"

"I knew you'd be feeling sort of strange." Mrs. Fulmer's eyes observed Jenny's tear-stained face and the un-eaten meal on the table. "I always think it helps to get acquainted with your neighbors."

"Oh, yes," Jenny said faintly.

Mrs. Fulmer seated herself without waiting to be asked. She was busy taking in the room and its furnishings. "Having a late meal, I see. The first day is always a problem. Out here we mostly finish supper by seven at the very latest."

Obviously newcomers were expected to conform to this routine. "Oh." Jenny waited.

"You'll hardly believe it, Mrs. Maxwell, but I've lived across the street for two years and this is the first time I've ever set foot in this house."

"Really?"

"The other doctor — well, his carryings-on!" She gave Jenny a significant look. "I can tell you no nice woman ever got asked in. Not that we wanted to come, of course, though you can't help being curious. Such a big house! Whatever did a widower want with so much room? Three bedrooms and two baths as well as all those rooms in the doctor's own suite. A mansion it is." She got up casually. "How is it laid out?"

Jenny stopped her before she could go through the house and see that beds were made up in two rooms. "I'd be happy to show it to you some other time but my little boy is a light sleeper and awfully tired from the trip."

"Mrs. Gates says you came all the way from New York."

"Mrs. Gates?"

"The woman who runs the motel. She was acting as caretaker for this place. The doctor left her in charge though I'm sure, as I was working for him anyhow, and just across the street, it would have been more natural for him to ask me."

"Oh, are you an office nurse?"

"No, I run the telephone answering service for this whole community right from my own house. I took the doctor's calls. That's one reason I came over tonight. I heard Mrs. Caldwell tell the doctor she wanted to see him, and she had to call the house when the office didn't answer, so I thought I'd just run over and ask if he wants me to carry on with his office calls. Save you having to answer when he's over at the hospital or something."

"I don't know. I'll ask him."

"If Mrs. Caldwell takes to him and he plays up to her he'll be busy enough."

"Oh?"

"A real money-maker for a doctor. Always thinks she is sick. Kept the other doctor solvent, if you ask me."

"Brad isn't like that!"

"Well, if it keeps a patient happy I'm sure I can understand it. Only human, after all, to look after your own interests." Mrs. Fulmer sounded indulgent.

"Do you know where he can get an office nurse? He has to have one."

"If you'd seen what I have seen of office nurses! They are all alike. If I were you, with a young and good-looking husband, as I could see from across the street, I'd take over the office myself."

"You don't think much of men, do you, Mrs. Fulmer?"

Her neighbor's lips tightened. "There's nothing personal about it," she said, and Jenny knew that this was untrue. "But I thought it was just as well to warn you, because people — well, you wouldn't believe the way scandal spreads in this place. I've never understood it."

Jenny thought she could understand it very well. "You needn't worry about my husband. He's a dedicated doctor."

After a few moments of unbroken silence Mrs. Fulmer got up. "Well, I'll be on my way so you can get your dishes done. I know how any good housewife feels about leaving dirty dishes. So slovenly. No man wants to come home to a house like that. You'll ask the doctor about the answering service, won't you?"

"Of course. And thank you."

Unexpectedly the older woman's harsh face softened. "You don't look to be much more than a baby. I expect you feel sort of lost and frightened, especially if you aren't used to being alone. If you want anything I'm right across the street."

"That's kind of you."

Mrs. Fulmer hesitated on the doorstep. "It's a shame, having that swell Lincoln. The sandstorms will ruin the paint job in no time. Why don't you trade it in and get a cheap little car, one that wouldn't matter? Anyhow, you know how it looks — sort of ostentatious." She switched on the flashlight and walked across the road to the white frame house.

ii

In spite of his blithe promise to arrive in thirty minutes it was nearly an hour before Brad found Hot Springs Canyon. Doubtless this was because there were no road signs until he had gone miles out of his way. As he drove slowly through the darkness, peering for signs at cross-roads, it occurred to him that a number of years had passed since he had lived in a land as unsettled and desolate as this. There might be more readjustments required than he had anticipated.

He remembered Jenny's panic when she had realized that she was expected to live in this empty land. He recalled her disconsolate face when she had set the dinner before him. If she expected to have a staff of servants out here, as she had had in New York, she was going to be disappointed. A staff of servants, indeed! For a moment he was inclined to be scornful of the idea. Then he recalled that, after all, she had paid for them. She had not been an idle woman; what she had she earned. And she had given up all that for Ricky. She would learn to manage a house in time but he wondered uneasily how much the learning would cost her, how much she would regret what she had left behind.

Ahead there was a house whose outside lights were burning. His headlights picked out the name Caldwell on a signpost. The door was opened before he reached it.

Against the light from the living room he saw a shadowy figure.

"Dr. Maxwell?"

"I am Dr. Maxwell."

"My mother was getting worried for fear you had lost your way because you did say half an hour. She is very nervous and —"

"I can speak for myself, Sarah. Bring the doctor in," called an irritable voice, and the figure in the doorway turned quickly. She was in her middle twenties, with a pale face, pale hair, a self-effacing manner, and a shy smile. She led him through the living room which, with a complete disregard for the climate, was furnished with heavy chairs and couches upholstered in plush, and a dark mahogany sideboard that took up one whole wall of the room and seemed to frown gloomily upon the whole place.

The bedroom into which she conducted him was unexpectedly luxurious. Brad took in the bedside table with its burden of medicine bottles, glasses, and its ominous little handbell. A hypochondriac.

Her faded blond hair had been cleverly touched up. Her faded complexion was delicately made up. She had a petulant mouth and a stubborn jaw, thick insensitive hands with thumbs that turned back, and unexpectedly beautiful eyes.

"Dr. Maxwell?" she said in a feeble voice that contrasted with the one in which she had summoned her daughter. "I won't need you for a while, Sarah."

"All right, mama. Just call me when you want me." She opened a door to an adjoining room, little more than space for a narrow bed and a chest of drawers.

Brad drew up a chair beside the bed and pulled out a

notebook. Name? Alice Caldwell. Married? Widow. Age? There was a pause. "Fifty-two," she said reluctantly, and mentally he added five years.

She unleashed a flood of symptoms, a heart that fluttered and pounded; exhaustion when she made the slightest effort; nerves that were a constant source of agony to her, especially when she was left alone; indigestion; and sleeplessness. She had always been high-strung, too absurdly sensitive. Sometimes she wondered how she had managed to survive so much nerve strain.

Brad took her pulse, her temperature, and her blood pressure, eying with awe the array of medicine bottles. Meanwhile Mrs. Caldwell had adroitly extracted his medical background, the fact that he was married and had one son.

"From New York! You can't imagine the relief it is to have a doctor here in town, especially a man from a civilized background."

This tribute to New York at the expense of the rest of America amused Brad but he made no comment.

"It makes such a difference! I often say that I live in a cultural vacuum."

"Why do you?"

There was an annoyed glint in the beautiful eyes. It was sympathy Mrs. Caldwell wanted and she was willing to pay for it. But she did not care for a cold shower of common sense. "This isn't where I would choose to be. I brought my daughter here because it seemed best for her sake." She had succeeded in surprising him. He had summed her up as a self-centered woman and a cannibal mother. "Sarah had formed one of those unfortunate attachments so I decided to keep her here. The man was a doctor, just starting out in San Francisco. Sarah was his office nurse. I put a stop to that, of course. He couldn't leave his job long enough to make the trip to see her here."

"And your daughter agreed to stay with you?"

The lovely eyes hardened. "Of course. What else would you expect her to do? I can't get along without her. Anyhow, he has married since then. That settled that."

It seemed more than likely that Mrs. Gates had been right. Mrs. Caldwell would never permit her daughter to be his office nurse if she could stand in the way, and she would be a formidable opponent. He wrote out a prescription for a mild remedy for indigestion and stood up. She rang the bell and the door opened promptly.

"Yes, mama."

"See Dr. Maxwell out and then drive in to the drugstore to get this filled." As Brad looked at his watch she explained, "The druggist lives over the store. He's used to filling my prescriptions at all hours."

I'll bet he is, Brad thought grimly.

"But hurry back. I might need you."

"Yes, mama."

"That's quite unnecessary," Brad said. "I can give you something that will do for tonight." He opened his bag and shook some pills into a sterile bottle.

"Thank you, doctor," Mrs. Caldwell said.

"Thank you, doctor," her daughter said slyly as she opened the door for him.

He dropped his voice. "She's quite all right, you know."

Her disillusioned eyes met his. "Yes, I know."

Then why the deuce do you put up with her? Brad bit back the words. Instead he asked, "Any possibility you could act as my office nurse? Mrs. Gates tells me you trained for it."

She smiled and he saw that behind the beaten woman

there lurked a wry sense of humor. "As long as you are married my mother might agree but she never likes being alone for long at a stretch."

"Perhaps we can work out something."

Brad drove back through the canyon and into the little town. Except at the lunch stand there were few lights. To his disappointment the house was dark when he drove into the carport. He had assumed that Jenny would be awake. He had looked forward to telling her about his first patient and her victimized daughter. There ought to be some way to shake a little fight into the girl before it was too late for her to escape, and some way to acquire at least a part-time office nurse.

As he walked to the house door he was aware of the chilly wind and remembered that nights on the desert are apt to be cool. He switched on the living room lights and turned off the air conditioning. In the kitchen he rummaged for bread and cheese and poured a glass of milk. It would be nice if he could share this hour with someone, share the excitement of his first private patient, even if she was an imaginary invalid.

He stacked his dishes in the sink and, aware of the dropping temperature, hunted for blankets. He put one on his own bed and then softly opened the door of Jenny's room. Light from the living room fell on her face on which he could see tear stains. She had pulled the sheet up to her chin and she was huddled up in a heap with Ricky close beside her for warmth. They would have to get him a crib.

Quietly Brad tucked the blanket in at the foot of the bed and drew it up over Jenny's shoulders. He bent over and kissed her hair.

VI

BRAD had been right about one thing. He was run off his feet. For the first ten days Jenny rarely saw him. Either everyone in Desert Winds had been saving up an illness for the new doctor's arrival or the people were curious to see for themselves what the new man was like. When he was not seeing patients in his office he was out on calls. Fortunately there was only one Mrs. Caldwell to make incessant and unreasonable demands on his time, but even so he had all the problems he could handle.

The Four Corners hospital was thirty miles away, over-crowded and understaffed. It could admit his patients only when an ambulance was available and the road was open and there was an extra bed. There were exasperating and sometimes dangerous delays caused by having all X rays, cardiograms, and laboratory work done at a distance.

But his frustrations were minor compared with the sat-isfaction of doing the work he had been trained to do and building a practice. He fell into bed exhausted and only one night out of four was his sleep uninterrupted. So far his search for an office nurse had been unproductive and he had been forced to require Jenny's attendance on several occasions, not only when he had women patients but when an emergency arose. At such times he seemed unaware of her as a person, issuing crisp orders as though she were a machine.

It was during those hours in his office that Jenny became aware of Brad as a doctor and gained respect for his work. She watched the gentle way in which he had soothed a frightened child, explaining patiently just what was going to happen so that when he had to hurt him the child was prepared and tried hard not to cry.

One night she was called into the examination room when two hysterical teen-agers carried in a boy whose leg had been badly mangled in a car crash. There were only two ambulances at Four Corners and both of them were out.

"I'll have to handle it here and you'll have to help me," Brad said.

Jenny leaned against the wall while the room whirled around her. "I can't," she whispered.

"You've got to, if we're going to save the boy." Brad ordered the terrified companions out of the room, scrubbed up, and ordered Jenny to bring clean sheets to cover the table while he sterilized his instruments.

"What is going to happen? Will he die?" Jenny asked huskily.

"Nonsense. The chief dangers were shock and loss of blood and infection, but I think I got him in time. If only those two idiots had handled him more carefully! Anyhow, I need your help, Jenny. Keep your head. This guy depends on us."

Standing beside him, handing him the things he wanted, trying not to see what his hands were doing, watching his face instead, Jenny fought back her sickness and revulsion. Brad was intent only on the job at hand. Seeing him like this she realized that it was no boy she had married; it was a man, a man who, at this moment, was concentrating all he had of skill and intelligence to save a life.

Then at last there were bandages and a white-faced, unconscious boy. Brad straightened his shoulders wearily and scrubbed up. Again he telephoned Four Corners and once more attempted to get an ambulance. Both were out on calls and neither could reach Desert Winds before morning.

"I'll keep him here until then," Brad said, "but when he reaches the hospital he'll need a blood transfusion at once. He had lost a lot of blood before the fools brought him here. I'll see him tomorrow afternoon."

He went out to the little reception room where two scared boys were waiting. He looked at them without sympathy. "How fast were you driving?"

"Ninety miles an hour."

"Come in here."

Reluctantly they preceded him into the examination room and looked down at the still body on the table.

"Is he dead?"

"No, but small credit to you. Remember that next time you think a car is a toy. You had better call his parents. Tell them I'll keep him here until morning when an ambulance will take him to the hospital at Four Corners. They can see him there."

"No, they can't. They live in Nebraska. He's just visiting us."

"Tough on him, isn't it? Now get out."

Once they had gone he came back to look down at the boy on the table. "I won't try to move him at all. In any case, he's not likely to wake up tonight."

"Will he be all right alone?" Jenny asked.

"Great Scott, no! I'll be right here."

"But you were called out twice last night."

"Sorry the phone wakes you. That goes with the job. Anyhow, I need some time to catch up on the medical journals." He looked at her face, almost as drained of color as that of the boy on the table, and saw the dark shadows under her eyes. "You're the one who needs the rest. I never meant to get you into anything like this, Jenny." He sounded contrite, as though he had not realized before how much he had expected of her.

She managed a rather wavery smile. "I didn't realize what it is like to be a doctor."

"Do you mind very much?"

"No. I'm proud of you, Brad. Very proud." Before he could recover from his surprise she had gone through the door to the main house and closed it behind her.

ii

There was one immediate result of that night's experience. Brad persuaded Mrs. Caldwell to let her daughter work in the office for two hours, three afternoons a week. A good deal of address was required to manage it. Mrs. Caldwell reminded him that she never knew when she might have an attack and need her daughter.

"I'm in a quandary," Brad told her. "If my wife assists me, it means that there is no one to look after my two-year-old boy. It comes down to this: I'll have to get a nurse here or I'll have to move on somewhere else to practice."

So Mrs. Caldwell consented, though grudgingly, and

only after having come to call on the doctor's wife to see for herself what the situation was and how much danger there was that Sarah might become involved with the good-looking doctor. She paid her call at a time when Jenny was in the swimming pool, teaching Ricky not to fear water. One look at the girl with the wide gray eyes, the golden-brown hair, and the beautiful golden-brown body in its brief bathing suit set Mrs. Caldwell's forebodings forever at rest. Her drab Sarah would never have a chance of interesting any man who was married to this girl with the vivid personality and the dazzling smile.

Jenny, who was fully aware of the woman's thoughts, was amused. "The doctor will be so grateful, and so will I, of course. I am always anxious when Ricky is left alone. He's just a baby."

So Sarah was installed as an office nurse for the few hours a week her mother would spare her.

"That poor little rabbit," Jenny stormed to Brad. "There's something about her that reminds me of my sister Louise. The same coloring, the same general appearance, the same sweetness. But Louise was radiant and Sarah is like a faded photograph. She lets that awful woman dominate her and she doesn't even know it."

"Oh, she knows it. Sarah isn't stupid. She just gave up all initiative, I think, when her doctor married someone else. She doesn't fight because she doesn't believe there is anything worth fighting for."

"Then it is high time she learns."

"Hey, don't scare away the only office nurse within miles."

"If I do I'll find you another," Jenny promised him rashly but, without consulting her, Mrs. Caldwell was already working on that. She did not fear that Sarah would become involved with Dr. Maxwell, but she might get some unfortunate ideas of independence. After going industriously through letters from old acquaintances — for she never threw away anything — Mrs. Caldwell wrote a long letter to a friend in San Francisco.

"If I were you," she wrote," I would advise my daughter not to keep Alma in her house any longer. It is absurd for her to give Alma a home just because she's a sister-in-law. I consider it very selfish of her husband to expect that of her. Alma is certainly old enough to look after herself. You remember that Alma and Sarah trained together. Well, I have an idea. Sarah is working again for a new doctor we have here — a married man with a child, thank heaven! Of course, she is only helping out in an emergency because I really need her. But if Alma would like to come here and take over the job — and there's no reason why a healthy girl shouldn't be earning her living! — she can live here in the house, rent free, and I know Sarah would be delighted to have her. Personally, I think your daughter should put it squarely up to Alma that she ought to go out and live her own life. The Demings have always thought only of themselves and you should tell your daughter so."

While Mrs. Caldwell was writing this letter Jenny was trying to write to Dr. Ferguson in reply to his note of inquiry.

"I feel responsible for your marriage, Jenny," it had concluded, "and my wife tells me roundly that I have been an interfering old fool. If she is right, how can I make amends? The truth is that I was under the impression that you two had been deeply attracted to each other from the very first. Your devoted if blundering old friend, Carl Ferguson."

Sitting beside the pool where she could keep an eye on Ricky, who was playing under a big umbrella, Jenny rolled her pen over and over in her hand, wondering what she could say to allay the anxiety of the kindly old man. It seemed to her that life had come to a standstill. In New York every hour had been filled with activity, with friends, with achievement; and well — be honest and admit it — with the gratification she got from applause, from being pointed out on the street, from being a celebrity.

Here no one noticed her except as the doctor's wife. Even with the difficult problems of learning how to run a house and prepare meals, drudgery which she tackled grimly but without enthusiasm or any sense of achievement, there were too many hours that were empty, too many nights when she cried herself to sleep in sheer desolation. And there was no one she could talk to. No one at all.

Ricky called, "Mama," and reached out his arms. Jenny ran to pick him up and to fasten around him a rubber contraption that would keep him safe if he tumbled into the pool, as he occasionally did. He was not often demonstrative but now he rubbed his head against her shoulder. "Swim," he declared and she went into the water with him.

That was one thing that had gone right. Ricky glowed with health. Daily he learned new words and new tricks. She pretended to scold him for being underfoot all day, but when he was tucked up at night in his new crib in the room between hers and Brad's the house seemed empty and silent. There were hours when she almost forgot that he was not her own child. Her love for him had become the most important thing in her life.

When Ricky had had enough of the pool she took him into his room and pulled the draperies to shut out the glare of the sun while he took his nap. She curled up on the couch in the living room, a writing pad on her lap, wondering how to reply to Dr. Ferguson and thinking about this strange marriage, which was no marriage at all.

Her relations with Brad were pleasant but remote. He was so busy with patients that she rarely saw him and even when he was free he spent most of his leisure in his office, reading medical journals and going over his equipment. She had come closer to an understanding of him during the days when she had served as his office nurse but they never became more than courteous strangers in their personal life. If she had not seen him with Ricky she would have felt that he was naturally cold, unable to feel any warmth or affection for anyone. But no one could mistake his devotion to the boy or his pride in him.

". . . Such a strange and desolate country," she wrote to Dr. Ferguson. "Not beautiful but unforgettable. And, of course, the very thing for Ricky. You would hardly know him. He is as brown as a berry, as healthy as can be, and he has no trouble with his breathing. How I wish Louise could see him now!"

Jenny turned the air-conditioner higher and went back to her letter. "Brad is terribly in demand and never seems to stop work. There is hardly a night when I don't hear the telephone ring. He has a lot of problems, of course, because he lacks the proper laboratory equipment. I understand from something the bank president let drop when he and his wife asked us to dinner last night that he has been inquiring about a loan.

"I have quite a lot invested in stocks and I could sell my apartment any time for more than I paid for it. Do you know what it would cost to install the kind of equipment a doctor needs when he is at some distance from a hospital: an X-ray machine, and I don't know what. And will you help me find some way of getting it for Brad without his knowing it because I am afraid, in the circumstances, he would not accept it from me. But something should be done, if not for Brad, then for the sake of his patients."

Jenny looked from the patio on one side of the living room to the closed office door on the other. There was no point in looking out the front windows. Except during the doctor's office hours no one moved on the road. There was nothing but Mrs. Fulmer's house and, beyond it, a line of gray-brown hills. Above was the relentless blinding brilliance of the cloudless sky. The desert still frightened Jenny but she had no wish to divulge her fear to Dr. Ferguson.

"I can't imagine," she wrote, "why you should think there is anything wrong with me just because Brad was silly enough to write you that I seem to be nervous and that I've lost weight. I'll be all right as soon as I get adjusted to the heat and I can sleep, but I've been used to such late hours and to the noise of New York, and here the town is dark by ten o'clock except on movie night, and it's so terribly quiet! Isn't it foolish to be kept awake by stillness? Love from Jenny."

"What did I tell you?" Dr. Ferguson's wife declared wrathfully, some three days later, when he read this letter to her. "I declare, I could shake you! And Bradley Maxwell too!"

"Why Brad? What has he done?"

"Obviously nothing. That's the trouble. He must be blind as well as stupid. Jenny's an enchanting girl. How he can help falling in love with her I can't for the life of me understand."

"He undoubtedly has," Dr. Ferguson said coolly. "In fact, I think he was bowled over at first sight. He never married that girl to ease his way into a practice, whatever he may say. It was his one chance to win her."

"Then why," his wife retorted, not cool at all, "doesn't the idiot tell her so instead of neglecting her, leaving her alone all the time?"

"The implications were that this was not to be a real marriage."

"Implications!"

"He's not the kind to try to force a change in their relations, my dear, when he's struggling just to get a toehold in his profession. Not fair to her."

"Rubbish," said Mrs. Ferguson.

iii

But while Jenny was still trying to write a cheerful letter to Dr. Ferguson, a letter which failed to deceive his wife, she was interrupted by two callers. The first, as she saw with a sinking heart, was Mrs. Fulmer, whose darting eyes took in the scanty bathing suit.

"Well, I've been anxious to pay a real call. Of course, with my answering service I can't often get away, even to do my shopping. But a distant cousin of mine is badly crippled and I've arranged for him to come here and he jumped at the chance. He had no job at all so he was terribly hard up and he was willing to do the work for me just for his keep. He can take over so I can get out now and then and he can handle all the night calls. I declare, with patients calling Dr. Maxwell at all hours I hardly ever get an unbroken night's sleep. But Bert can have that spare room of mine and I like having a man in the house. Not that Bert would be much good in an emergency because he can't get around without crutches, but at least no woman would ever bother with him so I can count on his staying where he can get three meals a day."

Jenny had slipped her unfinished letter under a cushion as she would not put it past her guest to try to read what she had written.

"You know I've never been right through this house," Mrs. Fulmer said.

"I just tucked Ricky up for his afternoon nap. Some other time."

"I see Dr. Maxwell got Sarah Caldwell to be his nurse."

"Yes, wasn't he lucky?"

"I never would have thought her mother would agree to it. She told me once that Sarah had made a perfect fool of herself over the doctor she worked for in San Francisco, and it took a lot of doing for Mrs. Caldwell to put a stop to it."

"But why should she stop it? I don't see what business it was of hers."

"I should think a mother might be assumed to know best." When Jenny made no reply, Mrs. Fulmer went on, "And I must say I think it was real nice of her to let Sarah baby-sit when you folks went to the Moss place for dinner. She never knows when she might have an attack."

But she wouldn't bother to do it without an audience, Jenny thought, remembering what Brad had told her about his most trying patient. She raised her brows in surprise. "How on earth did you know we were having dinner at the Moss house?"

"I heard Mrs. Moss when she called to ask you and the doctor to dinner. I notice they've called it dinner ever since the Penroses came out here to settle. Supper has always been good enough for us. But I suppose, next to Mr. Penrose, Mr. Ross is the most important man in town. President of the bank, you know."

"Yes, I know." Jenny tried to control the anger shaking her voice, to employ just the right shade of surprise. "But, Mrs. Fulmer, all you are expected to do is to answer Bradley's office calls when he doesn't do it. You aren't supposed to monitor our personal calls."

She was immediately aware of her mistake. She had made an enemy of the woman and Mrs. Fulmer could be a dangerous enemy. A doctor in a small community couldn't afford to have enemies. Caesar's wife, he had warned her. She must be Caesar's wife.

Mrs. Fulmer stood up. "I'll be going on but I'll say this first. I'm much too busy to listen in on personal calls. Much too busy, Mrs. Maxwell." She turned back from the door. "You're young and not experienced. You don't know much about men. Do you think you are wise to have a foolish and susceptible girl like Sarah working in your husband's office?"

"Not only wise but fortunate. She is sweet. She reminds me in a way of my sister Louise, except that Louise was a happy woman, and happiness made her beautiful. If

Sarah ever got another chance to be happy you would see what a difference it could make."

"Well, it's early days yet." This time Mrs. Fulmer closed the door behind her with a sharp click.

Before Jenny could find the pen she had laid down on Mrs. Fulmer's arrival she heard a car door slam and a moment later the two-tone chime sounded. A tall, slim woman in lavender slacks, a thin cotton blouse, and huge sunglasses stood smiling down at her. There was some silver in her dark hair and she had a lean, intelligent face with a wide, humorous mouth.

"I am Helen Gates, Mrs. Gates. I run the motel. I meant to call days ago and see what I could do to help you get settled but I've had a sudden rush of guests. I'm not complaining! This is about the end of the season here on the desert and every extra person is a godsend."

Jenny did not quite know how it happened, but within a quarter of an hour she was chattering as freely as though she had known Mrs. Gates all her life.

"But why a motel?" she asked suddenly. "You strike me as a person who could do almost anything and that must be awfully hard work. And a motel *here* at the end of the beyond."

Her tone was more revealing than she knew but, after a swift look at her, Mrs. Gates said lightly, "Well, it was just one more experience really, and all experience is interesting. And a challenge, of course. Anyhow, I do hate to go down in defeat and admit there are things I can't do. Don't you?"

From her breezy account, her life had been a series of gay adventures. Her husband had been a foreign correspondent and they had traveled widely. Then he had developed his own line of special reporting, a career that had taken them from one trouble spot to another. Behind the lighthearted account Jenny caught a glimpse of a life of hardship and danger and discomforts met with dauntless courage and determination to be a companion to her husband as well as a wife. There was no indication that Mrs. Gates had ever felt sorry for herself, simply annoyed when she had failed to meet a challenge.

Finally her husband had developed a serious respiratory illness and they came to the desert.

"Of course," Mrs. Gates said, still speaking lightly, "Colvin wasn't one to gather any moss. He came here two years ago, just when the hot springs were discovered and people thought something might come of them and the motel had just been built. We couldn't afford to pay rent so Colvin took over the management of the motel. And then — after all, we had moved around so much that we had no roots — when I was left alone I just stayed on. I'm still trying to make a going concern of that place and some day I'll hit on the right way or die trying!"

Before she left she looked around the drab living room. "How I envy you! Look at the possibilities of this room. In mine everything is built in so I can't make changes, but by the time you've put your own ideas to work and brought in some color to fight back at the desert, it's going to be a dream. Don't you love creating your own background? And speaking of creating —" She held out a thick package. "This is a marvelous cookbook, the start-from-scratch kind for people who don't know how to use a can opener or just pop frozen meals into an oven. If you can read you can cook, and such wonderful ideas for varied menus. It makes meal-planning a lot more interesting and the results much more palatable."

Jenny looked up at her tall guest, her head tilted a little on one side like an inquisitive bird's. New York audiences would have recognized the pose of her head and the mischievous smile that transformed her face. "And how would you know that I needed a cookbook?"

Mrs. Gates' eyes twinkled. "Well, I usually do my shopping at noon and I pass the lunch stand quite often and —"

"And what do you see but poor Dr. Maxwell, looking undernourished."

The two women looked at each other and laughed.

"I'm glad we've got someone so young and pretty and gay in town," Mrs. Gates said. "Call me if you need anything, or if you just feel in the mood to grouse about things."

Jenny shook her head. "Uh-huh. My telephone calls are monitored. I might just as well broadcast. At least I can't see Mrs. Fulmer being worried for fear Brad isn't getting the right food. She doesn't approve of men."

"Her husband walked out on her a year ago. The only wonder is that he stood her as long as he did."

"Oh, so that's why! The poor thing."

Mrs. Gates gave Jenny a sharp look but there was nothing in the girl's face but compassion.

VII

"**B**RAD!"

"Yes, Jenny?"

"A Mr. Penrose, Silas Penrose, called this afternoon and asked us to dinner day after tomorrow. Seven o'clock. He said he and his son were both looking forward to knowing us. I told him I'd have to ask you because I didn't know what commitments you have and, of course, that you are always on call. He said he quite understood."

Brad raised a lazy eyebrow. "What's your problem? I should think you could do with a little night life."

"Oh, nothing. I just thought —"

He grinned at her. "Out with it!"

"Well, he made the invitation sound a bit like a royal command, a come-or-else deal."

"A royal — oh, he's that Penrose! Yes, I suppose he would. We're to be on trial, you know."

"What do you mean?"

"He's the guy who plans to endow a hospital for Desert Winds when or if they get a doctor who meets with his approval."

"So I take it that we accept."

"We accept with bells on. I'll ask Sarah to baby-sit."

"But she isn't here today, is she?"

"No, but I have another patient in Hot Springs Canyon so I can stop by. The canyon is fascinating in daylight, by the way. You should see it sometime."

"I'd be glad to see anything."

Brad, who had been on his way out, turned to give her a long scrutiny but she was bending over her cookbook and making out a shopping list so she was not aware of it.

While he drove through the canyon he kept hearing Jenny's voice saying, "I'd be glad to see anything." Aside from dinner at the home of the bank president, she had not been anywhere except to shop. The car, except during office hours, was always at his disposal. And yet from the moment when she had betrayed her horror of the desolation of the desert she had made no complaint. He had had his chosen profession and its problems to occupy him but she had nothing at all except housework, which she obviously loathed and did badly. And Ricky, of course. She was learning to cope beautifully with Ricky. Still she had no adult companionship except for that odd woman who ran the motel and whom she appeared to like a great deal. After spending an hour with her she was always gay and in good spirits.

But what could he do about it? He had tried his level best to stick to the bargain they had made but he found the situation more difficult every day. He had gone down for the third time when he first saw her poised at the top of a flight of stairs, the spotlight on her face. As he had warned Dr. Ferguson he was a human being. Propinquity, he had said. God! He had stayed away from her as much as he could, even spending most of his lonely evenings in his office.

And now he realized that her evenings had been lonely

too. Was he such an egotist he could think only of his own problems? He would have to do better, that was all. He would have to find a safe line between ostracizing himself completely and managing to be with her without losing his head. A nice easy companionship, he promised himself. Keep it light and gay and impersonal. And when a way was found for Ricky to live a full and healthy life without Jenny's help and without danger from his uncle — and such a way simply must be found — she could pick up her career as though this interlude had never been.

Don't feel sorry for yourself, he thought savagely. You always knew she wasn't yours to keep. To keep? She isn't yours at all. Remember her saying she was only marrying you on Ricky's account? Suppose you could make her love you, what have you got to offer her compared to what she could get for herself? You should never have agreed to this arrangement; you knew from the beginning it couldn't work. *Agreed?* You jumped at the chance to be with this bewitching girl, whatever the circumstances.

When he had left his patient, after a few encouraging words to the man's anxious wife, Brad stopped with his usual reluctance at the Caldwell house, wondering what new symptoms his most trying and demanding patient would have thought up since he last saw her. He grinned to himself when he recalled her aggrieved complaint that Sarah refused to divulge anything about his patients. Sarah could not be dominated on one point at least, her respect for professional secrecy.

To his considerable surprise Brad found Mrs. Caldwell in high spirits. She was in her living room raptly watching color television and wearing an exquisite housecoat that looked wickedly expensive and was in sharp contrast with the faded blue jeans Sarah was wearing. The latter had been painting the guest room a delicate rose-pink and obviously had a headache from the fumes of the paint.

"Come in, doctor," Mrs. Caldwell said cheerfully. "What a nice surprise! Sarah, surely you can stop long enough to make some iced tea. I know the doctor would enjoy it."

"She seems to have enough on her hands," Brad said more tartly than he had intended, and Sarah gave him a startled half-frightened look.

"Well, she's going to have things much easier from now on, as I've just been telling her. A dear friend of hers, Alma Deming, is coming out to pay her a long visit and — guess what? She trained as a nurse with Sarah and she wants a job. Isn't that wonderful?" Mrs. Caldwell looked at him triumphantly. "Just the thing! She can take over for Sarah as your office nurse and give you as much time as you like, the more the better, because she needs the money, and it will be so nice for Sarah to see her old friend again."

Brad looked from the mother's face with its curiously triumphant expression to the daughter's, in which he saw a kind of defeat. The older woman was clearly up to something. In any case, he had no intention of pulling any chestnuts out of the fire for Mrs. Caldwell. Not if he knew it. Certainly not at Sarah's expense.

"I'll be sorry to lose Sarah, but of course if she can provide an adequate substitute I'll be able to make out. Sure this girl knows her job?"

"Oh, yes, she's good," Sarah said. "Very good." She brushed damp, straight hair away from her face and Brad was aware of his irritation. Why on earth did the girl let herself go like that? Maybe Jenny could help her.

"Odd time of the year for anyone to be coming to the desert, isn't it? I thought the season had about ended."

"I imagine," and Sarah met his eyes squarely, "Alma didn't have much choice. She has been living with her brother and his wife. He's very well-to-do and didn't want her to work, but I suspect her sister-in-law wasn't nice to her, maybe anxious to get rid of her. So when Mother wrote —"

"Oh, this was your mother's idea."

"I just suggested," Mrs. Caldwell seemed to be on the defensive, "that if dear Alma was tired of being dependent on her brother, Sarah would love to have her and I knew of a perfect job." She added thoughtfully, "Alma is very pretty."

And what she is up to I can't figure out, Brad admitted to himself as he drove home through the canyon, except that she will never let Sarah get out of her reach again. Personally I wouldn't trust that woman as far as I could throw her.

Then he remembered that he had forgotten to ask Sarah to baby-sit. He'd make a note to do that tomorrow because the Penrose invitation was one that he and Jenny must accept.

VIII

THE Penrose house was perched on a hillside, a square structure which seemed improbably large until one discovered that it was a hollow square built around a patio in which there was a kidney-shaped pool. Here at least the desert had been defeated. In sharp contrast with the sterile land outside, the patio bloomed with palm trees, lemon trees, flowering bushes, and bright-colored plants.

The houseman who admitted Jenny and Brad led them through a wide corridor with handsome rooms on either side to the patio. As she caught sight of the two men who had risen to greet them Jenny was glad that Brad too had worn a white jacket. Their host came forward to meet them, a spare, gray man of sixty, with hard and curiously colorless eyes behind horn-rimmed glasses and a mouth with a long, immobile upper lip which gave the impression that he grudged the words he spoke.

Jenny was aware in some amusement that he was hastily revising his original impression of them. A manner that had been a shade patronizing became more gracious as he smiled at her. Jenny, in an emerald-green Dior dress that left her shoulders and arms bare, her hair brushed back smoothly and fastened in a great coil on her neck, diamond eardrops shining like stars, was not the typical small-town doctor's wife.

"Mrs. Maxwell, I'm Silas Penrose. This is a very great pleasure. I don't know how long it has been since this house has entertained so lovely a woman."

"I can answer that. Never," declared the second man. "Do you realize that this is Jennifer Haydon?" He was as tall as Brad and perhaps a few years older. Thick blond hair was worn rather longer than Brad's and fell over his forehead. He had good features, a sulky mouth, and lines of dissipation under his eyes. To some people, Jenny thought, he might seem better looking than Brad.

"This is my son Wallace. And you, of course, are Dr. Maxwell."

Jenny, watching Penrose sum up Brad, saw that the latter, though courteous, was not adopting the deferential manner the older man appeared to expect, and she was pleased.

The contrast between the two young men could not have been more striking. Brad was alert, clean-cut, disciplined. Wallace Penrose had a cynical look of boredom as though he had experienced everything and found nothing worth the effort. His manner had a careless charm of which he was clearly aware. He took Jenny's hand and seemed reluctant to let it go, staring at her in incredulous amazement.

Penrose waved his guests to chairs near the pool. "I've been receiving glowing accounts of you, doctor."

"That's pleasant to hear."

Jenny wanted to withdraw her hand from the young man, who finally relinquished it and dropped into a chair beside her. "A miracle," he said. "And I'm the guy who didn't believe in miracles. To find you here — Jennifer Haydon in person! I'm almost afraid you'll vanish if I shut my eyes. I saw your opening night in *Heat Wave*. That was the last night of the last time I escaped to New York. I sent you orchids."

"How nice of you."

For a moment he was checked by her cool tone. He was not, apparently, accustomed to having his advances discouraged or disregarded. He was wealthy enough and good-looking enough to attract almost any woman who didn't have Brad to compare him with, Jenny supposed.

"Little did I think," Wallace went on, his voice sounding unexpectedly loud in a moment of silence, "when I heard you had made the great renunciation, that it would bring you into my orbit."

"Renunciation?"

"Left the stage. Disappeared. And now, of all places, I find the incomparable Jennifer Haydon buried in the desert."

Jenny saw that both Brad and the older Penrose were listening, Brad with a curious intentness. "Not buried," she corrected. "Married."

Wallace looked amused. "I've always understood that it was the same thing."

"Wallace," his father protested, "of all the graceless things to say!"

Jenny laughed. "It depends on the person you marry. Or maybe on the person you are. Some people just never come alive and some people can make a — a —"

"A garden in a desert?" Wallace suggested, his eyes mocking her. He might as well have spoken his thoughts aloud: *Who do you think you are fooling? The Broadway star satisfied to live in the desert? You are whistling in the dark, baby, and we both know it.*

Jenny could feel her color rising. She would have given much to retort to the confident, insolent man but she remembered the bait of the hospital. They were on trial, Brad had warned her.

She leaned forward. "You're laughing at me," she brushed aside Wallace's laughing protest, "but let me tell you — oh, not about myself but about a woman right here in town, and one of the happiest, most successful marriages I've ever heard of, though she settled here after a life of world travel and adventure and association with distinguished people."

She had learned how to hold an audience by the changes in her voice and by her gestures and the inner conviction which she was able so successfully to project. She used all her technique now while she told Wallace the story of Mrs. Gates. There was a moment of silence when she had finished, broken by Wallace's comment, "Actually, all you are saying is that the woman put up with the hell of a life, kept a stiff upper lip, and now she is running a motel which is on the downgrade."

"No," Jenny's eyes sparked dangerously, "I'm telling you how a person can have a rich and wonderful life if she just has the will and the imagination to do it." She added, "And the guts, of course."

"I wouldn't know," Wallace said. "So far I've never lived my life. Just my father's." He got up restlessly, lighted a cigarette, tossed the match into the pool.

"Wallace," his father reminded him, "all those matches have to be picked up."

"So you have often told me."

Brad began to speak hastily, asking whether it was true that sandstorms could seriously damage a car. Penrose answered in his usual dry voice. Wallace was about to toss his cigarette into the pool when he caught Jenny's eye, grinned as though in self-mockery, and came back to crush it out in the ashtray.

Later, seated at the beautifully appointed dining table on her host's right, Jenny looked at the exquisite damask, the crystal, the silver, the paintings on the walls, the three men in their trim white jackets. "Picture of the Beautiful People at Home," she thought, and she was uncomfortable. The hostility between father and son was almost a tangible thing and yet, when Penrose's eyes rested on his son's handsome, sulky face, his expression was one of deep affection combined with anxiety.

Taking advantage of a sudden spate of talk between the two younger men Penrose said, his voice cautiously low, "I had no idea that our new doctor was married to a famous actress. He is a singularly fortunate man but this must be a strange part for you to play."

Jenny's smile was grave. "Does that matter?"

He was taken aback by her directness. For a few minutes he devoted himself to his cold soup. "What do you mean by that, Mrs. Maxwell?"

This time her smile was mischievous. "Just what you meant, Mr. Penrose. Does it unfit me to be a doctor's wife?"

He was better prepared for her directness this time and he answered in kind. "You know the answer to that better than I do. What do you think?"

She waited while she was served with lobster thermidor, and when she looked up she was surprised by the intensity of his regard.

"All this time to think of a good answer?" he asked, and the underlying mockery in his tone reminded her of his son.

"No, to think of the true answer. Of course it doesn't help in the sense that, before I was married, I knew nothing about Brad's profession and I had no understanding of its demands. But that doesn't mean that I can't learn."

"And you want to learn?"

"There's no choice, is there? This is Brad's job and I've discovered how right it is for him. So the more I can understand about it the more of a help I can be, or at least the less of a stumbling block."

"No choice," he repeated thoughtfully and helped himself to tossed salad. "Westerners are convinced that a meal should begin with salad. Serving it with the main course is as far as we can go without causing a minor revolution. How has the doctor solved the problem of an office nurse?"

"He was lucky enough to get Sarah Caldwell. Do you know her?"

"I've seen her around as one sees everyone in this little community, and I've met her mother. A really terrible woman. A kind of octopus, tentacles creeping around you."

"Well, around her daughter, at least. She wouldn't let her marry; she brought her here to keep her away from people." Jenny was aware of a sharp look from Penrose. "Now she has found some other nurse for Brad so poor Sarah will have to go back to her slavery. If she could only fight for herself! Heaven knows she is old enough to be leading her own life." Jenny broke off, recalling Wallace's words about leading his father's life. The blood surged into her face and faded again. And there went Brad's big opportunity, because she had spoken impulsively before she thought.

Penrose did not seem to be aware of her confusion. He turned to address a comment to Brad and the conversation became general, though Jenny took little further part in it.

After dinner Penrose suggested that Wallace show Mrs. Maxwell his collection of snuffboxes while he had a little chat with the doctor. Wallace stiffened alertly and watched while his father and Brad went out of the dining room. Jenny sat with her hands clenched in her lap. What was Mr. Penrose saying to Brad?

Then Wallace asked, "Are you really interested in snuffboxes?"

"I don't know. I've never seen any except in a museum or, of course, in any movie or play about Napoleon. Except for thrusting his hand inside his jacket he never seemed to do anything but take snuff."

"Well, come along. If you are bored you don't need to look at them."

Jenny followed him into a small room whose walls were lined with lighted cabinets. "Oh, you really take collecting seriously!"

He smiled wryly at her revealing tone. She could not have made more clear her surprise at his having any genuine interests. "Oh, I have to do something, you know. We can't all be doctors and the saviors of mankind. At this moment my respected parent is doubtlessly telling your husband about his lung lesion that not only forces him to live in this godforsaken place but keeps me prisoner here too."

His tone was so savage that Jenny, after a startled look, turned her attention to the display of snuffboxes.

ii

At that moment Silas Penrose leaned back in a chair in his library, offered a cigar to Brad, who declined, and then made a ritual of lighting one for himself.

"I'm not supposed to do this so I never smoke except in this room."

"Lungs?"

"There is a general impression that I have a fairly serious pulmonary condition." Mr. Penrose drew on his cigar. "Actually I came out here because my son got into bad company and began to drink too much. Became a problem all around. I thought the best thing, the only thing, was to get him straight away from the people he was running with. My wife and daughter came along and I built this house. We needed a lot of room, of course, because we entertained a great deal and had house guests most of the time. Then my wife died, and Wallace —" He looked at the ash on his cigar. "He doesn't know, of course, that my health is perfectly sound. He mustn't know. He doesn't like it here because there is nothing for him to do, but I have to keep an eye on him. He's a wastrel. I don't understand it. He has had every opportunity and tossed every one away."

When Brad made no comment Penrose went on, "You may have heard that I have thrown out lures to get a good doctor here, that I promised to endow a hospital if we can attract a suitable man."

Brad nodded.

"I'm no philanthropist, doctor; don't make any mistake about that."

"I wouldn't have made that mistake, sir."

Penrose chuckled. "You and your wife are salutary in more ways than one. The point is that I don't need a doctor for myself. I want someone here who can find out what ails my son, why he drinks so much, why — to be blunt — he isn't worth a damn. You and your wife are just the ticket, far beyond my expectations. Young, attractive, and not run-of-the-mill. Wallace will take to you. He has already fallen for your wife in a big way."

"I noticed." There was nothing to read in Brad's face.

"Well, now we come to it. I asked you here tonight to size you up and, if I thought you were the right man, to ask you to have a talk with Wallace. Will you see what you can do for him? Or would you rather have time to think it over?"

The ticking of the clock seemed like a time bomb. Then Brad said, "If I told you what I really think you would throw me out."

"Go ahead."

"I'd say his chief trouble is that he can't escape from you and your demands. You keep him here under false pretenses. You're living on his sympathy and his sense of duty."

"Like Mrs. Caldwell. Your wife already made that point rather clearly. Go on with your instructive remarks, doctor."

"Have you ever tried to find out what your son's interests are and what he would do if he could follow his own bent?"

"The young fool doesn't know what he wants."

"He's not that young and he's not that foolish."

Penrose laughed without amusement. "What would you say if I told you he has no real interests except in the field of art? Art! What he would like is to be the curator of a museum or even work for one in any capacity."

"What you can find reprehensible about that defeats me," Brad said.

The houseman came to say that there was a telephone call for Dr. Maxwell. When Brad returned, Penrose was waiting for him in the corridor.

"Emergency?" he asked, looking in at the room where Jenny was bending over a display case, absorbed.

She turned quickly. "Something wrong, Brad?"

"A youngster has been bitten by a dog. They are afraid the animal may have rabies. I thought I had better collect you and run."

"Where is it?" Wallace asked.

Brad read aloud the address.

"But that's a good twelve miles south of here. You go ahead, doctor. I'll see that your wife gets home safely."

IX

THE cuckoo clock in the hallway sounded eleven times and Jenny raised her head in astonishment.

"Oh, I had no idea it was so late! I'm terribly ashamed of having strained your hospitality so far, but it has been such fun and so interesting. I never knew that snuffboxes could be so different and beautiful and have such fascinating histories!" She put down carefully the one she had been examining, a lovely thing of mother-of-pearl with an exquisite miniature of the Empress Josephine. "Did this really belong to Napoleon?"

"Supposed to," Wallace said. "I couldn't find anything but unsubstantiated claims." Jenny had noticed that this most casual of men was meticulous when he spoke of works of art. "I bought it simply because it is nice to look at, not because I was sure it was authentic." He put it in her hand, closing her fingers around it. "You like it. Keep it as a souvenir of a pleasant evening."

"I couldn't. Not possibly. It's much too valuable. But thank you very much."

He did not insist but returned the snuffbox to its proper place.

"I'm sorry you have to take me home so late."

Wallace laughed. "It's a pleasure, a real pleasure, and

there aren't many out here." He brought her coat and put it around her, his fingers tightening on her shoulders. She moved away and went to say good night to Silas Penrose who was reading in the library.

"Forgive me for staying so long. It has been such a happy evening."

"I know I can speak for my son as well as myself when I say it has been a happy occasion for us. It is one I hope will often be repeated."

When Wallace had helped Jenny into his rakish convertible he laughed. "My father always sounds as though he were a Victorian, or maybe he's straight Regency. It's good to get out of doors and blow the stuffiness out of our brains."

"It may be stuffy but I like it better than no manners at all. Good manners certainly make life a lot easier for everyone and a lot pleasanter. So even if your father is somewhat formal —"

"Stuffy," Wallace corrected her. "And speaking of stuffiness, how about having the top down and getting some fresh air. Will you be too chilly?"

"No, I'd like it."

"Better tie something over your hair."

Jenny pulled a long, silvery scarf out of her pocket and wrapped it around her head like a turban, with one long end hanging over her shoulder. Wallace glanced at her and said in a negligent tone, "There isn't a girl out here with style enough to do that. To them a scarf is a scarf is a scarf."

"Or a primrose by the river brim, though I must say I never saw why it shouldn't be just a primrose. That ought to be enough for anyone. Or Shelley's skylark. Why insist that it had never been a bird? What's so awful about that?"

Wallace laughed. "My God, you can read! You'd ruin yourself if people found out. Reading isn't 'in.' Anyhow, no one learns how any more."

"I used the speed-up system. Wonderful what it can do in six easy lessons. Now I can understand even the long words."

Wallace released the top and then turned the car. Before starting down the long, curving driveway to the road below he sat with his hands quiet on the wheel, looking out.

There was a full moon, high and white and serene in a sky that extended forever. Montana, Jenny thought, did not have any monopoly on the big sky. It seemed immense, unfathomable, as it must be to astronauts in space. But, she remembered, they did not see the moon like this.

The hills and the rugged, treeless land looked like some spent star that had burned out and held nothing living. A cool breeze touched Jenny's cheeks lightly, lifted the long, shimmering end of her scarf and let it drop again. No sound anywhere. It seemed to her that her breathing and the beating of her heart must be the only sounds in the world.

Then she was shaken out of her quiescent mood by a sudden blare of rock and roll from a car radio and she saw headlights on the road below. The car passed at a terrific speed. Wallace Penrose too was startled out of his quiet mood. He switched on the headlights and the car began to drop down the long driveway.

"A penny for them," he said.

Jenny let out a long sigh. "When I first came out here

the desert frightened me because it was so empty. By moonlight it's rather shattering, isn't it? A challenge. Not that you feel you could tame it or even want to, but as though it would be a tremendous victory to learn to live with it."

"Jennifer Haydon," Wallace began.

Jenny turned to look at him, twin moons reflected in the gray eyes. "Jennifer Maxwell."

"Is that the way it is?"

"That's very much the way it is," Jenny said and gasped. Why, it was true! She was so staggered by that moment of revelation that she almost forgot her companion until she heard Wallace laugh.

"Okay, we'll let that go. For now."

The challenge in his voice alerted her. A number of men had fallen in love with her and she had learned how to cope with them. She did not, in any case, intend to permit any emotional complications with Wallace Penrose. Anyhow, she was so startled by the discovery that she was in love with her husband that she had no time to think of Wallace. She didn't *want* to be in love with Brad. She didn't *want* to be married to a poor doctor who was just getting started, who was at his patients' call day and night. She wanted a husband to whom she would be the central interest.

She moved over as far as she could on her side of the car but Wallace did not attempt to touch her. Indeed, he did not speak again until he drew up in front of the house.

"No lights? Does that mean the doctor is still out on his errand of mercy or does he go to bed without making sure you get home safely?"

She did not reply but put her hand on the door. Before

she could open it he had switched off the motor and his headlights. He turned to her and took her in his arms, pulled her toward him and kissed her while she struggled to free herself, to prevent his lips from finding her mouth.

At length she wrenched herself free. "Never make that mistake again."

"Jennifer, I'm mad about you," he said thickly.

Jenny's hand fumbled with the catch and then she nearly fell out as the door was jerked open. A hand grasped her arm and yanked her out of the car. She was jostled to one side as Brad leaned in and lashed at Wallace's face. There was a moment of blank astonishment and then Wallace's head snapped back.

"Brad," Jenny said in a choked whisper, "you've hurt him."

"I meant to," he said in a voice she had never heard before.

"But, Brad —"

"Go into the house, Jenny, and stay there. I'll handle this."

"But —"

"You heard me."

She gave a little sob and went up to the house without a backward look, closing the door behind her. Sarah, who had fallen asleep on the couch, an open book tumbled on the floor beside her, sat up, startled.

"Oh, Mrs. Maxwell!" She yawned and laughed at herself. "I must have fallen asleep. I — somehow I had the impression that you came in some time ago. I thought I heard the car drive up and that you went in to look at Ricky."

"How has he been?"

"Perfect. The most adorable child I ever saw. I love being with him. Even if — that is, when Alma comes, I hope I can still baby-sit for him." Her voice changed. *"Is anything wrong?"*

"Nothing at all. I'm glad you had a nap. We didn't mean to keep you so late but the doctor had an emergency call." As Sarah stumbled sleepily to her feet, Jenny asked, "Wouldn't you like a glass of milk before you go?" But before pouring it she went into her own room and peered cautiously out the window. Brad was standing beside Wallace's car, speaking in a voice too low for Jenny to hear. Wallace, dabbing at his nose with a big handkerchief, made some comment. Then he switched on his headlights and Brad turned back to the house.

Jenny hastened into the kitchen, where she filled three glasses with milk and cut a chocolate cake she had made that afternoon, using Mrs. Gates's cookbook. She had intended to display this masterpiece proudly but now she set the milk and the cake before Sarah and Brad, without glancing at the latter.

"How was the boy who was bitten by the dog?" she asked.

"Okay. He's an only child so they were all hot and bothered. Nothing wrong with the dog."

"It's funny," Sarah said. "I thought I heard you come home half an hour ago, doctor."

There was a little pause. "I did." Brad looked at his watch. "I came in to see whether my wife was home and to take a look at Ricky. Then I thought I'd go back to collect Jennifer. Instead," he looked sheepish, "I fell asleep in the car."

"I didn't notice it in the carport when we got here," Jenny said.

"So I supposed."

Brad took Sarah out to her car. When he came back he watched Jenny stacking the used dishes in the sink. Her first cake and they had cleared their plates. She felt a glow of pride and she was comforted by something Mrs. Gates had said to her: "My dear, don't be upset and injured when your husband doesn't praise your cooking. The best praise is to see him eat it and enjoy it." Just the same, she thought, a little praise never hurt anyone.

"Jenny," Brad said, as she started toward her room, "when we got married —"

"I know. Caesar's wife. But I couldn't help it. He — it was just so unexpected. What did you do to Wallace?"

"I gave him a nice bloody nose, that's all. I didn't want to hurt him, just humiliate him. But next time he insults my wife —"

"That's enough, Brad!" Her voice was shaking. "You made a fool of yourself by fighting with Wallace Penrose and you are far more insulting to me in your attitude than he was. Men always think it's worth trying. You must know that. But if you believe for one minute I encouraged him you ought to be ashamed of yourself."

"Jenny!"

"What right have you to demand anything of me?"

"No right at all. Yes, by God! If you are going to kiss anyone it's your husband."

He jerked her around to face him and kissed her, eyes and cheek and lips and throat. She could feel his heart thudding. When at last his arms dropped she stood quite still, her eyes on his face.

"Brad?" she said at last, her voice questioning.

"I'm sorry. That was inexcusable."

"Yes." Her voice was flat, drained of emotion. "I'm sorry too. I had begun to think that I liked you very much." She went into her room and closed the door. For the first time she turned the key in the lock.

ii

Next morning Jenny was awakened by the sound of Ricky's infectious, chuckling laughter, and she realized that she had overslept and Brad was feeding the boy. The events of the night before came rushing upon her: the dinner at the Penrose house, the hostility between father and son, the revelation that she was in love with Brad, Wallace's tiresome lovemaking, and Brad's kisses. Caught in the strong circle of his arms she had been shaken by an emotion as strange to her as it was overpowering. When he had released her she had almost held out her hands. And then he had said that he had been inexcusable and she realized that his kisses had been without tenderness, almost a kind of anger. Well, at least she had been spared the shame of betraying her own feelings to him. It was small triumph but it was all she had.

She got up, showered, put on white shorts and sandals and a white blouse, brushed her hair until it shone, and tied it back with a white ribbon. Then, because it was so long and thick that it made her hot, she twisted it in a coil at the back of her neck. I'll have it cut short, she decided. This is no climate for long hair and it isn't as though it would ever matter for stage parts. That's ended.

Something nagged at her, something she had forgotten.

There was something different about this day. She tried to remember what it was. Some errand she had to do? No, not that. Perhaps it was the change in her relationship with Brad, who had been a friend and was now an enemy. And then she remembered. It was her birthday. She was twenty-two today. Odd to have a birthday and no one know — or care. In New York there would have been a party tonight after the performance and presents on her breakfast tray and a stack of cards and letters and continual telephone calls of gay good wishes.

By the time she reached the living room Brad had finished feeding Richard. He looked quickly at Jenny, and the sight of her set face checked what he was about to say.

"There's coffee made," he said, "and the cantaloupe is wonderful this morning. How do you want your eggs?"

"Just toast. I'm not hungry."

The telephone rang and Brad scooped it up. "Dr. Maxwell . . . Yes. Hang on." He turned to Jenny. "Long distance for you. New York."

It was Margaret calling to wish her a happy birthday, to ask about Ricky, and inquire how things were working out.

"Your letters always sound cheerful but I know you so well, Jenny, and I realize how difficult and uncongenial housework and cooking must be for you."

"I'm learning," Jenny said, "and yesterday I baked a chocolate cake. It's good too . . . Yes, he's blooming; you'd hardly know him; he's so brown and he has gained weight and he is learning to swim — well, at least, he kind of splashes around without being the least bit afraid. In fact, I can hardly keep him out of the pool. He just tumbles in as casually as though he were a frog, and I got one of

those lifebelt contraptions . . . No, we aren't celebrating
. . . No, honestly everything is all right, Margaret." She
laughed. "You just think I can't get along without you."

She put down the telephone and went to the dinette to
drink the coffee Brad had poured for her. "That was my
old housekeeper. She wanted to know how things are
working out."

Brad brought her cantaloupe and some toast.

"Shouldn't you be on your way to the hospital?"

"I have only one patient over there right now and he's
checking out today. Sarah won't get here until afternoon
and I've caught up on my records." He watched her, an
untouched cup of coffee in front of him. "Jenny," he began.

The two-tone chime sounded and with a mutter of annoyance at the interruption he went to open the door.

"Sarah! Great Scott, what's all that?" As he noticed the
girl behind her he stepped back. "Oh, come in, won't
you?"

Sarah came into the room followed by a tall girl whose
striking good looks underlined Sarah's pallid drabness.
Both of them had their arms filled with packages and letters. Sarah dumped hers on the table beside Jenny and her
companion followed suit.

"Mrs. Maxwell," Sarah said, "this is Alma Deming.
When I got home last night I discovered that she had
already arrived and my mother — that is, we wondered if
it might not be a good idea for Alma to start right away;
at least I can begin to show her the ropes. Oh, Dr. Maxwell, this is Alma."

He shook hands with her. "If you're as good as Sarah
says, you're hired. There's not a lot to do, of course, be-

cause I'm just starting to build a practice. The worst of it is having to cope with all the records and the billing and the forms to fill out and the stuff for insurance and Medicare and so forth."

"Chiefly 'and so forth,'" Alma agreed. She seemed to be supremely self-confident. She was appraising Brad not as a doctor but as a man. They made a stunning couple, Jenny thought, both tall and dark, both with a kind of arrogant assurance, both good looking. It was apparent that Alma Deming found Brad attractive. With his brisk, impersonal manner it was difficult to guess at his reaction to the girl.

"The reason we came so early," Sarah said anxiously, as usual feeling apologetic, "is that mother doesn't like to wait for the mail to be delivered, so I pick it up every morning. And they were simply swamped with all this stuff for Mrs. Maxwell so we decided to bring it along."

"What on earth —" Brad began, looking down at the packages, the magazines, the letters.

"I've had some things shipped out from my New York apartment," Jenny explained. "There is more stuff coming, furniture and all that. Then I had *Variety* forwarded and — the rest is just because of my birthday."

"Oh," Brad said blankly. Then his face flushed a dark red. He unlocked the office door and went in, closing it behind him.

While the two enchanted girls watched, Jenny opened her presents: a crystal vase from Steuben, as fragile-looking as spun sugar and etched with the exquisite figures from *Swan Lake;* an antique jade ring which opened to reveal a tiny pagoda, and inside that an infinitesimal miniature of Buddha; a diaphanous negligee of lemon lace with matching satin slippers; a music box with roses embossed on the cover, which played "Love sends a little gift of roses."

Sarah got up. "We'd better get going. We can look over the equipment and the books. Doctor won't be busy this afternoon. I'll just say hello to Ricky and then we'll go." She went to untangle a pull toy whose string was wrapped around a chair leg, her face soft as it always was when she looked at him. "A very happy birthday to you, Mrs. Maxwell."

"I think," Jenny suggested, "that from now on it had better be Jenny, don't you?" She smiled at the tall, glowing girl who was like a dark Viking. "I hope you'll like the job. It will be a great help to my husband."

Alma smiled at her, revealing magnificent teeth. "I'll like it. But if that isn't my luck! I find a really stunning man and he's already married."

When Jenny had settled Ricky under the big umbrella near the pool, well sheltered from the sun, she brought out her packages, magazines, and letters, and dumped them on the swinging couch with a canopy, which she had purchased for the patio. Once more she examined her presents and recalled Margaret's loving and anxious voice, which had been like a hand stretched out across the more than three thousand miles that separated them, to assure her of an unchanging and unchangeable affection.

She read her letters and birthday cards and then opened *Variety*. She already knew that *Heat Wave* had continued its long run with no abatement in public enthusiasm as a result of the usual summer doldrums or the retirement of the star. She was glad, she told herself; of course she was glad. But in spite of herself she felt a sharp pang. She was not even missed! Her understudy had managed the supremely difficult task of filling satisfactorily a part that had been written to fit another girl's personality and talent.

She flipped the pages of *Variety* with a feeling of nostalgia. How far away and long ago seemed the glittering life of the theater.

"Cinderella," she read, "lives again." She was about to turn the page when her own name caught her eye. She went back to the article. Hilda Harris, it said, had lived the dream of all young actresses. Hired as understudy for the fabulous Jennifer Haydon, she had replaced her when Miss Haydon withdrew from the cast of *Heat Wave* at the time of her marriage.

It was Miss Haydon whose insistence had led a skeptical management to give the girl a chance. It was Miss Haydon's patient hours of direction that had encouraged Hilda Harris to do the part not as her predecessor had done it but in her own way. Acts of generosity in sharing the limelight were as rare in the theater as elsewhere, almost as rare as in the political arena, but Miss Harris, who had achieved stardom almost overnight, owed an immense debt of gratitude to Jennifer Haydon, a debt she was most eager to acknowledge.

Much of this had already been communicated to Jenny in letters from her former understudy, but it was pleasant to have this public acknowledgment. It meant that she had not yet been completely forgotten, though the memory of the public is notoriously short. The paper dropped from her hands to the floor of the patio. She stared with unseeing eyes at the blue pool. She was pausing at the top of a flight of stairs, waiting for the applause to die down so that her first line might be heard. She was leaving the theater to smile at the admirers who waited in snow and rain to see her pass. She was in her luxurious apartment, ringing the bell for service.

And a bell did ring, the two-tone chime, and she went to open the door to the Penrose houseman. He handed her a bulky envelope. "Mr. Wallace Penrose sent you this with best wishes for a happy birthday."

Before she could speak he had returned to a big station wagon. Across the road a curtain dropped into place.

Jenny went slowly back to the patio, pushing her hair away from her eyes. How terribly hot it was! She looked at the thermometer. Over a hundred degrees already. She would give Ricky his dip in the pool and then take him back to the coolness of the house.

She dropped the envelope on the couch and turned as the boy peremptorily claimed her attention. She laughed, picked him up, and fastened his life preserver around him. Then, hurriedly, she went in and put on a bathing suit. She heard the door chime when the suit was half on and called, "Just a minute. I'm coming."

Mrs. Fulmer answered, "It's all right. It's just me. Oh, good heavens!" And she was running across the living room.

Jenny fastened her suit and ran out. Mrs. Fulmer was screaming and Richard was floundering in the pool, trying awkwardly to reach the beach ball he had thrown in.

Ricky, disturbed by the older woman's hysterical voice, began to whimper, and Jenny dropped over the side, laughing, and pushed the ball into his hands. In a moment his distress was forgotten and he tried to shove the ball under the water, chortling with delight when it popped up again.

After a few moments, aware of the sun blazing down on the pool, Jenny said, "That's all, little chicken. Out you come."

Ricky gave a perfunctory howl of protest, not that he expected it to make any difference but simply to assert his independence. Jenny took him into the living room, gave him some toys, closed the door, and returned to the patio.

"It's so hot out here, don't you think —" She broke off, staring in disbelief at Mrs. Fulmer, who was holding in one hand an open letter and in the other a mother-of-pearl snuffbox. *"What are you doing?"* Her voice sounded strange to her ears.

"The envelope broke open and the letter and this — this thing — fell out." Mrs. Fulmer's tone was half defensive, half aggressive.

"But that was private. People don't read other people's letters."

"Mrs. Maxwell, I came over here in the friendliest of spirits, as a neighbor, because I am an older and more experienced woman and I wanted to point out —" She became aware of Jenny's blazing eyes. "There was a full moon last night and I saw what happened when Wallace Penrose brought you home. Kissing you right in front of your house! No wonder your husband got mad. I think you might explain —"

"My wife owes you no explanation for anything she does, Mrs. Fulmer," Brad said as he came out onto the patio. "If I am satisfied —"

"You didn't seem to be last night," she snapped, goaded by his reaction to her interference. "And here he is, daring to send her a present, and valuable too, if I don't miss my guess."

"No, Brad," Jenny said hastily, seeing his expression. "She — she means well."

He laughed shortly. Mrs. Fulmer got up with what dignity she could. "I've tried to be a good neighbor but I have to admit I don't see how you two can fit into this community much longer. We're not smart New Yorkers, just plain, decent people. And when Mr. Penrose hears how his son is dangling after a married woman — and he won't put up with that for a minute, I can tell you right now — and when folks see that — that siren who is going to work in the doctor's office —"

Unexpectedly Brad exploded into a shout of laughter.

"Laugh if you like. Mrs. Caldwell told me all about her. Sent away from her brother's house. When your own family doesn't want you, then there's something mighty wrong."

Brad moved to one side and waited. Reluctantly she walked past him. The door slammed behind her.

"Well!" Jenny dropped onto the couch and looked blankly at Brad. "You really shouldn't have laughed."

"It didn't make things much worse. I came in here — I wanted to say —" He broke off, his eyes on the snuffbox. "Quite a work of art!"

"Oh, Brad, I do wish you wouldn't be such a fool. He offered it to me last evening because I admired it. He said it was a souvenir of a pleasant evening. I refused it then."

"So he brought it back."

"He sent it by his houseman and I don't know why. I haven't read his letter. No one but Mrs. Fulmer has seen it. Read it for yourself. Go ahead!"

After a look at her stormy face Brad picked up the note

to read it to himself. Then he looked down at her, an odd expression on his face, and read it aloud:

"Last night you refused this as a souvenir of a pleasant evening. Then I spoiled that evening for both of us. I took home a bloody nose, as your husband must have told you, which I think greatly amused my father, so this should even my score with your husband, don't you think, and wipe the slate clean. I told him last night he had my word I'd never bother you again.

"According to *Who's Who,* this is your birthday. Will you give a home to the Empress Josephine as a sign of forgiveness and acceptance of my profound apology? In the future I will remember that you are no longer, as you reminded me, Jennifer Haydon; you are Jennifer Maxwell. With sincere wishes for a happy birthday. Wallace."

For a moment Brad twisted the note in his hand. "It's a nice thing, isn't it? I hope you'll keep it, Jenny, if you like it. I wish I'd known about your birthday. When I heard you speak of it I felt — sick."

She didn't say anything, just watched him gravely.

"Look, Jenny, there's nothing pressing today and both girls are here to look after the office and Richard. Can't we — we haven't had a single day off — can't we drive over to Pasadena and just — celebrate a bit?" He held out his hand, a boyish grin on his mouth but his eyes anxious, imploring. "Mrs. Maxwell, may I have the pleasure?"

"Why, thank you, doctor, I'd be delighted." She put her hand in his.

X

JENNY picked up her small white handbag, put it down while she adjusted pearl earrings, and dabbed her best perfume behind her ears and on her throat. She picked up the handbag and set it down again in order to improve the line of her lipstick. She was taking a great deal of trouble over her appearance though she had rarely looked better in her life. Her skin had tanned to a pale gold that made her eyes seem wider and more brilliant than before. Her thin, sleeveless white dress fitted perfectly.

She remembered the day she had bought it in New York. A blustery day of drenching rain. News of her retirement and approaching marriage had been prominent in newspapers, on radio, and television. The clerk who sold her the dress had assumed she was buying a trousseau and assured her that the dress would be perfect for a midwinter honeymoon in a hot climate. How long ago that seemed! Only two months had passed, yet the girl who had bought the dress and the one who now wore it seemed like different people.

It was as if Jenny *felt* that she was happy, rather than *knew* she was. A day's outing in Pasadena! What was there in that to cause her heart to tumble over and over as it seemed to be doing?

She found Brad waiting for her in the living room, joking with Sarah, who was playing with Ricky. As a rule he had learned to conform to the casual style of southern California, which permitted a man, even a professional man, to go about without a jacket and even without a necktie. But today he wore his best white suit and carried his jacket over his arm. He was terribly good-looking, Jenny thought. How could Sarah be so absorbed in Ricky when Brad was in the room?

She gave some instructions which Sarah noted down. "We'll try not to be as late as we were last night."

"Take your time," Sarah urged them. "Alma will be with mother in the evening, you know, and that's the main thing. And there's no one I would rather be with than Ricky." As she smiled down at the little boy Jenny felt a queer jolt at the heart. When her face was alight, Sarah's resemblance to Louise was more apparent.

She was quiet as Brad helped her into the Lincoln. "We're off to see the wizard," he whistled. "The wonderful wizard of Oz." As Jenny made no response he asked quietly, "What's wrong, dear? Are you still — that is —"

"It's Sarah. She's so like Louise when she has any expression in her face at all. It always jolts me. Louise was special."

"Sarah really loves the boy," Brad said, his mood changing to meet hers. "And he loves her. She seems to know instinctively what a child needs. It's a shame she can't escape from that mother of hers and get married and have children of her own."

"You know, Brad, I have a suspicion that Mrs. Caldwell got Alma Deming here just to take Sarah's job and make sure she stays at home. I wish —"

"What do you wish?" There was gentleness in Brad's voice she had never heard in it before.

"I wish something could be done to help free Sarah."

"I've been thinking that too. It seems to me that together we could work something out."

Together. "Let's try."

Brad took one hand off the wheel and covered hers. For a moment he held it hard and then he released it as a gust of wind struck the car on the side, swerving it across the line. Ahead of them the road grew dimmer.

"We're running into a sandstorm and I wanted this day to be perfect for you."

And suddenly the day was perfect. "When we turn west up there we'll be moving away from the storm."

"Mr. Penrose," Brad sounded embarrassed as he mentioned the name, "tells me a bad sandstorm can ruin not only the paint job but pit the glass on the car to such an extent that the windshield has to be replaced."

"I was just thinking: The bill of sale is in the car glove compartment. I know that's careless of me but right now it might be useful. Why don't we go to a dealer in Pasadena and see if we can turn in the Lincoln: It's almost new, there aren't more than ten thousand miles on it, and we would be able to get a small secondhand car that sand couldn't damage much. At least it wouldn't matter."

"That's an idea, and it would certainly be cheaper to run. You wouldn't mind?"

"Of course I wouldn't mind. It would be better all round. We wouldn't have to worry about hurting this car. Why, if you are a good bargainer we might even get two little cars."

"Now that," Brad said alertly, "is definitely a sound idea."

"My ideas are mostly and nearly always sound," she assured him. "And I have another idea. Mrs. Gates has been telling me about the problem of getting people to come out on the desert in the summer. The motel is practically empty, month after month, so she loses most of her winter profits and barely gets by."

"I can't," Brad said humbly, "change the weather."

"You disappoint me, doctor. The fact is, there are hot springs of some sort here. No one has done any kind of job of exploiting them. They might attract people who can't afford Palm Springs but have arthritis or are recuperating from lameness or something and would feel a lot better in one of those hot baths with the gadgets that sort of churn up the water." As Brad laughed at her description she said, "You know what I mean. Well-being without effort; everyone's dream."

"Now and then I am afraid that I married an intelligent woman."

"Is that bad?"

"A fate worse than death. Don't you remember how careful Fielding was to assure his readers that Sophia would be a good wife for Tom Jones because she didn't have an idea in her head, or if she had she wouldn't dare express it before the superior male."

"Bring on your superior male, if you can find one," Jenny jeered. "No, honestly, Brad, isn't there some way to exploit the hot springs? I'm not just considering Helen Gates, though she is super. You'll like her immensely when you really know her. But think of Desert Winds.

Imagine how it would boom if it could attract year-round tourists. And people might even decide to stay, so the real estate man would really be in business and —"

"And where does the hard cash for this project come from?"

"You don't need to throw cold water on everything! If Mr. Penrose can afford to build a hospital he could finance a campaign to promote the hot springs and build, oh, whatever would be needed: pools and recreation rooms and I don't know what."

"Not to build you up too much, you've got something there, keed. Who's to break the big idea to Penrose? At this point I don't think he has a high opinion of me. We more or less crossed swords last night and after I sent Wallace home with a bloody nose I've probably cut my own throat."

For a moment the awkwardness was back between them and then Jenny said, "Well, that will be all right. At least I'm pretty sure it will be all right. When I left, Mr. Penrose said he hoped we'd have a lot more happy evenings together and I think he meant it. Perhaps you took the best way with a man like that, Brad. If you'd been a 'yes, sir' sort of person he'd have had no use for you. He likes to bully people but he doesn't like the people he can bully. But I don't think either of us should approach him about a thing like that. I'll talk to Mrs. Gates. After all, she's the one to whom it would matter most."

Brad laughed. "And after the way you built her up last night, her courage and her guts and all that, you are not only intelligent, you are chock full of guile, and that really alarms me."

"But I wasn't thinking of that at all when I spoke of

her. Why, we're on the freeway already! The time has gone so fast —"

Brad gave her a swift look and a little smile twisted his mouth, and then it was grave again.

"What do we do first? How about seeing what we can do with the Lincoln?"

"You're still sure that's what you want?"

She nodded emphatically.

It wasn't until after Jenny had parked her little Renault behind Brad's Volvo and they were sitting at lunch at the Stuft Shirt that she said blankly, "Brad, We've been so busy selling the Lincoln and getting those two little secondhand cars and registrations and California licenses and all, that we never thought that we'd have to drive home separately."

"It occurred to me, and on our one day out. Well, we'll have to make up for it another time."

When she had ordered and the waiter had removed the big menus she noticed that Brad had laid a small package beside her napkin. She opened it and sat staring at an old-fashioned gold locket on a gold chain. Inside there were two pictures: One was a romantic figure of a man wearing a big cowboy hat and with Brad's smile; the other was a girl with a small, heart-shaped face and a sensitive mouth.

"My father and mother," Brad said. "The locket was my mother's and had her parents' pictures; and it had belonged to her grandmother and it had pictures of her parents. You should have seen my great-grandfather's whiskers! Looked like some of the kids today. If — you won't want to wear it, of course, but I thought —"

Jenny's hand closed over it. "I love it."

"I wanted to give you something nice but there wasn't time to find anything."

"You couldn't have given me anything nicer." The glow died out of her eyes. "And, of course, when — that is, I'll give it back to you when — I mean —"

For a few moments the day was dimmed, then the waiter came with shrimp cocktails and in a few minutes they found themselves laughing.

An up-and-down sort of day, Jenny thought later. It was almost as though they both wanted to be happy but things kept happening to spoil it. The mention of Penrose had cast a shadow; then Jenny's reminder that this was not a real marriage had dimmed their gaiety. They had gone to the Huntington Library and wandered through the gardens and sat under the great mesa oak at the entrance and again found words tumbling over each other because they seemed to have so much to say.

Overriding her protests, Brad said they could stay on as late as they chose, so they left one of the cars in a parking lot and drove into Los Angeles, through the appalling traffic of the freeways, and threaded their way at length to Beverly Hills and the Brown Derby.

They were halfway through dinner when a young actress whom Jenny vaguely remembered seeing in a bit part on Broadway squealed, "Jennifer Haydon!" and came to the table accompanied by the other members of her party. Jennifer shook hands and laughed and answered questions and introduced Brad, but when they had gone on to their own booth Brad's lighthearted mood was gone and restraint built up between them. For some reason she could not understand he seemed to be resentful of Jennifer Haydon, to be made uncomfortable by the curious eyes that peered at them.

"Just celebrity hunters, most of them," Jenny explained, "or people who want to go home and say, 'I saw so-and-so today.' It's part of the job and I don't even notice it anymore. And if people get satisfaction out of looking at someone else and letting names drop, it's about all the poor things have to interest them."

Just as they were about to leave, a party of four passed their booth on the way to the back of the restaurant. One of them, Jenny noticed, was a well-known television actor. But it was the man who brought up the rear of the small procession who stopped short.

"My God!" he exploded. "And *now* you should change your mind and come out here."

Jenny laughed. "I haven't changed my mind. Mr. Prince, this is my husband, Dr. Maxwell. Brad, this is the celebrated Mayley Prince, who is a kind of king out here. I told you about him and his offer."

The egg-shaped man had to look up some distance into Brad's face as they shook hands. Then he leaned across the table and gave Jenny's cheek a noisy smack. "I suppose I ought to congratulate you, Maxwell, but I'm darned if I will." He looked at Brad again. "How did you lure this girl away from me?"

"I don't know."

After that there was no recapturing the holiday mood. Jenny was too accustomed to having her appearance in a restaurant create a stir to be at all affected by the heads that turned to watch while she and Brad walked out of the Brown Derby. The head waiter met her at the door.

"Miss Haydon, I didn't recognize you. I hope we'll often have the pleasure."

"Thank you." When they were outside she said, "I don't remember where you parked, do you?"

"This way." Brad took her arm, steered her around the corner. "You're chilly."

"My coat is in the car. What on earth — oh, I forgot we had sold the Lincoln."

He helped her into the little Volvo. "Seem pretty small to you?"

"Well, that's what we wanted, wasn't it?" she asked in surprise.

"There's no air conditioning."

"People have been known to survive that before, so I expect we can."

"You're quite a girl, Jenny. Let's go somewhere and dance, shall we?"

When they were seated at a small table in a night spot which was neither garish, noisy, nor vulgar, she discovered that Brad was an excellent dancer, better, in fact, than she was, a piece of information which failed to please her as much as it should have. He must have danced with a lot of girls to be able to do it so well, she thought, and she wondered what the girls had been like, and whether he thought of them now.

And then she looked up to see his eyes on her face, questioning her as they had questioned her during their brief wedding service, and she smiled at him.

"That," a man remarked to his wife, "is the best-looking couple I've seen in months."

She followed his eyes and nodded. "They're in love. Really in love. And what a stunning man!"

XI

THE birthday celebration outwardly made no change in the relations between Jenny and Brad. In the days that followed he still spent most of his evenings in the office, "keeping up with the literature," he explained. Now that she had a car at her disposal, Jenny devoted hours to exploring the desert, sometimes with Ricky strapped into the seat beside her, sometimes with Mrs. Gates, who was more satisfactory as a companion, while Ricky was left in Sarah's delighted care.

"How's the siren?" Mrs. Gates inquired one afternoon while they were driving through the canyon.

"Siren?"

"The mysterious dark beauty Brad has installed in his office. I understand that she is a dangerous woman with a dubious past and someone ought to warn the doctor's wife of what is going on." When she saw Jenny's outraged expression she laughed.

"Let me guess," Jenny said. "The local broadcasting station, Mrs. Fulmer."

"No credit to you for guessing."

"Do you suppose anyone believes that ugly nonsense?"

Mrs. Gates shrugged. "There may be a few, though most of them should know better, not only because they are familiar with the woman's poisonous tongue but because by now they know both you and the doctor and they should realize how absurd it is. If ever a man was in love with his wife it's your husband."

Jenny's heart leaped. Mrs. Gates was too astute to be mistaken. Could Brad be falling in love with her at last? Then she remembered his saying that no man wanted a prima donna in the house.

"I'm surprised she hasn't gossiped about me." Then Jenny's eyes opened wide in surprise. "She *has*. I can tell by your expression. But what on earth — oh, I suppose it's Wallace Penrose."

"Don't let that worry you."

"Did she," Jenny asked in a small voice, "say anything about Brad fighting with Wallace?"

"Did she! The original story was a corker. Dr. Maxwell almost beat young Penrose to death. But, since Wallace was seen the following day in good condition except for a swollen nose, no one took that seriously. Look here, Jenny, don't make too much of that. Wallace Penrose has a reputation for making passes, so there's no reflection on you."

"But I've never even seen him since that night," Jenny said. "Not a single time." She did not mention the snuffbox and the fact that, with Brad's approbation, she had written a note accepting the gift and the apology and promising to remember only a happy evening whenever she looked at it.

"That I can well believe!" Mrs. Gates was amused. "Every human being within fifty miles would have known about it before the day was out."

So it was unfortunate that, next time Jenny went riding

— driven out by loneliness and the silence of the house when Richard took his nap and Brad was busy — she encountered Wallace Penrose. She had been driving aimlessly, not caring where she went, simply seeking new sights to give her new ideas. But the faceless desert could not serve her need today, and the only thing she saw that moved was a large snake coiling its way across the road, leaving her, like Emily Dickinson, with zero at the bone.

She was on an empty road when the thing happened. Without warning the Renault swerved sharply to the right. She hauled hard on the wheel, slowing down, and again it swerved out of control. At first she believed that the steering column had snapped and then she realized as the car bumped along that she had a flat tire.

She had never in her life changed a tire. There was nothing moving in the whole desolate landscape. On this side road no help might arrive for an hour or two or even three. She looked hopefully through the glove compartment but the instruction manual was missing.

After looking carefully around for snakes she got out of the car. Immediately the scalding heat struck her bare head. There was some way of getting out the tire. The car dealer had explained it to her and had told her where to find the parts of the jack and how to assemble them. She had, she supposed, listened, but it had not registered. The idea of having to change a tire by herself was too monstrous to believe.

She was leaning over the trunk, half inside and half outside, when a pleased voice said, "My, my, what pretty gams."

She straightened up and dropped back onto the dusty road. In her relief she ignored Wallace Penrose's provocative expression. She held out her hand. "I was never so glad to see anyone in my life. Look!"

"I'm looking."

"Not at me, you dope!"

"The thing is —"

"The thing is," she interrupted, "do you know how to change a tire or don't you?"

"I have acquired that difficult knowledge," he said gravely, "and I will now proceed to demonstrate. I would like to show off for your admiring eyes but, on second thought, you get back in the car. You ought to know better than to come out without some kind of head covering. Sunstroke is no minor inconvenience, let me tell you!"

She climbed in obediently, grateful to be out of the blazing sun, though the car itself was scorching. When she had pointed out where the parts of the jack were stored and explained how to release the spare tire from its home under the license plate, he jacked up the side of the car, removed the flat, put on the spare, working with a minimum of effort and more efficiency than she would have expected of so idle a man. The huge Mexican sombrero that not only shaded his eyes but protected his whole body from the sun added a touch of glamour to his appearance. The only thing that had made him look ridiculous, she reflected, had been Brad when he had punched that very handsome nose.

When he had finished, put the flat tire on its proper compartment, and dismantled the jack, Wallace came back to the window, dusting off his hands and smiling at her.

"There you are, lady!"

"I'm terribly grateful. I can't tell you how grateful. I didn't know what in the world to do."

"You might," he suggested, "show your gratitude by driving me home. It's a fur piece and the temperature must be a hundred and twenty. You'd hate to have me drop in my tracks, especially after my Boy Scout deed."

She laughed and moved over in the passenger seat so that he could take the wheel. "Do you often walk in this heat? I should think it would be dangerous."

"So," he told her, "is stagnation. I swim. I knock around a few billiard balls. Now and then my father honors me by playing me at chess. I look at catalogues and see what new acquisitions the museums are making. But there are twenty-four hours a day to fill in. Twenty-four!"

He was driving very slowly, not more than twenty miles an hour. He tossed the sombrero into the back seat. "Do you come this way often?" His tone was casual.

She shook her head. "This is the first time I've taken this particular road. As a rule I don't go out alone."

He looked at her swiftly. "Afraid?"

She ignored the challenge in his voice. "No, I just prefer companionship though I suppose I'm afraid of a lot of things. There was a big snake crossing the road just before I got that flat. I don't like rattlers. They scare me stiff. And the wind — when it screams it terrifies me; something savage and untamed let loose. Somehow a danger you can see isn't as bad as one you just feel."

"How do you fill your days?"

"Housework and cooking and trying to think of new things to eat and learning how to cook them and planning to brighten up the house. And there's Ricky, of course. He takes a lot of time."

"Haven't you forgotten something?"

"What's that?"

"The estimable doctor."

"Oh."

He stopped the car and turned toward her, one arm across the back of her seat. "Look here, Jennifer, I don't know why you came out to the Mojave Desert. I don't know why you sacrificed a brilliant career. But I do know one thing: It wasn't for Bradley Maxwell. You're alone here, just as alone as I am. No, I'm not going to make love to you. I gave your husband my word. Oddly enough, I have a way of sticking to it. But we could be friends. I need one, God knows, and I think you need one too. Perhaps we could help each other."

"I don't need help."

"Oh, yes, you do. Any man who knows anything at all about women, and I, as you have doubtless been told, know a great deal about women, would know that you are not living a full, happy, normal woman's life. All right, don't say anything. I'll do the talking. Whether I can help you or not I'll leave to the future. But you can help me. How you can help me!"

"Well, how?"

"You must know the setup. Everyone knows the setup. My father has a serious lung condition and, because my mother and sister died a year ago, he feels I should stay with him, as he has only a few months to live. God knows that would be fair enough. But he keeps me on a short leash. He watches every drink I take. He raises hell and practically has a stroke if I get away for a few days to Los Angeles. I haven't been in New York since the night of the opening of *Heat Wave* when," he added without expression, "I saw you and fell in love with you for keeps. I haven't been in Europe in nearly three years. Once I had set up my cabinets of snuffboxes I didn't have one single thing to do. I'm going mad out here, hoping when I take a walk I'll die of sunstroke. For God's sake, help me, Jennifer."

"Well," she said, her voice matter-of-fact after his melodramatic outburst, "in the first place you don't really want to get sunstroke or you wouldn't protect yourself with that big sombrero."

In spite of himself his lips twitched.

"In the second place, I can't help you."

"You could."

She shook her head. "No one can help you but yourself. Your father keeps you on a short leash, as you say, because you drink too much. He's worried about you. He thinks you aren't trustworthy." She glanced at him and saw the stricken look on his face and realized, with a pang of pity, that more than anything else he needed his father's approval. "For heaven's sake, why don't you find yourself a job you like and fill up your days with something interesting?"

"I want to work in a really good museum, but that's out."

"You know, Wallace, I believe that if you could prove to your father that you can carry through a job — *any* job — and keep sober while you are doing it, he would back whatever you really want to do. Gladly."

"And what kind of job would you suggest I do? I could clerk at the Emporium, but unfortunately the owner doesn't need help. I could serve as a waiter at Kelly's but they need extra help only during the winter months when people are foolish enough to come here. I could assist Mrs.

Gates at the motel, except that she doesn't have anyone staying there in the hot months. Have you any other ideas?"

It was intended as a rhetorical question but to his surprise Jenny said promptly, "Yes, I've been thinking about it for a long time." In her excitement the words tumbled over each other while she outlined her idea of exploiting the hot springs and attracting tourists on an all-year-round basis. "It would take money, of course, but it would really make Desert Winds bloom."

It was some minutes before Wallace spoke and then, for the first time, it was without any undercurrent of flirting with her. "Well, I'll be damned! We'd need first to find out where the best springs are and we'd have to —" He fell silent again, ruminating. "Well, I'll be —"

A horn sounded and he started the motor and pulled the car farther to the right. A gray Chevrolet drove past slowly. When it had gone Wallace seemed genuinely concerned. "I'm sorry, Jennifer. Now I've really got you in trouble."

"Why?"

"That was Mrs. Fulmer. What a nice juicy bit for her! Here we are parked on a more or less deserted road. She'll add it up and get scandal."

"You aren't to blame," Jenny said reassuringly. "She can't really do any harm."

"She's not going to get a chance. I'll think of something. Oh, I know! I'll call your husband and tell him not to worry because you are late. I'll explain about the blowout and having to change the tire and say that you were kind enough to drive me home. That ought to take the wind out of her sails!"

"You mean she still listens to our private calls?"

"Of course she does. Well, there's nothing like using a wrestler's own strength to throw him." He stopped at the foot of the long driveway that wound up to the great, square Penrose house.

"Thank you, Wallace. I'd have been lost without you."

There was a curiously wry look on his mouth, as though he were laughing at himself. Then he said, "I'm the one to thank you, Jennifer. I'm off to clear your reputation and then I'm going to tackle the old man about the hot springs." He sketched a salute and then walked up the drive, the sombrero shading his body.

ii

Sarah looked up to smile when Jenny came in. Ricky, who had been dragging a pull toy around the room, ran to her.

"Been a good boy?" Jenny asked him.

He nodded emphatically. "Good," he assured her.

Sarah laughed. "He's been a little demon. He's been into everything he could get his hands on and when I was getting him some milk and a cookie after he woke up from his nap he got hold of the flour canister and turned it upside down. There was flour everywhere, walls, floor, stove, cabinets. You wouldn't believe two pounds of flour could scatter so far. I think I got all of it, though."

"Not what landed in your hair. Very becoming. Like an eighteenth-century French marquise."

Sarah looked at herself in the mirror. "Heavens, what a mess!"

"Look here, Sarah," Jenny began, "talking of — wait

a minute!" She ran into her bedroom and came out with a framed picture. "This was Ricky's mother, my sister Louise."

Sarah looked at her in astonishment. "But I thought he was your son."

"She died after she learned that her husband was missing in action in Vietnam. She gave him to me. No one knows but you—"

"It's safe with me." Sarah looked at the photograph. "How lovely she was. He's like her, isn't he?"

Jenny nodded. "So are you. That's about the first thing I noticed. Except that you don't care. You don't look after yourself or do your hair the right way or buy the right clothes or — or exert yourself!"

Sarah looked once more at the picture and then put it down gently on the table. "What's the use?" she asked at last. "A woman doesn't dress for herself, she dresses for the man she loves. And the man I loved married another girl."

"I heard about that. You walked out on him, didn't you?"

"Walked out!" Sarah protested. "I had to go with my mother, didn't I?"

"Did you? In that case, you deserved what you got. But, Sarah, there are other men and you are young and if you would exert yourself you could have a real life and maybe a son of your own. Sometimes I could shake you. You aren't really fooled by all your mother's symptoms. You know she wants to keep you around because she needs someone to boss. If you don't go to Pasadena and get your hair done — and pick a really good hairdresser even if it costs a fortune — and buy a new dress, I'll — I won't let you see Ricky again."

The two girls laughed and then Sarah said, "I might do it, at that. Someday. I have a little money in my savings account."

"Spend it."

"Perhaps. You look hot and tired. I'm in no hurry. I love being with Richard. You go ahead and get a shower before I leave."

When Jenny had taken a cool shower she slipped into shorts and a sleeveless shirt and sandals, and tied back her hair with a yellow ribbon. When she came out Sarah said, "I think you have the loveliest hair I've ever seen."

"It makes me so hot I'm thinking of having it cut short."

"Oh, don't do that! By the way, these just came in the mail. They look like belated birthday presents."

Jenny sorted out the personal letters — a thick one from Hilda Harris and one from Dr. Ferguson — and looked at the packages. She guessed by its size the contents of the one sent by Margaret. It was the book in which she had kept the notices of her performances. The second was big, heavy, and unwieldy, with Hilda Harris's return address.

"I'll just run into the office for a minute and speak to Brad," she said, "and then I'll take my time over these."

She tapped on the door and went in. Alma Deming, who was busy making out bills, looked up to smile at her. In her crisp white uniform she seemed even prettier than she had the first day they met. In the meantime Jenny had seen little of her though Brad had reported that she was better at her job than Sarah because she had more self-confidence and she had a quality that reassured nervous patients.

"Doctor's out, Mrs. Maxwell. Mrs. Brigg's baby isn't keeping to time schedule and the doctor has taken her to the hospital, following the ambulance. Thank God, there was one available. Doctor may be quite late." She looked down at the desk, straightening the bills, playing with her pen, "He works much too hard, and going back and forth in this heat —" Her voice trailed off. "Sometimes I wonder whether he eats enough. It's not always easy to eat in such heat, but he does use up so much energy."

She's in love with him, Jenny saw. Aloud she said, "I don't suppose anyone knows how hard a country doctor works."

"No, people don't realize." This time Alma looked directly at Jenny. "Oh, I'm glad you got home all right. Mr. Wallace Penrose telephoned to explain about the accident."

"But it wasn't an accident."

"No, I'm sure it wasn't." There was no mistaking the tone now. "I've left a note for the doctor about it, but this is a first baby so he may be very late getting home." She smiled dismissal at Jenny and returned to her bills.

As though, Jenny thought furiously when she had gone back to the living room, she was the one who belonged there and not me. Then it occurred to her that Alma did have the better right in Brad's office and that she was of far more use to him than Jenny could be.

When Sarah had gone Jenny settled down to her mail. First she read the letter from Dr. Ferguson. He cited prices, named dealers, made suggestions. "An X-ray room must be added on to the present building and I would suggest the following equipment if Brad is largely self-supporting there." A long list followed. "I can make arrangements at this end for shipping most of these things but Brad will have to arrange locally to have an annex built on to the office before there is any point in ordering supplies. An X-ray machine has special safety requirements, of course. It sounds to me as though Brad is doing a good job and building a sound practice. More power to him — and to you, my dear."

She set the letter aside, frowning. It had been her intention to have everything delivered without informing Brad, but apparently that would not be practicable. She turned to the letter from Hilda Harris. It was excited, exultant, and grateful.

"No girl ever owed so much to the generosity of another," she wrote. "If you haven't seen the article in *Variety* I'll send it to you. It would have been so easy for you to keep silent so the producer and the author would have looked around for another star name to replace you. Or you could have let me go ahead without the advice you gave me to play the part my way. All I have I owe to you, and how I know it! I hope you are as happy as I am. You deserve to be.

"I am shipping you the photographs that were hanging in the star's dressing room. You probably forgot them but I know you'd like to have them."

So that was the meaning of the big, unwieldly package. For a moment Jenny held it and then she put it down to open the third letter, which informed her that the furniture she had requested had been shipped and should reach her any day.

As Alma Deming had warned her, Brad was late that night, having helped a new baby into the world. Jenny saw Alma drive away from the office, and saw Mrs. Fulmer's curtain drop as the car turned the corner. She shivered. Having Mrs. Fulmer for a neighbor was like living on the edge of a gigantic spider web and having to watch every movement lest you be entangled.

After Ricky had had his bath and supper and been put to bed, Jenny took a quick dip in the pool and then, for the first time, looked through her wardrobe and put on the exquisite lemon lace negligee which had been one of her birthday presents. She brushed her hair until it shone and tied it back with a gold ribbon. In the kitchen she fixed herself a light supper and, remembering Mrs. Fulmer's comment about leaving dirty dishes, cleaned up from her scratch meal.

Back in the living room she opened the big package and looked at the photographs, one by one, with their glowing inscriptions: "For darling Jennifer," "To our Fabulous Jennifer with love," and, from her leading man, "With devoted love," and his name scrawled in big letters. As he was a happily married man and devoted to his children, Jenny accepted the inscription in the lighthearted mood in which it had been written.

The two-tone chime sounded and she scrambled to her feet. Before she could reach the door it opened and Mrs. Fulmer came in, her eyes missing nothing from the sheer negligee to the photographs.

"I heard about your accident," she said, "and I wanted to be sure you got home all right."

"But you must have known that," Jenny said gently.

Mrs. Fulmer was impervious to sarcasm. She came to

look at the pictures. "Actors!" she exclaimed. "Stage actors. I knew people collected pictures of movie stars, but stage actors — oh!" The sound was jolted out of her as she looked at one of the photographs Jenny had not yet had time to examine. It was of Jenny herself, at the climax of the second act of *Heat Wave*. She was wearing red velvet lounging pajamas designed by Mainbocher, and she was clasped in the arms of the leading man. Beneath was pasted a notice from a New York newspaper. "One of the most unexpected and delightful moments in this altogether delightful play is the impromptu love scene at the end of act two. Leon Grant has never been more witty. Jennifer Haydon reached her peak in a ruefully gay scene in which she restrained any temptation to overplay the part."

"Well," Mrs. Fulmer said, and looked at Jenny as though she had never seen her before, "so you were an actress. I must say I never dreamed — but I suppose their ways aren't like ours."

Jenny held on grimly to her temper.

"My, the Four Corners paper would sure like to know about you. They run stories about people who aren't half that important. Well, I just wanted to be sure you were all right." She looked around the silent room. "Doctor has to be away a lot of nights, doesn't he? And that Deming girl can come and go as she likes."

When she had gone, Jenny swept together the pictures, those she had looked at and those she had not, and stacked them at one end of the couch. Mrs. Fulmer could imply more evil in a phrase than anyone else she had ever heard of.

To take her mind off the annoying woman she unwrapped the package Margaret had sent. As she had supposed, it was a book of newspaper notices of her performances. For a few moments she turned the pages idly. She had expected to feel a wave of nostalgia but she found that she was barely skimming the lines of print that once had so delighted her. Her mind was on two women: Mrs. Fulmer with her disgusting ideas, and Alma, who seemed to have set herself up to be a guardian angel for Brad. Alma indeed!

Jenny slammed shut the book of clippings, and went to switch on the television set, saw part of a western, and shut it off. With all the wonder of the West, why were the western pictures so unlike the truth, such a travesty of it! How long the evenings were. Twenty-four hours to get through, Wallace had said bitterly. And every hour like twenty-four, she thought.

Without any particular plan she went into the kitchen, where she put a clean napkin on a tray, poured milk, put on a plate some brownies she had baked, and then made a ham sandwich. After looking at the tray she made coffee and filled a thermos. She went into Brad's office and put it on his desk, because it was to his office he would return and not to her. On the desk she saw a neat transcription of Wallace Penrose's telephone call. For a long moment she looked at it. Then she began to smile. It was what he called her guileful look, the one he most distrusted. She chuckled to herself. I've got guile I haven't even used yet, she warned him silently.

XII

JENNY climbed gingerly to the top of the ladder and tried to screw the fixture into the wall. "Careful," Mrs. Gates called. "Watch your balance."

Jenny steadied herself with one hand against the wall and then tried again. She leaned backward to wield the long screwdriver and slipped. For a moment her arms flailed as she tried to find some support and then she was falling backward. She heard Mrs. Gates scream, heard running feet, and then, miraculously, she was caught before she struck the floor. Brad's arms held her firmly. She let her head rest against his shoulder, felt the thudding of his heart, and looked up into his white face.

"What the hell were you trying to do?" he shouted furiously, and Jenny smiled to herself. He had been afraid. Terribly afraid. She made no attempt to free herself, resting comfortably in the circle of his strong arms. Then he released her and stepped back. "You all right?" In spite of himself he could not conceal his fear. "You should know better. What were you up to, anyhow?"

"Mrs. Gates has been helping me remake the draperies, the ones I had sent out from the New York apartment to brighten up the room. The old fixtures wouldn't hold them so I was trying to put them up."

"I'll do it." Brad went up the ladder and adjusted the new fixtures. Then, following the anxious instructions of the two women, he lifted the heavy rod that held the draperies, climbed carefully up the ladder, and, with a good deal of grunting, managed to fit the two ends safely into their sockets.

When he had climbed down the women sighed with relief and busied themselves in adjusting the folds of the draperies, drawing them tightly closed, pulling them open, studying the effect.

"Well?" Jenny said expectantly.

"What?" Brad asked.

"Well, do you like the room?"

"Oh. Oh, sure." He had started toward the door and then turned back to say, "Oh, I forgot what I was going to tell you. Alma's car is in the garage being serviced so I said I'd drive her home."

"Why not let her take my car? She can bring it back in the morning."

Mrs. Gates caught her lower lip firmly between her teeth and busied herself in adjusting a fold in the new draperies.

"And remind her that we are expecting her for dinner."

"She knows. Mr. Penrose is going to pick her up." Brad reached the door of the office and turned back. "You keep off that ladder."

"Yes, doctor," Jenny said meekly, but when he had gone she wasn't meek at all. "All day long we've been slaving, moving in the new furniture and hanging pictures, and remaking those draperies, and washing the crystal and polishing the furniture so this house will look brighter and prettier, and what does he say? He says,

"Oh sure," and he didn't even look around him. Not one look. Sometimes I'd like to take an ax to the man."

Mrs. Gates laughed. "That's what you say. Well, if I'm to dress properly to do you proud at this dinner party I'd better get back to the motel. You're sure you understand about the roast? And better use that canned hollandaise — it's quite good — until you've practiced a bit more with making it from scratch. That has to be last-minute stuff. That's a good rule: Never serve anything to guests until you've tried it out for yourself."

"I have it all written down. I'm so grateful. Without your help I'd never have managed."

Mrs. Gates smiled at her. "You're an odd person."

"In what way?"

"In some ways you are completely self-possessed and self-assured. In others you are oddly humble. You're the rare person who does things for other people and isn't aware that she is doing them."

Jenny was surprised. "You have taught me how to cook and how to manage the house. You encouraged me to brighten it up and make it nicer to live in. And most of all you've taught me a little about having guts, and being cheerful no matter what happens. What on earth have I ever done for you?"

There was a twinkle in Mrs. Gates's eyes. "At the moment you've arranged a dinner party to enable me to follow up Wallace Penrose's approach to his father about developing the hot springs. What an engaging fellow he is! And knows it, of course. I wouldn't trust him an inch, for all his charm."

"You could trust him, though, if he said you could. He hasn't much strength but he has his own code of honor and he'd stick to it. Anyhow, this means as much to him as it would to you; that is, if Mr. Penrose agrees to help him exploit the hot springs."

"Don't tell me that Wallace the Wolf wants a steady job!"

"Not this one, but this is just a stopgap. What he really wants, though he doesn't know it, is his father's approval."

Mrs. Gates smiled. Jenny seemed so young and frivolous and yet she constantly surprised by her insight, by the gentleness of her judgment of other people — with the notable exception of Mrs. Fulmer and, Mrs. Gates thought in amusement, the lovely Alma Deming.

"Was there any awkwardness about inviting Alma tonight without asking Sarah and her mother?"

"Of course I'd have liked to have Sarah but if I'd asked her without her mother, she'd have been called home in the middle of dinner because Mrs. Caldwell had a spasm of some sort. And I definitely didn't want Mrs. Caldwell. There would have been no chance to talk about the hot springs project because she would have taken over the conversation and spoiled everything."

Although she had been in the habit of keeping her personal worries to herself Mrs. Gates could not help saying, "Jenny, do you think it will work?"

"I don't know. I hope so. Just don't let Mr. Penrose's manner get you down. And you could kill two birds with one stone, if you cared to try. Mr. Penrose is awfully fond of that son of his, but he disapproves of the fact that Wallace isn't just like him. You might drop some comments to show how impressed you are with Wallace's ideas."

"Wallace's ideas?" Mrs. Gates's eyebrows rose. "Wallace is simply brimming over with your ideas, so don't try to pull the wool over my eyes, but I'll try to build him up with his father. And talking about two birds with one stone, I realize it was only in order to keep your table balanced that you asked Alma Deming tonight. You wouldn't be throwing bait to the wolf, would you?" She winked at Jenny and went out to her car, laughing.

ii

Jenny, flushed from cooking, had never looked prettier than when she opened the door to welcome her guests. She had worked hard over the meal and her table gleamed with the silver and crystal and linen she had unpacked that morning. Sooner or later she would have to tell Brad that she had sold her New York apartment, or perhaps, if he didn't even notice the new furniture, the subject might never come up. In any case, this was no time to tell him. Tonight things simply must go well. So much depended on it. And Brad was in an unpredictable mood. From the time when he had come in from his office, after giving Alma the keys to Jenny's car, he had been in a foul temper. She knew that he was deeply angry and assumed it was because she had prevented him from taking Alma home.

After all, she had no right to object to Brad's friendliness with Alma. They had mutual interests that she could not share. Anyhow, he was free, wasn't he, to like another woman. And Alma was so lovely!

She would have been surprised, when she opened the door to greet her guests, if she had known that Alma's heart sank when she saw Jenny in her simple but exquisitely cut dinner dress, the kind that only an inspired couturier can produce. How lovely she was! And she generated a kind of excitement around her through sheer vitality. No girl could compete with that.

The Penrose men had brought Alma with them, and Wallace, after a rueful and half-mocking look at Jenny, which showed that he knew what she was up to, devoted himself gallantly to the dark Viking. When Helen Gates arrived, a few minutes later, Jenny scarcely recognized her. For the first time she saw her without a slack suit. She wore a severe dinner dress of black with silver, with an antique silver bracelet on one wrist and no other jewelry except for her wedding ring. With her black and silver hair she was easily the most distinguished person in the room, in spite of the competition of two younger and prettier women. A glance at Mr. Penrose showed Jenny he was surprised and impressed by her. Just what he expected of a motel keeper she did not know, but it was certainly not this woman with her sophistication, her easy flow of good talk, her polished wit.

Silas Penrose looked around the room at the furniture, the paintings, the lamps on gleaming tables, the lemon satin draperies that shut out the desert. "You have really made the desert bloom, Mrs. Maxwell, and you've created a perfect setting for yourself."

His words attracted Brad's attention and for the first time he studied the transformed room, recognizing colors and pieces he had seen in Jenny's Park Avenue apartment. He shot her a look she could not interpret, but fortunately his manners were too good for him to betray any sign of bad humor and the evening became, without apparent effort, the most spontaneously gay that Jenny had spent since her marriage, except for the one night when she had danced with Brad in Los Angeles.

She had left it to Wallace to decide on the right time and the right method in which to introduce the subject of the hot springs development, but, instead, it was his father who took the initiative.

He turned to Mrs. Gates. "My son seems to have come up with quite an idea and he tells me he has discussed the possibilities with you in a tentative way. What do you think, Mrs. Gates?"

She brought her hands together with a quick movement. "I think it would transform this place, bring in people, improve business, develop the whole community."

"You think that, do you?" His face was never expressive, and his upper lip, which rarely moved, concealed any sign of what he was thinking. "Have you considered the question of costs?"

Her eyes twinkled at him. "As I haven't a red cent to invest in anything there would be no point in my considering costs."

"I've gone into it a bit," Wallace said. His voice was still lazy but his eyes were more alert than Jenny had ever seen them, without his usual cynical boredom. "I've talked to more men in more departments than I ever knew existed, but I finally found the ones who could supply the answers. It's a big project. We need to find the location of the hot springs. Then there's the question of providing the right kind of pools, which is quite a project in itself, with costs what they are today. Then, if the place is to prove a tourist attraction and persuade invalids to stay on here for any length of time, perhaps even to rent or build houses, we'd need additional electrical power for air conditioning, and more attractive accommodations, and considerably more in the way of entertainment than the present weekly movie."

"And that would run into how much?" Penrose asked.

"I have the figures at home."

Alma Deming leaned forward. In ice blue that left her arms and back bare, she was like a statue of Aphrodite, Jenny thought. Apparently the men thought so too. Certainly they were all watching her when she said, "But, Mr. Penrose, this is terrific! If you can carry this through, some day you'll have your statue set up here in the town square, as the founder of the community, and very handsome it will look too."

Silas Penrose was about to make one of his tart comments when he realized that she was not addressing him but his son. He looked quickly from one to the other.

"I'll probably be older than the town fathers by the time I've carried this thing through," Wallace said.

"By the time *you* have," his father ejaculated. "Using what for money?"

Wallace grinned at him. "When I went to Pasadena and Los Angeles to get specific information on this project I also talked to a couple of banks. I can raise enough to get the thing started, at least. After that, when I have some publicity going, I can probably get other people to come in on the deal." He looked at Alma. "You're wasted in a doctor's office," he told her with an impudent glance at Brad. "Wait until I've started operations and I'll send you around to publicize the project. One look at you and there will be a stampede."

"That," she laughed, "is definitely an idea."

Jenny, aware of Mrs. Gates's amused eyes on her face, refused to look up.

"You've given this matter a good deal of thought," Penrose said in surprise.

"If it's worth doing at all," Wallace said, deliberately sententious, "it's worth going at in the best manner I can. And so far as raising the initial amount is concerned, I think I've got it made."

"I'll go over your figures when we get home," Penrose said. "I never turn down a sound investment."

Jenny saw the quick clenching of Mrs. Gates's hands and the way they relaxed in sheer relief. If the project were to succeed she would be assured of an adequate annual income.

When the Penrose men had left, taking Alma with them, Mrs. Gates held out both hands to Jenny. "My dear, how can I thank you? If this thing should go through — do you think there is any chance it will? I suppose that depends on Mr. Penrose."

"No, it depends on Wallace. If he can keep sober and stay on the job I'm sure his father will provide the financing. He wants to be proud of Wallace. He needs to be proud of him. Just as Wallace needs his father's approval. Aren't they stupid not to see each other's point of view?"

"People often don't, even those who love each other very much; perhaps most often those who love each other. Good night."

"I'll see you to your car," Brad said, and picked up a flashlight to take her out onto the dark road.

By the time he came back, Jenny had removed her dinner dress, and in shorts and halter, covered by a big apron, she was tackling the dinner dishes.

When Brad returned it was from his office and not from outside.

"Well?" she asked anxiously. "How do you think it went?"

"You did quite a job on the old man, didn't you? Little Miss Fixer-Upper."

"Brad!"

"Let the dishes go. I want to talk to you, Jenny."

"Just a minute." She finished stacking the dishes, delaying the moment when she would have to face Brad's smoldering anger. She was sick with disappointment. She had worked all day to make the house bright and attractive for him, and struggled to make her first dinner party a success; she had sparked an idea that might well prove to be helpful in solving personal problems for Mrs. Gates and Wallace Penrose, and that might even have a long-range effect on the whole community. She had transformed the house and made it beautiful. And instead of a single word of commendation Brad was glaring at her, calling her Little Miss Fixer-Upper. It was because of Alma, of course. He was as aware as Wallace himself that Jenny was deliberately trying to bring the two of them together.

But when she had come back to curl up in her favorite chair from the Park Avenue apartment, with its down cushions, Brad had no reference to make to the dinner party. He pulled a letter out of his pocket, a crumpled letter, which he had apparently read and reread.

"Why didn't you tell me that you had sold your apartment?"

She was so astonished that she could think of nothing to say.

"When you said, some time ago, you were having stuff shipped out from your apartment to make this place more attractive I believed you."

She was bewildered. "But that was true, Brad! Don't you like it at all?"

"What did you get for the apartment? And," he went on without waiting for a reply, "just how much did you get for the stock you sold? You pretty well wiped out all you had, didn't you? But if you think for one minute I'm living on your charity you have another think coming."

"Brad!"

"And don't try to sidetrack me by going all helpless and appealing. It won't work, my girl. Nothing you can say or do has any effect on me."

"Yes, I know that."

He looked at her suspiciously but her subdued tone seemed genuine enough. The radiance that had kept her face alight all evening was gone now. She looked tired and curiously defeated and almost plain. He stifled an impulse to say: "I didn't mean it, Jenny. Don't look like that.

"What's wrong?" she asked. "I've never seen you like this before."

"This," and he held out the crumpled letter, "is from Dr. Ferguson. It seems you sold your apartment and practically everything else you had to buy an X-ray machine and other equipment for my office, and build on an annex. Dr. Ferguson said I must arrange locally for the building of the annex to house the X-ray equipment. He said you hadn't wanted me to know you were paying for it but he felt I should be informed. I should darned well think so! Did you assume I was the kind of heel who wants his wife to support him?"

In her relief that Brad's anger had not been aroused about Alma Deming Jenny almost laughed aloud. Then she said, "Aren't you being egotistical as well as bad-mannered? I wasn't thinking about you except as this community's doctor. I was thinking how far people have to go for X rays, and for a lot of laboratory work you could do here."

She hadn't been an actress for nothing. She didn't dare reveal her relief at the cause of Brad's anger. She whipped up a spurious air of indignation. "If you don't care for the welfare of your patients I do. This is just a — a sort of investment in human beings. Turn it down if you like, but you'd be a bigger person if you went ahead. You can pay me back some day, with interest, if you like, and if that helps convince you that you're a big, strong man who can stand on his own feet."

As she spoke she rose to her feet and made the gesture that was so effective in the last act of *Heat Wave*. Brad's surprise at her counterattack was followed by an appreciative grin. "Okay, spitfire. We'll call it a loan, but just the same you're a little finagler." He took a step toward her and then stopped abruptly. "Here, you've worked all day and I'm not sleepy. I'll finish the dishes. You must be worn out. Go to bed."

"I'm not sleepy either."

They worked in companionable silence. When the last of the silver had been restored carefully to its felt-lined chest Brad said, "How about a dip in the pool? Help you sleep."

He was already standing beside the pool when Jenny

came out in her brief suit, her hair hanging loose, a cap in her hand. This is a mistake, he thought. What was wrong with him tonight? He watched her pull on her cap and slide over the side of the pool and plunged after her. They swam the length of the pool half a dozen times.

"Had enough?" he asked as he pulled himself up. He stretched out his hand and drew her up beside him and smiled down at her. "It was a grand party, Jenny," he said gently. "A successful party. The house is transformed; it looks wonderful, and I never expected to have you turn out to be such a marvelous cook." There was no moon but the sky was brilliant with stars. "Don't go in yet."

There was something in his voice Jenny had never heard before. "I'll get us a snack," she said breathlessly. "Some milk and ginger cookies I baked yesterday."

When she came out with the tray he took it out of her hands. "I haven't thanked you for leaving a tray in the office."

"I thought — you're up so late — and you don't often come into the house — I'd better leave it there."

He turned to her abruptly. "You must know why I don't come in, Jenny. It's because —"

The telephone rang shrilly and Brad, muttering something under his breath, went to answer it. In a few minutes he came to the door. "A man named Wister on Crest Road. His wife says he is having some sort of attack. See you in the morning," and he ran into his room to change.

Jenny toweled herself dry, changed to thin pajamas, and went for a final look at Ricky, who was sleeping soundly with his head at the foot of the crib and one foot on the pillow. She turned him right side up, pulled a sheet over him, and bent over to kiss his cheek. Leaving the door open between his room and hers she went to bed and lay staring out at the star-spangled sky until she saw Brad's headlights sweep across the ceiling. He was home and all was well. She turned on her side and slept.

XIII

SOMEWHAT to everyone's surprise, Wallace did not lose interest in the project after his first burst of enthusiasm. Even while the desert grew hotter and hotter and occasional sandstorms made life miserable, the little community began to buzz with activity. For the first time Mrs. Gates was going into the summer season with every room at the motel filled with engineers and specialists in various fields who had come to study the situation, make plans, and draw up estimates. The lunch stand was doing a thriving business and expanding. Kelly, who served only dinners, was beginning to seek extra waiters and he planned to provide lunches as well. Wallace himself seemed to be everywhere, escorting his experts around the desert and supervising the construction.

Brad was busier than ever. The newcomers seemed to have a propensity for getting themselves bitten by rattlesnakes or spraining ankles or suffering from sunstroke and severe sunburn. He was a racehorse harnessed to a plow, Jenny thought, and she knew that Desert Winds could not offer him the scope he needed. So far he had been too busy to go ahead with work on an annex to house an X-ray machine and an enlarged laboratory and, in any case, while work was being done on the hot springs development there were no accommodations to house more workmen.

There was nothing more Jenny could do. She had turned almost all the money she had received from the sale of her apartment over to Dr. Ferguson to purchase the equipment Brad would need. From now on she would have to be more careful about the money she spent. She had assumed responsibility for supporting Ricky and herself, and it was going to be more difficult to keep her bargain. She had some money, of course, but how she could earn extra income in Desert Winds she could not imagine. Anyhow Brad would raise the roof if he knew she was thinking about getting a job.

As she had fallen into the habit of doing, she took her problem to Helen Gates, whom she found in a small lounge beyond the pool at the motel, deserted at this time of day. It contained a cold-drink machine, hot coffee in a thermos, ice in a small refrigerator, canvas chairs, and a rack of magazines. She was lying on a deckchair, sipping iced coffee and flipping the pages of a woman's magazine.

"Picture of a hard-working woman," she called gaily. "Fix yourself some iced coffee. I'm too lazy to stir."

"How are things going?"

"I actually had to turn down some man from San Francisco, one of the countless specialists it takes to get this job rolling, I thought the poor devil would have to commute from Four Corners until Wallace rushed in to the rescue and offered to put him up at the Penrose house."

"Without asking his father?"

"So far as I can make out, Silas Penrose is taking a new lease on life. Wallace hasn't had too much to drink since this thing started." She sipped her iced coffee and waited for Jenny to explain why she had come.

"Suppose," Jenny began, "you wanted to earn some money and you lived in Desert Winds, where there weren't any jobs for women, and anyhow you didn't want anyone to know you had to earn money. How would you do it?"

Mrs. Gates sorted this out without difficulty. "Ever since the Four Corners weekly ran that article about 'Famous Actress in Our Midst,' people have been wildly curious about you. In your position I think I'd sort of casually drop the idea that you'd like to contribute something to this charming community of which you are now a part."

"Cynic!"

"Quiet! I'm struggling with an idea. Oh, of course. The annual church fair. You can produce a play, using local people. And," Mrs. Gates added triumphantly, "with her usual generosity Mrs. Bradley Maxwell, the former Jennifer Haydon, will also conduct a class in speech and take private pupils. Her purpose is not only to teach people how to speak well and effectively but also to arouse interest in creating a permanent repertory theater, as part of a developing cultural center in this rapidly expanding community and blah, blah, blah. Fill in the rest yourself."

Mrs. Gates went on in the artificial tone of one reading a commercial. "Realizing that people prefer to pay for what they get," and she broke off to say in her normal voice, "and what a liar that makes me!" Then she continued with her commercial spiel. "Mrs. Maxwell will make a nominal charge of ten dollars a lesson for speech pupils and will, of course, charge more for private instruction. There is a growing demand for well-trained young people for the stage and television at a time when there are fewer schools. In fact, the day of the professionally trained child actor has almost vanished and there is a real need to be met."

She set down her empty glass. "And if that doesn't bring half the town beating a path to your door I'll eat my hat! Everyone — but everyone — thinks his child can act."

"You are the most wonderful woman I know," Jenny told her. "You are the most wonderful woman in the whole world."

"Why, of course. Now run along. I've got to see about the laundry and order more soap for the bathrooms and call Henkins about that light switch in room four."

ii

Jenny's offer to produce a play to raise funds for the church, using local talent, brought an immediate response. So did her decision to start a speech class. Mrs. Gates had understated the case. Not only half the proud parents in town dragged reluctant children to Jenny for lessons, but an incredible percentage of adults showed up to try out for parts in the play. A long-distance telephone call to Beaver brought his agreement to let her produce *Heat Wave* for charity without paying royalties.

"It's your play, after all, Jennifer, even if you did walk out on me, *and* queer my chance on television."

"I'm sorry."

"Well, the truth is that what Mayley Prince wanted was you. I was just being taken along for the ride."

"I'm sorry," she repeated.

He laughed. "It's okay, darling. Don't fret. While *Heat Wave* is bringing in the cabbage I can keep the wolf from the door. So you want to produce *Heat Wave* out there in the desert. What are you using for actors? Rattle-snakes?"

"I don't know yet."

"Good luck to it."

Somewhat to her surprise Jenny was besieged, but she had always been at her best when she was involved in her own profession. Within a week she had established a routine. Mornings she held classes, both private and general instruction; in the afternoons she took care of the house and did her shopping and planned meals; in the evenings she auditioned for the play. It took some persuasion to get Wallace Penrose to try out for the leading man. Alma Deming was chosen for the leading lady. Helen Gates, though she claimed bitterly that she was being blackmailed, tried out for the part of a sardonic aunt of the leading man. A garage mechanic, one of the young engineers, a serving boy from the lunch stand, the real estate dealer, the banker's wife, every girl between sixteen and thirty, appeared to read a part. Some of them were unexpectedly good. Most of them were terrible. But the most unexpected applicant was Mrs. Caldwell.

"I feel," she explained to Jenny, "that exertion in some art form would be good for my nerves."

Jenny's heart sank. "You understand, Mrs. Caldwell, that rehearsals must be regular and the cast dependable."

"That's just it. Having something worthwhile to do and stimulating people to be with would be just the answer."

Stimulating people. Mrs. Caldwell had heard that Silas Penrose had offered the use of his big living room for rehearsals. The part Jenny asked her to read was that of a busybody neighbor, not a big part but one that had considerable bearing on the plot. It was not a flattering role but, to Jenny's astonishment, Mrs. Caldwell did it well.

So it happened that, in a season when the desert normally baked, silent and ugly, with no one stirring out of doors except on the most necessary errands, Desert Winds became a whirlpool of activity. The engineers and workmen were stripped to shorts, sandals, and Mexican sombreros. They swarmed like ants. They blasted and hammered and excavated and tunneled and drilled. Temporary barracks were set up for the men whom Mrs. Gates's motel could not accommodate. A drive-in Pup and Taco stand appeared and a drive-in stand for cold drinks and ice cream. Business in the liquor stores boomed.

In the mornings Jenny coped with her classes, teaching her pupils how to articulate clearly, how to stand and speak without fidgeting or falling back on the tiresome "you know."

Afternoons she devoted to Ricky and the running of the house and shopping for meals. And in the evenings she took Ricky with her and drove to the Penrose house, where the cook put him to bed, and she began to drill her cast in the play. For the first week they sat around a table and read their lines while Jenny suggested different readings, explained the characters, and worked with timing because most of them believed there should be a considerable pause after each speech to give the audience time to digest it.

One of the young engineers who had come to work on

the hot springs project proved to be a natural comedian though Jenny took him severely to task for hamming. Wallace was adequate and his good looks and fine voice compensated for a lack of any real acting ability. Alma was the worst disappointment. She was lovely to look at but her delivery was flat, and though she tried hard, she could not do the part well. Helen Gates simply played herself, which was all her part required. Mrs. Caldwell was good. Jenny's only objection was that she tried to get too much attention. All this violent effort was directed at Silas Penrose, who sat in the background, making no comment, watching the progress of the play.

"Monday," Jenny said at the end of that first week, "we'll begin walking through the parts. You can have your books handy, of course, but I do hope you'll have learned most of your lines by then." She went to collect the sleeping Ricky.

Mrs. Caldwell seized the opportunity to talk eagerly to Silas Penrose. "Don't you find it stimulating, all this creation going on?"

"Very." He was laconic.

"Such a lovely house you have, Mr. Penrose. I always feel so — so at home when I come here."

"Oh?"

Alma touched her arm. "Hadn't we better be on our way? We are keeping Mr. Penrose up."

"Oh, I wouldn't want to do that. Good night, dear Mr. Penrose. Perhaps when the play is over you'll let me return your wonderful hospitality and dine with us."

Observing his father's expression, Wallace said hastily, "I'll see you out." He met Alma's eyes, brimming with laughter, and found himself sharing her secret mirth. It was the first time he had noticed her with any interest. A striking-looking girl. He'd been so besotted with Jenny that he had had no attention to give another girl. But Jenny had made it clear that she was not for him. Being a philosopher he accepted the comforting fact that there were other fish in the sea.

He watched Alma drive the car slowly down the long, steep road to the highway, saw the headlights disappear around the side of a hill, and strolled back to the house, whistling thoughtfully to himself. To his surprise he found his father still up. He had set out a game of solitaire.

Wallace sat down facing him, watching him put a red nine on a black ten. As a rule solitaire was an indication that Silas Penrose was working out some problem in his mind.

"Are these rehearsals too much for you?" Wallace asked.

"I enjoy them. We've been too quiet here. Maybe we needed to be shaken up a bit, needed more social life."

Wallace grinned wickedly. "Like Mrs. Caldwell?"

"That poisonous woman!"

Wallace laughed. "There's gratitude for you! How many men your age have a charming widow displaying her winning ways for your benefit?"

"Winning ways!" Penrose snorted. Then he said, "A man of my age. I suppose it seems ridiculous to you that a man of my age might want some companionship."

"Not at all. It was the idea of Mrs. Caldwell becoming my future stepmother that disturbed me."

Penrose swept up his cards, shuffled them, then pushed them away and got up.

"Look here, I was only joking," Wallace said. In recent weeks his relationship with his father had changed. Apparently Jenny had been right. The fact that he was sticking to the project and keeping sober had made a big difference. Things were nearly restored to the way they had been in the past before his father had developed the lung condition. "I honestly forgot that you aren't well. We can drop this whole business of the play if you like."

Penrose came back to his chair, let himself down slowly. His hands closed over the arms, gripping them. "I think it's time I told you the truth."

"Is it — serious?"

Seeing Wallace's alarmed expression, the way the color drained from his face, Penrose realized that his son was devoted to him and genuinely afraid something would happen to him.

"I've been lying to you all along, Wallace. You got to running around with that arty set and I couldn't understand it. I thought men had to have other, more practical, interests. When I put a stop to it you began to drink. So I brought you out here to get you away from bad company and bad habits. I offered to build a hospital if I could get a good doctor here. What I was after was a man who could help you.

"Maxwell came along and I tackled him about it the night he and his wife came to dinner. He turned me down cold because he said you were the one to help yourself. He said he didn't see what was wrong with art. He blamed me. I said you were such a young fool you didn't know what you wanted and he said you weren't that young or that foolish. Well, then you set up this project and you've stuck to it. So I was wrong. If you want to go back East or wherever, and work in a museum, you go ahead. And forgive me, if you can, for deceiving you. I did it for the best."

There was a long, anxious silence while Penrose waited for his son to speak, watching the changing expression on his face, from surprise to bewilderment. Then Wallace leaped to his feet.

"You mean you're *all right!*"

Penrose nodded. Wallace was laughing, pounding his father's back, laughing again.

"Why," Penrose said, "you're *glad!*" After a moment he held out his hand.

To break the emotional tension, Wallace said, the old mocking look in his eyes, "And now perhaps you'll explain that comment about men of your age. If the lady isn't Mrs. Caldwell it — good lord, it isn't Alma Deming, is it?"

Penrose ran a finger under his collar, swallowed. "Don't be ridiculous, Wallace. I was simply thinking we should have a little dinner party; perhaps the same congenial group Mrs. Maxwell assembled."

"Including," Wallace said, enlightened, "Mrs. Helen Gates."

His father returned the mocking look. For a moment there was an uncanny family resemblance between father and son. "Including Helen Gates," he said.

iii

Brad was in the living room when Jenny came in. He took the sleeping Ricky out of her arms and put him in his crib. When he returned he went to the kitchen to fix Jenny a cool drink and put it in her hand.

"How long do you think you can keep this up?"

"Heavens, I always worked harder than this in New York! It's just the heat. At least the days go faster this way. They rush past."

"Has it been so terribly dull for you?"

Jenny met his eyes honestly. "I've been lonely, of course."

He got up to pace the room, running his fingers through his crisp, short hair, whose curl was so sternly controlled. "I lie awake nights trying to think of some way out for you."

She clasped her hands tightly on her lap. Otherwise she did not move.

"The essential thing, of course, is Ricky."

"Of course." Her voice was flat.

"Sarah loves him and takes wonderful care of him. Suppose you were to return to New York and the theater —"

"And depose the girl who has taken my part and made a success of it? I wouldn't do that even if I could."

"Other producers would jump at you, as you must well know. And Sarah could be paid to keep Ricky, and I'd be here to make sure he was all right."

"And Joe Colfax would find out I'd turned his nephew over to someone else and —"

"I'd forgotten Joe."

"Had you?" She pulled herself out of her chair. "Thanks for that cold drink. Good night, Brad."

"Wait, Jenny! Wouldn't it rest you a bit to take a quick dip?"

She nodded and went in to change. When she came out Brad was in the pool. She walked down the steps, feeling the water just slightly cooler than the atmosphere creep up her body, thighs, hips, waist. Then she dove under, found herself beside Brad, felt his lips on her cheek and then on her mouth and came up for air.

"So sorry," he said, though he watched her anxiously. "I mistook you for a mermaid."

"What could be more natural! People are always noticing the resemblance." She swam away from him and then floated on her back, looking up into the black vault of the sky. She shivered.

"Cold?" Brad's hand touched her arm.

"No. That black sky. Space. Awful, infinite space. All black except where the light of the sun reaches." She climbed up the steps and took off her cap, shaking out her hair in a shower over her shoulders.

Brad had pulled himself out. He lifted her hair. "It's so beautiful, Jenny. So beautiful." He bent over, resting his face against it.

"Brad! Brad!"

"What is it, darling?"

"Listen! What's that?"

It was a queer, rattling sound. Brad leaped past her, running to Ricky's room with Jenny at his heels. The little boy was sitting upright, his face swollen and congested. The rattling sound came from his throat.

"He's choking!" Jenny screamed.

"Quiet!" Having upended Ricky, Brad probed the child's throat, and then he pulled out a tiny block. "A piece of that building toy, though how he managed to swallow it is beyond me. Okay, boy. You're all right now." He held him up and slowly the boy's choked breathing rasped less, and finally became normal. Then he howled in memory of his fear and suffering. Brad settled him back in his crib, talking quietly until the tears stopped rolling down his cheeks. His eyes closed but even when he slept the small body was still occasionally shaken by a sob.

Brad nodded to Jenny, his lips shaping the words, "Good night."

"Suppose," she said, "just suppose we hadn't been here."

XIV

"I regard you," Mrs. Gates said, "as an extremely immoral woman."

For the third time since her arrival there had been telephone calls from ambitious mothers asking Jenny what chances their children would have in the movies.

"They are the immoral ones, trying to exploit their children. At least I am teaching those kids to stand up and speak plainly without being flustered, and articulating so they can be understood and not going 'uh — you know — uh — I mean to say — you know.' My pupils are going to do me proud, you just wait and see. I'm not promising to make them actors, but whatever jobs they do later they'll handle better; they will even be more at ease socially if they know how to come into a room and speak clearly and move around without bumping into the furniture."

"And I gather you are teaching a little in the way of manners. I audited that class yesterday, remember?"

"Why not? If they imitate the kids who have discarded all civilized values they can't be anything but destroyers. I want them to feel so sure of themselves they won't have to ape their inferiors."

"Good girl. You stay in there pitching." Mrs. Gates kicked off her shoes and stretched out on the couch. "You must be sick of the sight of me but I had to get away from the motel or go out of my mind. They are tiling the first of the big pools today and it sounded as though they were pounding tiles into my skull. And when I went shopping there were so many people milling around I had to park blocks away with the temperature 110. It's absurd that there should be no space to park in the desert!"

"You break my heart, you with your motel filled to the bursting point."

"At least I am the bearer of good tidings so perhaps that will help you to put up with me. But it mustn't go farther than you — and Bradley, of course. I promised Silas faithfully."

"Silas?"

"Silas Penrose. He's been dropping by quite often with ideas about improving and enlarging the motel and — oh, lots of things. And don't get that knowing look on your face! Anyhow, here it is: Silas is going to endow a hospital for Desert Winds, a kind of hospital and sanitarium combined, to correlate with the hot springs spa development."

"How wonderful!"

"Isn't it? But he doesn't want any rumor to get out until the night of the play. By the way, it looks as though there may have to be several performances, the way the demand for tickets is coming in. People from all over. Of course, if you were taking the lead the town couldn't hold them . . . Why didn't you?"

"It is intended to be a local project. Anyhow —"

"Out with it. You know you'll confide in me sooner or later."

"Well, I don't think Brad likes to have me act or to be

reminded of Jennifer Haydon. I don't know why. I'm sure it's not prejudice against the theater itself. But when we had dinner in Beverly Hills and people recognized me he wasn't — well, it sort of spoiled the evening."

"What's spoiled is your precious husband. Oh, I know you won't hear a word against him but he's jealous of your career and your success."

He doesn't care enough about me to be jealous, Jenny thought. She remembered his voice when he said, "Nothing you say or do has any effect on me."

When Helen Gates had gone Jenny tapped on the office door and Brad called, "Come in."

There was no one in the office. "Where are you?"

"In the laboratory. Come on in. No one here. I've just got to finish a job."

He was bending over a microscope and making notes. He spoke without looking up. "What is it?"

"Sorry to bother you."

"You aren't. Just ten minutes more." It was nearly twenty before he straightened up and saw her expression. She had been watching his face, his deep absorption, and her own expression was unguarded. His lips parted to speak but he pressed them together. Only his breathing quickened as he saw her heightened color.

"Where's Alma?"

"She took the day off to get a permanent wave and went to Mark's in San Marino for it. It's a wonder to me she works as often as she does, what with being leading lady in *Heat Wave* and in Wallace Penrose's life as well."

"What!"

"If," Brad informed her, "you hadn't broken off social relations with the local broadcasting station across the street you would keep up with the gossip. But I get around. I keep my ear to the ground." He stood looking down at the top of her head. "And what's more I'd be willing to bet all the cash now in my billfold — four whole dollars — that Little Miss Fixer-Upper's was the hand that wrought this miracle." There was no anger in his voice, no jealousy, only a kind of affectionate teasing.

"Like what?" she asked.

"Like," Brad said, "bringing them together at a dinner party, arranging to have them take the lovers' parts in a play."

"You are getting to be as bad a gossip as Mrs. Fulmer."

"Don't you agree," he asked, "that a husband should have no secrets from his wife? The moment I heard this juicy bit of news I ran to share it with you."

"Secrets! That's what I've come to tell you. Helen Gates was just here and she told me — only it's a solemn promise and you aren't to breathe a word — that Mr. Penrose is going to build a combined hospital and sanitarium here to sort of fit in with the hot springs project and turn the place into a real spa."

When Brad said nothing she added in a small voice, "I hoped you'd be pleased."

"I am. God knows it is needed. And in that case, there will be no need for the equipment that was to be installed here. We'll have to get your money back, Jenny. I've never known how much you put at Dr. Ferguson's disposal but, thank God, you can get it back! You don't know how I hated accepting that from you, even as a loan."

"I'm sorry. I didn't mean it to be that way. I'll write to Dr. Ferguson today."

The look he had detected for one unguarded moment on her face was gone now. She was a courteous stranger. Now what had he done wrong, Brad wondered.

ii

"Come in," Wallace said. He added with exaggerated surprise, "Dr. Maxwell in person! We've been writing our own mystery about The Case of the Missing Husband. Have you come to applaud our efforts?"

"I come to scoff and I shall remain to sneer," Brad said loftily.

"Fine. Just what we need. Have a seat beside my father, will you? The most encouraging factor is that you won't suffer long. You'll find yourself getting numb. Take my father; by this time he is almost past feeling any pain."

Silas Penrose shook hands with Brad. "Glad to see you, doctor."

"Where do I park this?" Brad asked, looking down at Ricky, who was asleep against his shoulder.

The cook came in, smiling, to carry him away.

"All right," Jenny said crisply. She sat at the far end of the room, an open script and a colored pencil on the table beside her. "We're going to start with act two. Take your places, please."

The young engineer and Mrs. Caldwell moved onto the improvised stage.

"Curtain."

The scene progressed smoothly, at almost a professional pace, and Brad was impressed. It lacked the polish of the New York performance but the engineer was a natural and Mrs. Caldwell proved to be an excellent foil for him. For one thing Brad was exceedingly grateful. Ever since she had begun to act, Mrs. Caldwell had been without symptoms that required the house calls of an overworked doctor and the attentions of a slave. Watching the action Brad realized that Mrs. Caldwell was playing to an audience of one, the silent and unresponsive man who sat beside him. A sidewise glance informed Brad that Penrose was sardonically aware of her activities.

"No," Jenny interrupted. "Remember, Mrs. Caldwell, you are speaking to John. You must look at him and not at the audience."

Mrs. Gates came on and a couple of minor characters whom Brad recognized as townspeople but could not identify. Then Wallace appeared with Alma.

"No," Jenny said again. "Mrs. Caldwell, by moving upstage you are forcing Wallace to turn his back to the audience when he addresses you. Let's take that last speech again . . . No, remain where you are, Mrs. Caldwell."

Up to this point, with the exception of Mrs. Caldwell's single-minded determination to hold the limelight, all had gone surprisingly well for an amateur performance. But now it lost pace, though, in the Broadway performance, this was the moment when it had built to its high peak. There were two causes for this. One was that Wallace, though an engaging actor, kept forgetting his lines and substituting others that threw the cast off. But the most disastrous one was Alma. She looked lovely, she moved well, but she was wooden. She could not project gaiety or poignancy or any other mood. Brad remembered Jenny in the part. How she must long to play it, to bring it to life.

"Let's try that again, Alma. Wallace, cross left before you speak your line, and if you don't get your part memorized by the opening I'm going to wring your neck."

He gave her a lazy smile, crossed the makeshift stage, looked at Alma, and spoke his line: "All right, you've done everything but tell me the truth. Is that so hard to do?"

"It would be harder on you than on me."

Jenny interrupted. "You sound sorry for him, Alma. You're supposed to be challenging him. Try it again."

"It would be harder on you than on me."

Jenny shook her head. "Now you're threatening him."

"I don't know how else to say it."

"Like this." Jenny took her place and turned to Wallace, her expression mocking but with a tiny gesture of the hand as though irresistibly drawn to him. "It would be harder on you than on me."

Alma tried again.

"That's better," Jenny lied. "Go on."

iii

While Jenny went to collect Richard, and Wallace was ushering out part of the cast, Penrose was talking to Helen Gates.

"Pleased, was she?"

"How could she help it!" Mrs. Gates's thin, clever face was alight with enthusiasm. "It will mean so much not only to her husband but to the whole community. And you can count on the Maxwells not saying a thing until you make the announcement at your reception after the play."

"That reminds me, Helen, would you mind very much acting as hostess for me that night or is it too much to expect after you have just appeared in the play?"

"I'd be happy to."

"Of course, any ideas you might have — food, rearranging the house or whatever — don't hesitate. A bachelor establishment must need a great deal of improvement."

"I'll consult with your cook about the buffet, if you like, and make some suggestions, though I doubt if she'll need them. But the house is so beautiful I can't imagine improving it."

"I'm glad you think so. I want you to like it, Helen."

Before she could answer, Mrs. Caldwell had laid her hand confidingly on Penrose's arm. He disliked clinging and helpless women because they were demanding and, from his standpoint, dangerous, but he said courteously, "A very good performance tonight, Mrs. Caldwell. You are becoming quite professional."

"Well, of course," and she smiled sweetly, "Mrs. Maxwell was a professional, wasn't she? A good director, I don't say she isn't, but perhaps just a teeny bit harder on the women than on the men, don't you think? But I suppose that's only human."

"I noticed that she was sounding off at my graceless son for not knowing his lines."

"But nothing *mean*. Oh, I don't intend to say —"

Jenny came back with Richard, and Brad took him from her. When they had gone, Mrs. Gates left, and only Alma and Mrs. Caldwell remained. The latter seemed to be in no haste to take her departure.

"We must go," Alma told her.

"Are you working tomorrow?" Wallace asked.

"In the afternoon."

"Would you come to the rescue and let me practice my second-act lines on you in the morning?"

"If you don't come too early."

"Ten o'clock. And we'll lunch at Kelly's. After which I will deliver you to the doctor's office." Wallace waved good-by and waited until the car had made the long driveway safely before he went inside.

"We ought to do something about that driveway. It's much too steep to be safe. Anyone with bad brakes could have a serious accident."

"People with bad brakes shouldn't drive."

Wallace grinned at his father. "People with bad tempers shouldn't throw stones."

"It's that confounded Caldwell woman! I can't endure her. Always pawing me and telling me she only feels spiritually at home when she is in this house."

"You look out or you'll have her in this house. Permanently."

"Want to bet on that?"

"I'm turning in," Wallace laughed at his irate father. "Tomorrow I have to see a man about putting up a new motel. We're going to have to buy more land. That ten-acre tract east of town seems to be the best bet. And there's an up-and-coming guy with an idea of setting up a small and very smart shopping mall for desert wear, high-priced negligees, expensive gifts. I told him he'd better wait a year and see what happens but he said he'd take a chance on getting in on the ground floor."

"And you've got to rehearse your lines."

The two men exchanged an understanding smile.

XV

IT was late on Saturday afternoon when Jenny returned from shopping and brought in the big brown paper bags of groceries. There was no sign of Brad.

"Doctor," Alma said in the impersonal tone she always adopted in the office, "is out on call."

Sarah was in the pool with Ricky. When she saw Jenny she brought him out quickly. "It was only for a few minutes and the pool is shaded for about half an hour at this time of day."

"I never worry about him when you have him." Jenny looked at Sarah without favor. "That bathing suit looks like something out of a Mack Sennett comedy."

Sarah shrugged. "Mother got it for me so I feel I ought to wear it."

"If you ask me, she got it at a rummage sale. You're an idiot to wear a thing like that. You have a pretty figure and you make yourself look like a sack of meal."

"Oh, well!"

"I could shake you."

There was a little smile on Sarah's lips. "You're beautiful so you don't know what it is to be plain."

"I'm not beautiful. Actually there are not many beautiful women on the stage, but you can learn to give the illusion of beauty if you can make yourself believe it. Take a day off and splurge. Look, we could go to Pasadena together — I wouldn't trust you by yourself — and buy some clothes and have your hair styled in a more becoming way. We could take Ricky with us," she added, throwing out the most enticing bait she knew.

Sarah shook her head, regretfully but firmly. "It isn't worth the fuss it would cause. Perhaps I'll do it after the play. Right now mother is more contented than I've ever known her to be. I guess she just needed an interest. If you can find something else equally interesting for her when the play is over she probably wouldn't mind so much letting go of me."

Jenny made no comment on what she guessed to be Mrs. Caldwell's real interest. She wanted to be installed as the wife of Silas Penrose and hostess at the big Penrose house. Undoubtedly she saw herself snubbing people who had avoided her in the past, and being gracious to people she had always longed to know. At this point Jenny wouldn't have given a penny for her chances of fulfilling her ambition.

The office door opened and Brad came in, looking hot and tired. He nodded to Sarah and went to toss a shrieking and delighted Ricky in the air.

"I'm going to take a cold shower. Then how about going out to dinner for a change, Jenny? Let's go to Kelly's. Will you stand by, Sarah? And don't tell anyone where we are. I need some time off."

Sarah laughed. Laughter always transformed her face and made her look much prettier. "Of course I'll stay. But if you think for one minute that Mrs. Fulmer won't know where you are you're —"

"— living in a fool's paradise," Brad finished for her.

When Jenny had changed, she found Brad waiting in the Volvo. She got in beside him.

"Hard day?"

"No, just little things. Sorry if I sound disagreeable."

"You can't help it," she consoled him, and he began to laugh.

"Little Miss Fixer-Upper," he said, but without rancor. "You always coax and beguile me out of a bad temper. I suspect I'm being managed, but though I should resent it, I rather enjoy it."

Dinner was a leisurely affair interrupted by a stream of people, stopping to talk to them, one with a jovial comment about the doctor who kept his lovely wife hidden away, afraid of competition.

"Good lord," Brad said in contrition when the man had gone, "this is the first time we've come here! You have no life at all, except what you are building for yourself with your classes and rehearsals. I ought to be shot."

"Not a bad idea, but I can't really see that it would improve matters."

"He was right, you know," Brad said, looking into the dark-fringed gray eyes, seeing the face that had become so familiar to him and yet was always changing as her moods changed. "The loveliest woman in town and I keep her under wraps without showing her off."

"Not under wraps. Just submerged, like the Dormouse."

He laughed. "Were you brought up on *Alice in Wonderland* too?"

"Of course. Only the best company."

"There's so much I don't know about you, Jenny."

She bit back the words she wanted to say, but in her

expression there was something he had seen once before, when he had looked up from his microscope to find her watching him.

After dinner he said, "I don't have any serious cases who are apt to need me tonight, and Mrs. Caldwell, thank God, has other irons in the fire, so she doesn't need any symptoms to keep her amused. Shall we just drive?"

Once in the car he asked, "Which way?"

"How about Four Corners? Perhaps they have a movie every night. We could really live it up."

He turned the car obediently. "I've made this trip so often to the hospital I think the car could do it by itself."

"I was just thinking how the desert is changing," Jenny said. "Only a few months since we came. Remember how still the town was at night? Now it is filled to bursting. Business is booming. There are cars all over the place. People from outside are pouring in, looking for work, and they'll find it. Even when the spa is finished there will be service jobs and then work will start on the hospital and sanitarium. That means that people will come here to live and that will require more houses and more stores and then —"

"You know what made the desert bloom, don't you, Jenny?"

"What?"

"A small girl with big gray eyes and golden-brown hair who had an idea. One idea and so many lives will be changed, so many people helped."

"But it wasn't I!"

"Wasn't it? Because Helen Gates had a problem in making ends meet; because Wallace Penrose had a problem in dealing with his life; because the hot springs were here but everyone else just stood there and you did something about it."

Unexpectedly the car jerked as though a giant hand had sideswiped it. Brad pulled it back on the road.

Jenny sat up suddenly. "Flat tire?"

"Wind. I guess we had better turn around and high-tail it for home, while we still have a road to follow. And be sure to close your window."

"We'll stifle."

"Better than what you'll get otherwise. Close it tight. Just leave the side window open a little bit. There's a lot of power in that wind." His voice was so casual that Jenny was not alarmed. Obediently she closed her window, and at once the car was airless and steamingly hot.

"I can hardly breathe."

"Take it easy and relax or you'll just get more overheated."

Jenny peered through the windshield. "What's wrong with the lights?"

"Nothing. That's sand."

"Brad!"

"It's okay. We're fairly well sheltered by the cliff. Not much chance of our turning over. Just the same," his voice was still even, unhurried, "it might be a good idea to take off your safety belt in case —"

The car gave a violent lurch, leaped like a skittish horse, hurling Jenny against the door. Again Brad pulled it back into its own lane.

There was no road ahead now; it had been completely obliterated by blowing sand. Sand? It sounded like points of steel as it bit into the windshield and into the frame of the car. The air was almost black and there was no visibility. And the wind screamed like a woman in terror or an animal in pain, thin and high and relentless, on and on.

Inside the closed car the air was hot and it was difficult to breathe. Brad shut off the motor and put his arm around Jenny, trying to protect her from being bruised as the car jolted from side to side. She was a little Trojan, he thought tenderly. Not a sound out of her, though she must be terrified. He began to tell her of a blizzard he had experienced in North Dakota. "And there, of course, we had the extra threat of freezing to death, which is one problem we won't have here."

As the fury of the storm increased he kept his voice low so that she leaned closer to hear his words, until her cheek brushed his. The car staggered like a drunkard but though it was shaken and shoved helplessly across the road, it did not turn over.

"What happens if someone crashes into us?" Jenny asked once.

"That would be quite a mess, but no car is likely to be moving. I doubt if even a heavy truck could keep going on this road, what with the force of the wind and no visibility. Traffic is bound to hole up the way we are doing and wait until the wind dies down. Try not to be afraid."

She was surprised. "I'm not afraid. At least I would be if you weren't here, but —" As the car rocked she buried her face in his shoulder. He heard her muffled voice. "Talk to me. Tell me more about when you were a boy."

He talked, building up an outrageous parody of his childhood and his adventures, in all of which he was the hero. "But you know me," he said, "brave to the very core. So I . . ."

Now and then she chuckled in response to his stories, but finally invention flagged. "From now on," he told her, "you've got to do the talking. We can't sleep in this inferno and I've run out of ideas."

So Jenny recited all the women's speeches she could remember in Shakespeare, ranging from Lady Macbeth to Portia, from Cleopatra to Rosalind. The words began to falter. "How many fathoms deep I am in love," she said, almost in a whisper, and then she was asleep.

Brad turned her head gently, kissed her cheek, kissed her lips. All through the night he held her, unmoving, listening to the fury of the storm, protecting Jenny from being knocked about as the car lurched and swung across the road and, once, rose off the ground on one side, canted toward the other, and after what seemed to be an eternity settled back with a jar on all four wheels.

Daylight came, a dirty yellow daylight, with the sun a pale disc behind a sullen, sulphur mist. The wind had died down and Brad peered ahead where a road had been. It was completely obliterated by sand. Nothing moved in the whole landscape. Eventually sweepers would come along, as snowplows did in the north, and uncover the road. But meantime he had patients to see and he had been out of touch for many hours.

Even with the car closed sand had sifted over everything: sand in the interior of the car, sand on their clothes, sand on their hands and faces, sand thick in their hair.

Brad opened the window on his side and then leaned

over to open Jenny's. Immediately she was wide awake, staring at the havoc wrought by the storm.

"How on earth do we get home?"

"I'll drive very slowly so that, if I get off the road, I'll realize it at once. It's fairly straight here, if you remember, and no ditches. We'll make it."

"I feel as though we were all alone in the world. There doesn't seem to be anything alive but us."

"Adam and Eve."

"But this isn't my idea of Paradise."

"I'm with you there. You know, whenever I try to get some time alone with you I seem to be jinxed."

There was all the time in the world, Jenny thought, but she could not say so. "Well," she sounded practical, "at least we don't need to worry about ruining the Lincoln."

"You're a wonder, Jenny. Any other girl would be howling her head off and blaming me."

"How vain you are! You don't have that much effect on the weather."

It was broad daylight by the time the Volvo limped into the filling station. The startled attendant asked, "You folks come far?"

Brad grinned. "It just seemed far. Spent most of the night with the car across the Four Corners road hoping it would stay rightside up and that no one would hit us."

"But, doc, that road has been shut off all night. You're the only people to get through."

"I believe you," Brad said wearily. "Fill it up, will you? At least we had enough gas to get us back."

When they drove up before the house Sarah flung open the door, a heavy-eyed, weary Sarah.

"Oh, thank goodness! I've been terribly worried. I've followed the weather reports all night and I was afraid you'd been caught in the sandstorm."

"We were," Jenny said, "but it's all right, Sarah." She added belatedly, "Do you mean to say you kept awake all night waiting for us? You haven't slept at all?"

"I was worried. I'll put on some coffee."

"But there was nothing to worry about. Brad was with me," Jenny pointed out, as though his presence solved everything, and Brad looked at her swiftly, a question in his eyes.

"Old Faithful, that's you," he said. "I'll get a quick shower and change and start on house calls. Any messages?"

"Yes, that's why I waited up for you."

"An emergency?"

"I don't know. He didn't call the house. He said he had called the office. And then —"

"He *said* he had called the office? You mean he came here to the house when he must have been told by Mrs. Fulmer that I was out?"

"Yes. Well, it seems before he came here he saw Mrs. Fulmer. It was her suggestion. In fact he's there now."

"He saw her *first?*" Brad was baffled.

"I didn't like him at all," Sarah said. "Not a single bit."

"What did he want, Sarah?"

"He wanted Ricky."

XVI

JOSEPH Colfax pushed back his chair so violently that it fell to the floor with a crash, making his wife start and spill her coffee. Nervously aware of her husband's angry eyes on her face she lifted the cup in a shaking hand. The coffee dribbled down her chin.

"Wipe your face," he shouted at her. "You look ridiculous."

She wiped her face with her napkin. Something must be very wrong. Joe's temper was never reliable but she had seen him this angry only twice before; once when he learned the terms of his father's will, and the second time when a judge had given Jennifer Haydon custody of Richard's small son.

For her own sake, Mildred Colfax would have welcomed her husband's nephew. He was the most enchanting small boy she had ever seen and she needed someone to love, someone who could give life back something of the sweetness it had had before she had married Joe Colfax. All that seemed an immense time ago though she was now only twenty-eight, still a young woman. Seeing herself in the small mirror in the kitchen she wondered how many people would believe it. She looked forty. Her youth had faded without having bloomed.

Sometimes she wondered, in a kind of bewilderment, how it had happened. For one thing she had rarely been away from her father's farm in upper New York State, and she had known few boys of her own age. When Joseph Colfax appeared — he was selling farm machinery at the time — she had thought him the most charming man in the world. It was not until after their runaway marriage and their return to the farm that she began to question her judgment. Her father was a sensible man who, though he would certainly not have approved of her marriage with a man of no stability and no ambition, accepted the *fait accompli* with as good a grace as possible and took Joe into the family. It was Joe's idea to give up his job and devote himself to helping on the farm.

The questions began to arise little by little. There was her father's death, which followed her marriage within three months, and the discovery that Joe had known of his condition before their marriage. There was the half-veiled warning from the banker that she should insist on looking after her own financial interests, for, unexpectedly, her father had left several hundred thousand dollars about which Joe had also known, and which he had ideas for increasing. So before long Mildred was certain that Joe had married her only because he knew how much money her father had and that his health was precarious.

Not until she met Joseph's older half-brother Richard did she realize this was the kind of man she had believed Joe to be, the man Joe was not. Even before she became too afraid of him to fight, she had learned to accede blindly to whatever he demanded. She had made a mistake and she ought to pay for it.

But she was glad on little Richard's account that he

had been placed in Jennifer Haydon's care. The actress had given up her career for the child and she had not asked for any part of his father's estate. Now and then Mildred had thought wistfully that it would be nice if she and Richard's lovely wife Louise could become friends, but Joe resented his half-brother so intensely that they rarely met. Since his father's death, when he learned the terms of his will, Joe had come to hate Richard, even when he was lying dead somewhere in the jungles of Vietnam — or, worse perhaps, still living in a Vietcong prison.

For a time Joe had seemed to acquiesce to the judge's decision but recently he had become increasingly violent. The banker, meeting Mildred on the street, urged her not to let Joe squander away all the money that had been acquired by such hard work. "Take a stand," he told her.

Take a stand. It was years since Mildred had done that. She knew that Joe had been plunging on the stock market and had already lost more than half of the money her father had left. Then, on the advice of a friend, he tried to recoup with an unknown stock, a "sure thing," which could not fail to rise sky-high and make his fortune. By that morning's mail he had learned that his investment had been wiped out and only a tenth of the original estate was left.

"Joe," she began timidly.

Without replying he went out, slamming the screen door behind him. She watched him walk across the neglected fields to the barn, which he had converted into a garage, saw him back out the Chrysler which he had bought to replace the old Chevrolet, heard him drive away with a racing of the motor and scream of brakes when he reached the highway.

Late that afternoon she came in from feeding the chickens to find Joe in the old-fashioned sitting room with its organ and horsehair sofa and the whatnot in the corner, which he had called so amusing when he first came here; now he said it looked like something out of the Ark. He had put on his best lightweight suit and he had a suitcase at his feet. He was coolly going through her handbag.

"Forty dollars," he said discontentedly. "That's not enough."

"Where are you going?"

"Some one-horse town on the Mojave Desert."

"But that's clear across the continent!"

"So what?"

"But why?"

"Ricky. My lawyer has been keeping tabs. There's where Jenny took the kid. My lawyer knows a guy who runs a gossip column out there. He has a few leads. Said he thought we could make a good case against Jenny and have the custody order revoked. I'm on my way."

"But, Joe —"

He shrugged off her restraining hand. "Where do you keep the money you've been holding out on me?"

"I'm not holding out."

He laughed. "I got a look at your checkbook the other day. You've been withdrawing fifty dollars a week. What are you doing? Hoarding it?"

"Just keeping it safe. We'll need it. When you've run through everything else we'll need it."

His face darkened. He could not endure having his

judgment questioned, no matter how often he was proved to be mistaken. "Where is it, Mil?" When she did not answer he twisted her arm and she gave a shrill cry. "Where?"

He released her and she went to the couch, unzipped the cover of a sofa pillow, and thrust in her hand. He snatched the money away and counted it. "Eight — nine — one thousand — one thousand and fifty. That's more like it." He put the money in an inside pocket, patting the bulge it made approvingly. He picked up his suitcase. "You'd better get that spare room ready for the kid. I'm not coming back without him."

ii

The heat was like the blast from a furnace and the air was heavy, presaging a storm. Joseph Colfax got out of the bus and went into the drugstore to find a telephone. He dialed the number of Bradley Maxwell, M.D.

While he waited for an answer he looked out at the desert. What had possessed Jennifer Haydon to give up all she had for this dump? One thing must be clear to anyone; no actress made that kind of sacrifice for another woman's child. He thought he might soon learn what lay behind her fantastic action.

Anything he could pick up would be grist to his mill. And he wanted Ricky. He must have Ricky. All his father's money. *All* of it. And into the hands of a two-year-old. That is, if Ricky lived until — well, they had to wait seven years, of course, unless proof of his half-brother's death could be established before then. Three million and very likely more. And I was the older son, Joe thought.

My own father acted as though I could not be trusted to handle money.

His anger built up again. The sense of bitter injustice. His own father. His own money. Over three million dollars. On that he could live as he had always wanted to live. And with his flair he could double it, quadruple it. And in the way stood a two-year-old.

On most subjects Joe was capable of defining the situation to himself. There were only two on which he did not think at all. He skirted them as though they did not exist. One was his personal failure to handle money. The other was the ultimate fate of young Richard. Someday he'd be gone. Something would happen. Something was bound to happen.

The woman who answered the telephone said that Dr. Maxwell had gone out for the evening.

"That you, Jennifer?"

"This is the doctor's answering service. If you will leave your name and telephone number, the doctor will be informed on his return."

"My name is Colfax. Joseph Colfax. I can't give you a number because I just got off the bus from the airport and I haven't found a place to stay. I suppose there's a motel in this dump."

"It's filled. I do know that. Is this a personal call?"

Joe laughed. "It sure is."

"What message shall I leave? It may not reach him until morning and he does his house calls first, so I don't know when he can call you."

"Tell him I want the boy. That ought to bring him running."

"The boy?"

"Richard. Richard Colfax."

"Richard *Colfax!*" Mrs. Fulmer sounded bewildered.

Joe laughed again. "Is that the story? Richard isn't Maxwell's son."

"Well! You don't say." After a moment's agitated thought Mrs. Fulmer said, "As you have no place to stay you might come here. It's an easy walk from the drugstore. Just tell the druggist it's Mrs. Fulmer and anyone can direct you. I can put you up on the couch in my sitting room. It's real comfortable and I'm sure I don't know where else you could go, and it's whipping up for a real bad storm, if I know the signs."

A quarter of an hour later Mrs. Fulmer turned over the switchboard to her cousin and sat down facing Joseph Colfax. A real nice-looking man, she thought. "Jennifer," he had said, as though he knew Mrs. Maxwell quite well. Something mighty wrong here, mighty queer.

"You could have knocked me down with a feather when you said Richard wasn't the doctor's son," she began eagerly.

Joe was not intelligent about money because he was too greedy, but he knew a lot about human weakness. He summed up Mrs. Fulmer in a couple of minutes. The village gossip, he thought, and she hates the guts of Maxwell and Jennifer. Mentally he shook hands with himself. You never knew what the spin of the wheel would bring.

It didn't take him long to get the story. Jennifer Maxwell was flighty; she had seen that from the start, long before she had ever suspected the girl was an actress. With her own eyes Mrs. Fulmer had seen her sitting right outside her house in Wallace Penrose's car and he was kissing her like mad. Doctor hadn't liked it and he had had a terrible fight with young Penrose, half killed him. But it hadn't stopped the affair. Mrs. Fulmer knew for a fact that the girl accepted expensive presents from him, like jewelry, and she had seen her with Wallace parked along a road that was almost always deserted. Now he was trying to cover up the affair by pretending to play around with the doctor's office nurse, who was no better than she should be.

Joe, concealing his jubilation, shook his head dolefully. "I was afraid of it. I once found her at one o'clock in the morning with a couple of men in her apartment. You can't bring up a child properly in such surroundings."

"Of course not. And she neglects him. I can tell you that for a fact."

Joe leaned forward eagerly. "Sure of that?"

"I went in one day and there that dear baby was, all alone, and he had fallen into the swimming pool. Why, if I hadn't run like mad, he'd have drowned."

"Well, well," Joe said. "Well, well! Would you be willing to go on a witness stand and testify to that? In the interests of justice, of course, and for the child's own sake."

"I certainly would."

Hearing the vindictive tone in the woman's voice Joe wondered in some amusement what Jennifer had done to make her so angry.

"Of course," she said, "what can you expect with an actress?"

"That's just what I always say," Joe agreed. "Where do the Maxwells live?"

"Right across the street. They're out now, of course, but their baby-sitter is there. They leave the poor boy with her half the time."

"I think," Joe suggested, "I'll just run across and leave a message. Then, if you really mean it about letting me sleep here — Jennifer would never ask me to stay even if I had to sleep on the ground, though I am the boy's own uncle."

"Of course. I'll leave the front door unlocked. No one locks up here. My cousin will tell you where the bathroom is and I'll lay out some clean towels and bedding for the couch. I'll just say good night then."

Mrs. Fulmer went into her bedroom but not to sleep. She sat in the dark, watching. She saw Joseph Colfax cross the street, saw Sarah open the door and admit him after a brief parley. It was nearly half an hour before he returned and by that time the storm had struck and he ran across the street. But though she watched for a long time she did not see the Maxwell car return.

iii

When Joe had persuaded Sarah to admit him — "It's all right. I am Joseph Colfax, Ricky's uncle"— he looked around the living room, recognizing pieces he had seen in Jennifer's Park Avenue apartment: the same colors, the same atmosphere of gaiety and brightness.

With the total lack of courtesy he had fallen into since his marriage, he settled himself in a chair without waiting to be asked. "I am Joseph Colfax, as I told you. Are you the baby-sitter?"

"I am Sarah Caldwell."

"Got a drink in the place, Sarah?"

"I have no idea. I'm not the hostess here, Mr. Colfax."

"Just the hired help?" He saw the small flame of anger in her eyes. "Do you have to do this often?"

"Do what?"

"Look after the kid while the Maxwells are gallivanting."

"I love looking after him. He's such a darling. But I've not been asked more than twice before to stay in the evenings. Doctor works so hard that they hardly ever go anywhere, and she works mornings teaching children and in the evenings she is directing a play for the benefit of the church fund, but she always takes Richard with her. And he's not," Sarah added sharply, "kept awake all evening. He's asleep when he goes and he rests just as well as he would here, and there is someone to look after him at the Penrose house."

This was not the kind of information Joe wanted to hear and besides there was something in the girl's patent honesty that would make a far better impression in court than Mrs. Fulmer's unconcealed animosity.

"How is the boy? I've not seen him in a long time. Sickly kid. Sort of pathetic. I've worried about him a lot, I can tell you."

Sarah, not being as vulnerable as Mildred Colfax had once been to Joe's dubious charm, was not taken in by this spurious air of affection and concern. "He's splendid and he simply glows with health. He has a tendency to bronchial asthma, as you probably know, so this climate is perfect for him. If you haven't seen him in some time you'd hardly know him, he's so brown and he has put on so much weight."

"I feel that a child should be with his own kin, don't you?"

"It depends. Where there is enough love tempered by common sense I think a family is the best thing there is. In Ricky's case, I don't see what more he could have than the love and care he gets. Dr. Maxwell takes a firm stand on discipline, of course."

"Hard on the boy?" Joe was alert again.

Sarah laughed. "They adore each other. Come take a look, but do be quiet, won't you?" She led the way into Richard's room, with its crib and toy bin and colorful furniture for a small boy. She turned on a lamp whose light was shielded from the boy's face. Joe bent over the crib to look at the sleeping child. His hair seemed fairer than ever in contrast with the brown skin; his lips were red, his body sturdy. He exuded a sense of well-being.

When they were back in the living room Joe asked, "What time do you expect Jennifer and her husband to return?"

"I don't know. They had no plans. They so rarely take off time together."

"Oh?"

"And I don't mean," Sarah said, with a sharpness that was alien to her, "that they take off time with other people, because they don't. All that is bothering me tonight is the weather report. There's a big storm blowing up near here so they could be in trouble." As though on cue, the windows rattled suddenly. "Here it comes. You'd better be on your way. Staying at the motel?"

"No, at Mrs. Fulmer's across the street." He explained how he had happened to call on her. "So she was kind enough to take me in."

"She wanted to find out what you were doing here." Sarah opened the door and a gust of hot wind made her stagger. "By the way, Mr. Colfax, don't believe everything Mrs. Fulmer has to say. Lying is practically a profession with her. Good night."

He heard the warning in her voice. He looked at her in a way that would have made his spineless wife quake, but the mouselike baby-sitter merely said, "What do you want me to tell them?"

"Tell them I want Ricky."

XVII

"YOU see," Sarah explained, "I wasn't afraid of him because where Richard is concerned I could — I could —"

"Fight your weight in wildcats," Brad suggested. "You keep right in there pitching, gal."

"What do we do now?" Jenny asked. She and Brad had showered and changed and the three of them were now having breakfast. "It's hard to believe that Joe Colfax is right across the street, and at Mrs. Fulmer's, of all places."

"Mrs. Fulmer's finest hour," Brad commented. "If I were to follow my inclination I would go over and smash Joe's face in, but I don't suppose that would help the situation much. What do you suppose that woman told him?"

"Plenty," Sarah said gloomily. "I warned Mr. Colfax not to believe her, but anyone could see he wants to stir up trouble."

"But why?" Jenny asked.

"I suppose," Brad said, "he hopes to create enough scandal so he can reverse the custody order."

"Surely he can't do that!"

Brad covered Jenny's cold hand with his warm one. "You aren't afraid of Colfax, are you, dear?"

"He mustn't have Ricky, Brad."

"No," Sarah chimed in firmly, "that man must not have Ricky."

"Now isn't that just too bad!"

Joe had walked in without knocking, leaving the door wide open. Across the street Mrs. Fulmer had pushed aside her curtains and she was frankly watching. Joe stood, hands in his pockets, his eyes mocking them. "Now isn't that just too bad! My lawyer has been in touch with an old friend of his in L.A. who says we've got quite a case. Very juicy, in fact. Richard isn't going to be left in the hands of a cheap little actress who —"

Brad's chair fell over as he jumped and Jenny cried, "Brad! No!"

Seeing Brad's blazing eyes and that he was kept in check only by Jenny's restraining hand on his arm, Joe stepped back, angry because this man could frighten and humiliate him as he had done once before at Jenny's apartment.

"Apologize," Brad said, his voice hoarse with the restraint he was exercising.

"I've got facts, Maxwell."

"Apologize to my wife."

Brad took a step forward and Joe fell back. "Okay, okay, I apologize. And now let's get down to brass tacks. I want Ricky. I'm not going to leave him here. Why, if it hadn't been for Mrs. Fulmer across the street that poor, neglected kid would have drowned, and she's willing to testify to that. And to a lot of other things, too, if you make it necessary. So I'm taking the boy home with me."

"You aren't taking him anywhere."

It wasn't Brad who had spoken. It was the man who stood in the doorway, a man with a marked resemblance to Joe except for the firm mouth, the steady eyes, and a deep scar on his forehead.

Joe wheeled around, staring as though he had seen a ghost. He thrust out a hand as though to push the apparition away. "No," he said almost in a whisper. And then, "Richard! My God! Richard!"

At last Jenny was on her feet, running toward him, dragging him into the room, flinging her arms around him, laughing and crying. "Richard! Oh, Richard! What happened to you? We thought —" She stopped short. "You know about Louise?"

"Yes, I heard. When I was finally released from the hospital they flew me home. I looked for Ricky and at last I discovered that you had him. I came out to get him." Richard turned to his half-brother. "I see you had the same idea." His voice was quiet but his expression was dangerous.

Joe held out his hand. "Rick! How wonderful! How marvelous! I never hoped for this."

There was something sardonic in Richard's eyes. "That I can well believe." The heartiness faded from Joe's face, leaving a look of uncertainty. "What did you have in mind for my son, Joe?" His voice was deadly. Its very lack of stress made it frightening.

Jenny intervened hastily. "Sit down, Rick. I'll bring you coffee and fix you some breakfast."

He looked away from Joe and smiled, making apparent the profound difference between the half-brothers. When Richard smiled even his eyes laughed. *"You'll* fix breakfast?" he asked in mock amazement.

"Of course. I've learned to be a cook, haven't I, Brad?"

"And a good one too. This scatterbrain of mine seems to assume we know each other. I take it you are Richard Colfax. I am Bradley Maxwell, Jenny's husband."

The two men shook hands, each liking what he saw of the other.

"I know," Richard said. "I saw our old housekeeper Margaret who told me Jenny took over Richard and gave up the theater in the middle of a smash hit to bring him out here because the poor little tyke seems to have inherited my asthma. I'll thank you both adequately some time when I can find the right words. But — can I see him now?"

"Of course. It's time for him to wake up anyhow. This way." Jenny led him to the door, saw Richard go to bend over the crib, looking at his sleeping son, touching the soft cheek with one gentle finger, and then she went back to the living room, leaving them together, wiping away her tears.

"Lazarus," Joe whispered, "back from the dead." He added, "Of all the rotten luck!" He looked from Sarah to Brad to Jenny, turned on his heel and went out, slamming the door behind him.

Mrs. Fulmer, who had been lingering over her housework in the sitting room where she could keep an eye on the Maxwell house, turned in surprise when Joe came back for his suitcase.

"You are leaving without the boy?"

"His father just came." Joe's voice was still dull with shock.

"His father!" Mrs. Fulmer was avid for more but Joe did not explain. "Are you going back home?"

"Yes. When is the next bus?"

"There are only two a day. The one Richard's real father must have come on. It leaves in half an hour for the airport. The other leaves about four in the afternoon."

Joe picked up his suitcase. "I'll be on my way then. Thanks for putting me up for the night."

"But is Richard's father going to stay *there?*"

As her meaning dawned upon him, Joe gave a short bark of laughter. Whatever happened to young Ricky now, at least some scandal about his birth would haunt the Maxwells for a long time to come. He had wasted a lot of money and lost his best chance, perhaps his last chance, of gaining a fortune, but at least he had been able to retaliate to some degree. As he headed for the bus stop he felt better.

ii

That night when dinner was over and the small boy had been tucked into his crib, Jenny and Brad and Rick Colfax sat drinking coffee and talking.

"So all the time, instead of being dead, you were lost in the jungle," Jenny said. "I don't understand how you survived all those months."

"I had been in a helicopter that was shot down. The other guys were killed. We'd been working together for two weeks by that time and I knew them better than I'd be likely to know anyone else in a lifetime. Well, I got shot in the head and was discovered by a Vietnamese. When he saw I was alive he took me to his place. Just a hut. The man and his wife had three little kids but they gave me their only bed and slept on the earth floor. They nursed me back to health, shared what little food they had with me, and hid me from the Vietcong who were always raiding their village. That took guts. My God, what guts!

"The chopper had come down a long way from any possible communication with our troops and the man didn't dare leave his helpless family long enough to reach them and tell them about me. I'd blanked out completely. I might as well have been born the day I finally woke up in that hut. I didn't know who I was or how I had come there.

"Well, there was one of those lulls in the fighting and the guy who saved me got through to the Americans somehow and they came for me and I was taken to a hospital. My memory came back then but they decided not to fly me home until the head injury had healed completely."

Brad was watching him closely, aware of the emotional strain under which he was laboring. "Sure you want to go on with this?"

"Let me tell it now and then we'll forget it. I cabled Louise, of course, and that's when I learned . . . After that I didn't care so much what happened to me. But the first thing I did when I got home and out of the service was to try to find Richard. I couldn't discover what had happened to you, Jenny, except that you had sold your apartment, had married a doctor, and gone west somewhere. I was about crazy until I ran down Margaret, our old housekeeper, who told me about you and Joe and the custody suit and what you had done for Ricky.

"Well, all I wanted was to get my hands on Joe. There could be only one reason for his wanting my boy and I was feeling pretty violent. Anyhow I went up to his wife's farm and saw the poor girl. She was terribly glad I had come. She was worried about little Richard. She said Joe had run through ninety percent of her father's estate and he — well, I guess he wanted mine — and my son's." That deadly note was in his voice again.

"I think so too," Jenny said. "He was going to try to get the custody decision revoked because he was going to claim I wasn't fit to have him."

Richard Colfax had always been a good-looking man. Now, while all the boyishness was gone, he had gained a quality that would make him stand out in any group. His mouth was harder, his eyes more disillusioned, but his smile was still, as it had always been, irresistible. Whatever might happen to him, he could cope with it. He went on speaking of his half-brother.

"Joe has always been a bad egg. I tried hard but we never got along. And his poor wife!" Unexpectedly Rick laughed like a boy. "I settled Joe's hash, anyhow. I shook some courage into Mildred. She closed out what money she had left and her farm has been snapped up by the next neighbor. She took the Chrysler and right now she is driving out to Reno for a divorce. Not that she would ever want to marry again but at least she'll be her own woman and free to go her own way. Joe is in for a big shock when he gets back."

Seeing the blazing anger in his face Jenny asked quickly, "What do you think of your son?"

"He's going to be a lot like Louise, isn't he?"

"Are you going to take him away at once?"

Rick rubbed his forehead, frowning. "I've been thinking about that all day, of course. It was my first intention but you've given him wonderful care and he thrives in this climate. I — guess maybe the best thing for him would be for me to disappear again."

Jenny was aware of a flash of gladness at the idea she

might keep Ricky, and then she was ashamed of her monstrous selfishness. "You know what I think?" she said impulsively. "Why don't you stay here with us? We could put up a bed in Ricky's room until you can make some plans and have a chance to get to know your son all over again. He's such fun now, learning new things every day. He's your boy, not ours, and you ought to have the deciding voice in the way he's brought up. And then when you've had time to think things out, after you get used to being a civilian again, you can begin to plan for the future. You might even decide to settle here permanently; after all, you need this climate too. If you wanted to set up your own establishment you could find some woman to look after Richard so you could keep him with you. What do you think?"

There was a little pause. Then Rick said, "There's nothing I'd rather do, but this seems to me a terrific imposition. You and Brad are still honeymooners. You won't want someone else in the way. But there may be some suitable place near you."

"We both want you to stay," Brad told him.

iii

By the end of a week most of the tension had relaxed and Rick seemed more like himself. Brad kept a watchful eye on him, made sure that he did regular swimming on the pretext that he could teach his son, and saw that he had long hours of rest. Everyone in a hot climate, he assured Rick gravely, took an afternoon siesta, and Rick, sleeping heavily through the heat of the day, was unaware that his example was not followed by others.

Day by day his tension relaxed; the recent past was

already receding; his delight and pride in his son became the core of his life; he began to take an interest in his surroundings. Because of Jenny's morning classes he was out for hours at a time, often taking Ricky with him, viewing the changes that were being made at Desert Winds.

"It's like Jack's beanstalk in the fairy tale," he told Jenny. "You can see it grow before your eyes."

There were moments when something tickled his fancy and Jenny saw again the brother-in-law whom she had adored: his charm, his gaiety, his bedrock dependability. If her heart was wrenched with pain that Louise could not see him like that too, she forced herself to accept the fact that if the past cannot be regained, there is always a future to build.

"You," Brad accused her one day, "are up to something. Little Miss Fixer-Upper has an idea." He grinned at her air of bland innocence. "Okay. I suppose I'll find out eventually."

Jenny made no reply but she was planning a bold move. The first step came when she telephoned Sarah, whom she had not seen since the morning of Richard's dramatic arrival and Joe's ignominious departure.

"Come to Pasadena with me tomorrow. Mrs. Gates will baby-sit. I've got to get some stuff for the play."

She planned in advance, made an appointment with Mark in San Marino to give Sarah a permanent and restyle her hair. When Sarah emerged from the beauty parlor, her pale hair shining and more becomingly arranged than Jenny had ever seen it, her eyes sparkling with a new sense of confidence that came from the awareness that she looked well, Jenny dragged her, helpless and protesting, through Bullock's and I. Magnin's and made her buy half a dozen dresses and a bathing suit that startled Sarah and then made her laugh impishly.

"When Mama sees this."

When Richard sees this, Jenny thought. Attractively dressed and looking her best, her face glowing with a kind of inner excitement as she became aware of her own unsuspected potentialities, Sarah's resemblance to Louise was almost startling.

On their return to Desert Winds, they stopped to collect Ricky from Mrs. Gates. The latter took a long look at Sarah and another at Jenny. "I never would have guessed she had it in her," she confessed. "What will you be up to next? Mrs. Caldwell is going to have a fit."

"I didn't do it for Mrs. Caldwell."

Helen Gates laughed. "You don't believe in waiting for the mills of the gods, do you? May I ask for the meaning of this transformation?"

"You'll see."

"That is what I am afraid of."

Jenny smiled at her. "You aren't really afraid. I don't do things to hurt people."

Sarah had scooped up a delighted Ricky, who behaved as though they had been separated for a year instead of a week. She let him sit on her lap in the car as Jenny drove away from the motel, and when he had tired of this exuberant reunion and wriggled to be free she lifted him over into the back seat.

"When is Mr. Colfax going to take him away?"

"Not at once, in any case. This climate is as good for him as it is for little Richard and we've been sort of talking about his settling out here. He was in advertising before he went into the service and now he's at loose ends. He doesn't have to work, of course, but he's the kind of man who never would be satisfied just idling. I've been hoping that Wallace Penrose could get him interested in the spa, perhaps even persuade him to invest money in it. It's always exciting to help something grow. And, of course, if he should stay here we wouldn't lose Ricky altogether."

"That would be wonderful. Then I could see him sometimes. I don't think I could bear to lose him altogether. When will Mr. Colfax make up his mind?"

"I haven't said anything about the spa. But I thought if you mentioned it to Alma and she mentioned it to Wallace —"

Sarah turned to look at the girl at the wheel of the little Renault. "What is it about you, Jenny? Things go on and nothing ever happens and then you come along and change things. The town is different. The people are different."

"Well," Jenny said, almost apologetically, "I can't just stand there when I see things that can be done. Come in for iced coffee before I drive you home."

By the time Jenny had served the iced coffee a car door slammed. "Visitors," Sarah said. "I'll be on my way."

"Nonsense, you aren't going to walk home carrying all those suitboxes. Anyhow, stop running away from people. You're a knock-out, whether you realize it or not. Stay where you are. I think it's only Richard."

He came in, nodded a greeting to Jenny, and went, as usual, to pick up his son. When he had set him down, Jenny said. "Iced coffee? Oh, I don't think you know Sarah Caldwell. She's Ricky's good angel."

Richard noticed Sarah for the first time. On his arrival he had been so absorbed in his son and his half-brother that he had paid no attention to the drab colorless girl who had been in the room. He had barely been aware of her existence.

Ricky came rushing to Sarah, wanting to play a favorite game. Her face lighted up as it always did when she was with the boy. Seeing her through her brother-in-law's startled eyes Jenny knew that he was seeing another Louise. She felt a sharp pang for her sister and then told herself that Louise would want her son to have a devoted mother and her husband to have a wife who would be loved in her own right but also be a memory of her.

XVIII

"YOU," Wallace Penrose said, "must be Richard
Colfax."

Richard had left the comfort of his car to stroll to the
site where dressing rooms were being constructed beyond
a large pool. The man who addressed him appeared at first
glance to be a Mexican. Then as he lifted his head Richard
saw the blue eyes.

"And you," Richard said slowly, taking in the man's
good looks, his air of command, "must be Penrose, the
man who planned all this." He made a vague gesture to
indicate the extent of the activity that was going on.

Wallace held out his hand, smiling. "Yes, I'm Penrose
but I am not, unhappily, the one who planned this project.
That was the work of Jennifer Haydon. I mean Jennifer
Maxwell. Jennifer is quite a girl, Colfax."

"So," the other acknowledged, "I am just beginning to
realize."

"I owe her quite a debt," Wallace said.

"So do I. How great a debt I can hardly calculate. She
— if it weren't for Jenny and Brad, my son —" He made
a helpless gesture. "You can't really pay the big debts, can
you?"

"I suppose not, but there are some things —" Wallace broke off to give a direction to a waiting workman and turned back.

"Am I interrupting?" Richard asked.

"Not at all. I've been wanting to talk to you, for several reasons."

"By the way, how did you know who I am?"

Wallace laughed. "Everyone in Desert Winds knows who you are. You are little Ricky's father."

Something in his tone made Richard say grimly, "Just what are you getting at, Penrose?"

Wallace made a placating gesture and then took off the big sombrero to wipe his forehead. "If you aren't busy, how about taking a little ride? Get out of the sun and cool off while we talk."

After a quick look at him Richard got into his car and Wallace joined him. When Richard had switched on the air conditioning he asked, "Any special direction?"

"If you want to get an idea of the scope of what we are doing here, I'll show you around. What I really want is to talk to someone about Jenny and what is being said. I won't risk Maxwell. He'd go out and break someone in two. The thing is — I got the story from Sarah, or rather she told Alma who told me — that your half-brother believed you were dead and he came out here to get your son. Shenanigans about an inheritance. Your appearance drove him off but he left a nice little piece of scandal for Mrs. Fulmer to spread about your son's parentage."

"I see. Well, I can clear that up without any difficulty."

"It occurred to me — we plan to give a reception after the opening of *Heat Wave*. You know about that?"

"Sure. Jenny is rehearsing you people every night."

"There will be a nice public opportunity to get in your version of the story."

"I hadn't figured on going to any receptions."

"It's the least you can do for Jenny. The thing is that trouble is brewing. Jenny has made an enemy of the Fulmer woman; Sarah's mother resents her because she is trying to help Sarah escape her clutches. I wouldn't put it past them to do something unpleasant and we can't let that happen."

"No, we can't let that happen. I'll be there and primed for trouble."

"Good man. I understand your war experiences were really something."

Richard forestalled any further comment about his personal life by saying, "Tell me about this project of yours, Penrose."

"We have a big slice of desert here, land that lies dead all summer and can't support itself even in winter because it hasn't the soil to grow things or minerals or oil or power for manufacturing. It has stayed more or less like this for a million years or so, since the seas finally drained away. But it has warm weather in winter, it is dry, and it has hot springs. In other words we have a climate and hot springs that are good for certain conditions.

"What we are trying to do is to turn these hot springs into a paying proposition, build proper motels and housing, provide some entertainment, and get people not only to visit here but to want to stay. If it works it could transform the whole community. Whether it works or not, it is, at least for the time being and for many months to come, providing a good deal of employment, because, when work on the spa is finished, my father is going to build a combined hospital and sanitarium."

"A long-range project," Richard said thoughtfully. "You seem to have everything under control."

"Not everything. What we need, as of now, is a big advertising campaign to tell people what is going on here, what the future possibilities are for investment. The trouble is that I can't swing it. Everything I could get my hands on through the banks has gone into the building operation."

For some time they rode in a silence broken only when Wallace would give directions and point out the excavations for the new motel, the site of an entertainment center, the temporary shelters for the workers.

"You know," Richard said thoughtfully, "I have a friend on *See*."

"The big picture magazine?"

"Yes. This sort of thing on a wide-scale plan that is providing work when men are being laid off, a start-from-scratch idea to remake a whole community, is just ready-made for a feature story. There is plenty of action in it and it has a note of hope that's typical of America at its best."

"Would you care to write to him about it?"

"Write? I'll call him today. I'll get at it right away and see whether I can stir up some action." Richard added casually, "I used to be in advertising myself. If this interests *See* you'll get all the publicity you want and it won't cost you a cent."

ii

"So," Wallace concluded, "at this very minute Richard Colfax is probably selling his friend on running a feature article on the Desert Winds spa. National publicity that won't cost us a cent, which is just as well. I've run through most of the money I borrowed to get this thing started."

"Can't your father help?" Alma asked.

They had been swimming in the big pool at the Penrose house and now they lay in long chairs on the patio. Wallace had turned to face her, the tall, slender, dark-haired Viking. There was a quality of assurance about her that came from an inner sense of balance and serenity. She was — no, dependable was a dreary sort of word and Alma was not dreary. But safe. *Safe* was a good word. With Alma around you'd always think the world was on an even keel.

"I suppose he could help out but I would much rather not ask him. In the first place, the hospital will be an enormous expense. In the second place, I'd like to carry through what I started. I don't want my father to think I've failed at everything."

"But you haven't," she said quickly. "You've proved that you can do this. And no one can be expected to carry on without money."

"True, O Queen. Anyhow, if Colfax makes his pitch to the friend of his on the staff of the magazine we'll have publicity to burn and maybe even get some financing from people who like to get in on the ground floor when they make investments."

"I thought you were going to send me out to do publicity for the spa."

"Would you do it?"

"Of course."

"Even if it would mean giving up your job with Dr. Maxwell?"

"Of course. It would be much more interesting than being an office nurse."

"I thought — now and then I've had an idea that you rather liked the good doctor; in fact, that you liked him a lot."

Alma's eyes met his squarely. "I did. Quite a lot. But he is a very much married man and I don't like women who try to smash up marriages." She laughed. "Even if I could — which I couldn't. That marriage was made to last."

"The job I have in mind for you might not be as steady as being an office nurse."

Alma smiled at him. "Is that so important?"

He got up suddenly and went to stand beside the pool, staring down, his back to her. "My father believes it is important. Anyhow, a public relations job isn't what I had in mind for you. That is something that Colfax can possibly do spectacularly well."

"And I couldn't?"

He turned to smile at her. For once he was wholly serious and not conscious of his charm. Indeed, he seemed almost diffident. "I had another idea for you. I don't know how good it could be. I want to pay off my bank loan and get out, find a job in a museum somewhere. It wouldn't pay very much. There will never be much money. My father and I talked over the hospital project and he explained it wouldn't leave much more than a comfortable income. Nothing spectacular. No crown jewels. No duplex penthouses. I could feed a healthy girl with a healthy appetite. But no yachts. I — it's not much of a job I am offering you, is it, darling?"

"It might help," Alma said, "if you told me what the job is."

"Oh, I thought you knew that. I want you to marry me."

"Then what are you waiting for?"

It was a long time before either of them found it necessary to say anything. Then Alma drew away from Wallace's arms, held his protesting hands away from her, and said, "There is someone coming. I must go and dress. Anyhow, it's high time I get back to the house. Mrs. Caldwell will be champing at the bit."

"That's Dad with Mrs. Gates. If you must go I'll change and drive you home."

"No, don't go," Penrose called from the doorway. "Won't you stay for dinner, Miss Deming? I've persuaded Mrs. Gates."

"Another time, if I may. I promised Mrs. Caldwell I'd help her with her costumes tonight."

"You do enough for that woman," Wallace grumbled.

"At least it gives Sarah a break now and then. Since Jenny has transformed her, Mrs. Caldwell is terrified that she'll get away. If I know anything about women, as soon as the play is over she plans to have the granddaddy of all relapses, and she'll need Sarah day and night."

"If I were Sarah I'd take an ax to the woman," Mrs. Gates declared.

"And hit her forty whacks? But she might not be as lucky as Lizzie Borden," Penrose said. "Oh, Wallace, when you can get a few free moments will you look at the rock garden and see what can be done? Everything is burned to a crisp."

"I'll get into some clothes and take a look at it now," Wallace said, hoping to detain Alma for a few more minutes. "Come and give me your opinion, Alma."

"I don't know anything about rock gardens."

"Then it's time you learned."

"All right. Ten minutes."

It was actually only ten minutes when she came out dressed in a shirt, shorts, and sandals, a broad-brimmed hat on her dark hair.

Wallace reached for her hand. "Alma is going to marry me, Dad."

His father, beaming, kissed her on both cheeks and shook hands with his son heartily. "Welcome to the family, Alma. We're very lucky to have you and you'll make Wallace a happy man. I congratulate you, Wallace."

"I was thinking," Alma began when they were out of earshot, "that —"

"For God's sake don't move! Don't stir!"

At Wallace's horrified voice Alma instinctively turned, saw the huge diamondback rattlesnake coiling its way into the rock garden. She gave a convulsive leap and fell, twisting her leg under her. Wallace, white-faced, lifted a large stone and dropped it on the snake, which seemed to thrash around a long time before it lay still. Then he came to bend over Alma.

"Are you hurt?"

"I don't think so."

He helped her to her feet and she staggered. "My ankle!"

He picked her up and carried her into the house.

Mrs. Gates helped him place her on the couch and felt the ankle which was already beginning to swell. "Wallace, call Dr. Maxwell and tell him she may have broken her ankle."

It seemed only minutes before Brad arrived. He examined Alma's ankle and said it was only a severe sprain.

"But it will probably hurt just as much. And she is to

be kept off it." When he had strapped the ankle he said to Wallace, "I'll help you get her home."

"Mrs. Caldwell wouldn't lift a hand for her," Mrs. Gates said.

"She must stay here," Penrose decided. "There's plenty of room and my cook —"

"Thank you very much," Alma said. "I'd honestly prefer to go back to the Caldwell house if you can get me there without too much trouble."

"Then you'll only have Mrs. Caldwell to rely on," Brad warned her, "because if you are laid up I'm going to need Sarah."

Mrs. Gates's face lighted in amusement. "Tell Mrs. Caldwell that Alma is engaged to Wallace Penrose and she'll act like Florence Nightingale."

Penrose laughed. "My dear Helen, I'm afraid you are a cat."

"Of course I am," she said cheerfully.

iii

"So," Sarah said, "you'll have to take the lead yourself. Can you manage it?"

Jenny looked surprised. "There's no choice, is there? At least I have the costumes. I could never wear Alma's. Mine were shipped out with my other things and I've never even unpacked them. How are you managing with Alma?"

"Mama is looking after her. Alma's a good patient, as you might expect. She says she loves having a legitimate excuse to lie around and plan for her wedding. She's going to marry Wallace, you know, and I think they'll be good for each other. Alma will give Wallace the stability he needs and she's the attractive kind of woman a man like that wants to display as his wife. And she is genuinely fond of him. He's terribly good-looking, of course."

"And so they lived happily ever after," Jenny said.

Sarah laughed. It was hard to believe that this self-confident, glowing girl was the drab and lifeless creature she had been a short time ago. "You know, when people tell me after this that a marriage was made in heaven I'll wonder if somewhere in the background there isn't someone like you arranging things."

"Like me!"

Sarah laughed. "You and your innocent surprise! A female Machiavelli, that's what you are." She turned as Richard came into the room and dropped wearily onto a chair.

"Hello, Jenny. Hi, there, Sarah." The scar on his forehead was less noticeable now that he was so bronzed.

"You've been doing too much," Jenny scolded him. "Brad warned you not to overdo at first."

"Don't blame me. I've been walked to death by Wallace Penrose. I have a suspicion he'd like to unload this project of his on my shoulders because I made the mistake of saying that I was thinking vaguely of going into business on my own; I have some capital to invest and I'd rather gamble on myself than on someone else."

"It's a marvelous idea," Jenny said.

Her brother-in-law eyed her with open suspicion. "It's probably your idea, if I know anything about you. Oh, I suppose you know Wallace is going to marry the glamorous Alma, so there goes Brad's office nurse."

"Yes, Sarah told me."

"Was that your idea, too!"

"Don't be absurd."

"I also understand that because of the Deming girl's accident you'll be taking on your old role in *Heat Wave*. Talk about perfect timing."

"What do you mean? Good heavens, you don't think I had anything to do with Alma's accident, do you?"

Richard gave a shout of laughter. "I wouldn't put it past you but I'll give you the benefit of the doubt. No, I think the timing is perfect because my friend on *See* leaped at the idea, like a drowning man at a straw. The story they were working on blew up in their faces, the account of a new giant airplane, but the thing crash-landed on the test flight. They were hunting desperately for something to replace it. He called again this morning to say he has gone into action and he is flying out a crew of cameramen, researchers, writers — in fact, the works. And they'll get here tomorrow in time for the opening of *Heat Wave*. You'll be back in the news, Jenny, and a godsend to the magazine, which could use a glamorous and famous woman in its illustrations."

"I hope Brad won't mind too much."

"Why should he?" Rick looked at her troubled face and remembered the two bedrooms. He fell silent. As a ball plopped down at his feet he started and then tossed it back to the small boy. "Hi, son."

Ricky scrambled after the ball. "Hi, Dad."

$\mathcal{A}$ week had passed in such a whirl of activity that Jenny dropped into bed in a state of exhaustion every night. Aside from at breakfast she rarely saw Brad. And now she had to take her old role without a rehearsal. There were a dozen things to attend to at the big church annex where the performance was to be held: inexperienced scene shifters to be instructed, her costumes to press, her makeup kit to be unearthed from a box in storage.

Because she had so much responsibility and so many details to handle, Jenny was only dimly aware of the curious eyes that watched her. It seemed almost as though the friendliness she had always encountered was shadowed by something — suspicion, hostility? She pushed aside the impression to concentrate on the performance, running through her lines when she dared take the time.

That morning the crew of *See* magazine arrived, settled in a motel at Four Corners, and commuted the thirty miles to Desert Winds, which they turned at once into bedlam. Those who were not taking pictures were talking to the inhabitants. When they learned what was happening, the women of the town swamped the only beauty parlor, recently installed and with a single operator. This was the most excitement Desert Winds had ever had.

There was, of course, the inevitable dissident voice. The owner of the lunch stand slammed a hamburger and an order of French fries in front of Brad and glared at him.

"You see that guy going out? Know what he asked me? Was I a *native?* What they think we got out here? Right surprised when I told him to scram. He said other people — other natives, I suppose — was glad enough to talk. And they are, too! I haven't been able to get Gladys to put her mind on the job all day. And primp! The only customers she even sees when they come in here are part of that bunch of people from New York. She serves *at* them when she isn't waiting on them. Just stands there and poses with her hand on her hip and bats her eyes."

He stopped to catch his breath. "What's got into the people here? A nice quiet town with nice quiet people and now they've gone crazy. All they can think of is crowding in front of a camera and answering fool questions. Go around clucking like a bunch of chickens. I tell you, doc —" The owner broke off as he saw Brad, and he grinned reluctantly.

"Okay! I guess I got sore and sounded off. My wife talked to one guy as though she had been born under a piece of cactus and played with rattlesnakes as a baby, and she never saw the desert until she was twenty-five. Came here from San Francisco. But you just wait until it happens to you and your wife. Oh —" He broke off awkwardly.

"What's wrong?"

"Oh, nothing." After a moment the proprietor asked, his tone elaborately casual, "Ever come across a fat guy with little eyes and a big mouth? Says he's a columnist — gossip, I'd guess. Calls himself Chatty Charlie?"

Brad shook his head. "No time to read that stuff."

Later in the afternoon when he returned from the hospital Brad found a reporter and a cameraman waiting at the office.

"Hold it, doc," one of the men called, and when Brad turned to face him the man snapped his picture. "Thanks a lot. Now can I get one of you with a patient?"

"You cannot."

"Okay, but it never hurts to ask."

The cameraman waved cheerfully and got into the waiting car while the reporter said, "I'd like a few minutes."

"I haven't time."

"Just a few minutes. Your brother-in-law set up this deal, you know, and —"

"Then talk to him."

"I have, Dr. Maxwell. I certainly have. The thing is that there's a nasty undercurrent here and I don't like it. I talked to the boss, too, who's a friend of Colfax. Chatty Charlie has come here from L.A. There are some rumors about Miss Haydon —"

"Mrs. Maxwell," Brad said, and his expression was dangerous.

"Look here, doctor, just for the record, I've seen every play your wife ever appeared in. I fell in love with her at first sight. I still think she's tops, the loveliest person I'll ever see. I'm on her side. But someone ought to know what's going on."

Brad stood aside. "Come in."

ii

The big annex that had been built on to the small church for meetings was already packed. In the back there were standees. The demand for tickets, now that it was known Jennifer Haydon was to take the lead, was so great that it had been decided to give performances for five nights.

After swallowing a cup of soup Jenny came out to find Brad waiting for her.

"Where's Richard?" she asked.

"He's taken the boy over to the Penrose house and then he's going to see the crew and give them some background stuff about the spa, and how you came to take part in the play, and all that. He seems to be a demon organizer. Wallace must be delighted with the publicity he has cooked up. Have any photographers bothered you?"

Jenny was startled by something in his voice, trying to sense his mood. He hates this publicity, she thought, and her heart sank. But she had to see the job through now. At least the church would benefit by all this.

"Oh, they followed me around for a while and wanted pictures. I didn't really mind. And they promised to wait until after the performance tonight to get me in costume and until the end of the week for other pictures. The way I looked today they wouldn't have wanted to get a picture."

"How about reporters?"

"There were a few."

"What did they have to say?"

Jenny was surprised by his insistence and annoyed at his keeping at her. She had a dozen things to see to and a virtually unrehearsed performance to give with a green group of unpredictable amateurs. If it were to be, as had been planned, a performance for Desert Winds people only, any breakdown would not matter, but tonight they would be playing for the Big Time. She knew that *See* had flown out their drama critic.

"What did they say?" Brad repeated.

"Oh, the usual things. Why did I leave the stage? How do I like the desert? Do I miss New York? Do I plan to return to the theater? Will I be happy just raising a family? Things like that."

"And what did you tell them?"

Jenny looked at her watch. "Brad! We've got to go. There are half a dozen things to do before curtain time, as well as make up the women, and at least a few of the cast are bound to be in a dither."

When Brad had put her makeup kit, a big mirror, and her costumes in the back of the car she began to laugh. "When I think how careful I always was to rest before a performance and how I had a dresser and everything ready — and here I worked until three this morning and ever since seven I've rushed without a pause. I can't imagine how I'm going to go on tonight."

When Brad had parked behind the annex, after a surprised look at the jammed parking lot in front, Jenny turned to him impulsively. "Brad, wish me luck!"

iii

The curtains had been pulled apart rather jerkily and the first lines of *Heat Wave* were spoken, too softly, too uncertainly. Sarah sat behind the curtain, holding the book, ready to prompt if anyone broke down, her finger following the lines, her heart pounding. It was going all wrong. The play creaked along, without life or tempo. It was going to be a colossal flop, a turkey to end turkeys. Anyhow, the audience seemed to be in an odd mood. All that day her mother had looked like the cat that stole the cream and she had spent a lot of time on the telephone talking to Mrs. Fulmer, breaking off when Sarah appeared. People were whispering. She wished the whole thing were over.

Then Wallace Penrose's voice rose angrily and he banged on the table. There were no stairs but a curtain at the back of the stage was thrust aside and Jenny appeared. There was a moment of silence and then some scattered, rather tentative applause. If she was aware of the hostile atmosphere, Jenny gave no indication of it. For a few moments she held her pose and then she flashed her famous smile, and ran across the stage and spoke her first line.

In some way the action semed to quicken, the actors were speaking more clearly, more confidently. A quality of electric excitement had been generated. Sarah was so engrossed in the action, in the way Jenny seemed to draw the best from the whole cast, that she forgot to watch her book until she heard Wallace falter for a line and she turned pages rapidly.

Now and then, particularly in the spirited exchange between the young engineer and Mrs. Caldwell, the audience burst into delighted laughter. It was Jenny, however, though she never attempted to steal a scene, who held the audience in the hollow of her hand. They watched for her smile; they responded to a laugh; they found her, as New York audiences had found her, irresistible.

Brad, in the back row, watched intently and somberly. Not even the avid reporters could read anything in the unrevealing face. It seemed strange that the only person to remain impervious to Jennifer Haydon's enchantment — and tonight she was Jennifer Haydon — was her youthful husband. Something odd there. Could be the rumors might have some foundation. But everything was submerged in the magic of her performance.

And then the final lines were spoken and the curtains were pulled together. In response to the applause they opened again and again, on the bowing cast. The houselights went up and still the audience remained seated, determined not to be cheated out of a bow by the star herself.

"Stand back," Wallace said, his voice low. "This is for Jennifer alone. Understand? Don't bow or smile." He herded the cast back against the wall and as the curtains opened again Jenny stepped forward, bowing and smiling. Then, to her shocked surprise, there was a giggle, followed by an outburst of laughter. What on earth could be wrong? She bowed again, saw Sarah behind the curtain with her face buried in her hands, and then realized that Mrs. Caldwell had come forward and was sharing the curtain call with her.

And the play was over.

Jennifer, still in the black velvet evening gown of the last act, went out of doors to keep her promise to the photographers. In a moment she was surrounded. "Mrs. Maxwell, you were wonderful. Absolutely wonderful. Miss Haydon, come back to New York. We miss you."

Someone said, "Did you see the Caldwell woman? Funniest thing I ever saw."

Jenny turned to find Mrs. Caldwell within earshot and went to say, "You gave a fine performance tonight. Your

234 FORSAKING ALL OTHERS

very best." Her voice was warm but it could not dim, in Mrs. Caldwell's ears, the sound of the audience laughter or of Sarah saying in distress, "Mama, how could you?" Her own daughter. Well, she'd show them. The wonderful Jennifer Haydon Maxwell wouldn't feel so smart when the stories got out. And as for Sarah, who had neglected her lately, trying to make a swan out of the ugly duckling she was, she'd be surprised. That was all. At the dress rehearsal Silas Penrose had told her in a confidential tone that he'd have something interesting to say after the performance. Her moment of triumph. No one would laugh then.

From the moment she had learned how rich he was she had felt a kind of bond between Silas Penrose and herself. She was never as happy as when she was in his home. To be the lady of the house there would be something. If she married Silas she wouldn't care what Sarah did. Actually she wouldn't want a grown daughter around.

Jennifer Maxwell was surrounded by admirers, as though she were the only member of the cast. Well, what could you expect? Across the parking lot Mrs. Caldwell saw Mrs. Fulmer talking to that famous and delightful man whose column she'd been reading for months. Chatty Charlie, they called him. She had been friends with him at once, just as she had felt at home with Silas Penrose. "Call me Charlie," he'd said in his engaging way. No doubt about it. She was more at home spiritually — she was sure it was a spiritual matter — with people who were rich and famous.

For a moment the two women looked at each other, smiling. Then Mrs. Fulmer got into her car and drove away.

Richard came up with Sarah. "Ready, Mrs. Caldwell? I've already hoisted Alma into the car, with Wallace's help. He suggested I take you home to change."

"How thoughtful of the dear boy to take such good care of me," she said.

There was a curious expression on Rick's face but he made no comment as he opened the back door and started to help her in beside Alma.

"Oh, I always prefer the front seat," she told him. "Sarah can sit in back."

Without comment he opened the front door for her and Sarah got in back with Alma.

"Sarah," Mrs. Caldwell said as Richard drove toward the canyon road, "weren't you rather careless, dear? Poor Wallace had quite a time before you gave him his line. So embarrassing for the dear boy. I suppose you were wool-gathering again."

Richard swallowed a word and kept his eyes on the road.

"I was so excited by Jenny's acting I forgot everything else," Sarah said. "I never realized how marvelous she is. Incandescent. And so generous. She made the whole cast seem better somehow."

"Well, after all, that was her job once, you know. But I'd like to see you less intimate with her. From all I hear —"

"Just what have you heard, Mrs. Caldwell?" Rick asked.

"Here we are," Sarah broke in anxiously. "Are you all ready for the reception, Alma?"

"Of course. I'll just wait here with Mr. Colfax while you change."

"That won't be necessary," Mrs. Caldwell said firmly. "Sarah can drive us over when we are ready. You needn't wait."

"Really, Sarah," she burst out, when Richard, after a protest, had driven away with Alma, "there are times when you make a downright fool of yourself. First it was that impoverished doctor in San Francisco, who obviously didn't care a rap for you or he wouldn't have married so soon; now you are throwing yourself at the head of this Colfax man, come from who knows where and he's who knows what, but from the stories I hear —"

"I know who he is, mama, and where he came from."

"You'd believe anything the Maxwell woman told you. But I do beg you not to make yourself conspicuous tonight, running after him."

"I —" Sarah gave up. *Conspicuous.* She remembered her mother stepping forward to share the limelight with Jenny and her face burned.

Seeing the blush Mrs. Caldwell laughed indulgently. "All right, dear, don't take it too hard. I just wanted to give you a teeny hint. I wouldn't like anything embarrassing to happen tonight. And I mean it when I say I don't want you to see that man again."

"Why?"

"You'll find out why." Mrs. Caldwell went into her room to dress, leaving Sarah staring after her.

XX

WHY didn't Brad come? Jenny had turned and smiled and gestured obediently while flashbulbs exploded. Then a small, ovoid man thrust his way through the crowd and kissed her noisily.

"What on earth are you doing here?" She was astounded.

"You're news, dear. Didn't you know? There are two Hollywood agents here as well as the drama critic from *See*."

As people crowded around her he said, "We've got to talk."

"I can't tonight. I'm going on to a reception."

"Then I'll crash the party. I've got news for you, Beautiful. That offer is still open. Tonight, after this clambake we'll get down to the nitty gritty."

Because of his height Brad loomed over most of the people who surrounded her and she turned to him in relief. He stood beside her, his eyes on the people near her, almost as though he was warning them to keep off.

"Anything to take home?"

"Nothing. We're going to do four more performances, you know, so I'll leave the makeup stuff here, and the costumes. Oh, I forgot the cream."

"What does it look like? Okay. Stay where you are. I'll get it."

When they were driving home Jenny, realizing that Brad was not going to say anything, asked him, "What did you think?"

"About what?"

"Why, the play, of course."

"Wonderful. But you always were."

"I didn't mean me. The play itself. How did it go?"

"It was all to pieces until you came on and then darned if you didn't run up a seam and sew it together again. They were all good from then on." He laughed in the dark. "Until that curtain call."

She gave a gurgle of laughter. "Wasn't that awful! I heard the laugh and I couldn't imagine what had happened, and then I saw Sarah cover her face with her hands and there was Mrs. Caldwell, bowing like anything. She did everything but blow kisses. Poor woman. She'll never live it down. Not in a small place like this."

"Serves her right. Wasn't that odd-looking man who kissed you the one I met over near Hollywood?"

"Yes, Mayley Prince."

"Television?"

"That's the one."

"What did he want?"

"Oh," Jenny tried unconvincingly to yawn, "I'm dead for sleep. I don't know what he wanted. He said he'd crash the Penrose party."

Brad sounded rather tart. "He looked capable of it."

When Jenny had removed the heavy stage makeup and changed for the reception to a dress like a white cloud, in dramatic contrast with her last-act costume of black velvet, she was so tired she felt as though her whole body had been beaten with rods. Then she squared her shoulders, forced herself to smile, and went out to find Brad and Rick waiting for her. They had been talking in low tones and broke off as she appeared.

"Ready?" Brad asked.

"Yes, I'm ready. I thought Richard was going to take care of the Caldwells."

"Mrs. Caldwell had other ideas. She doesn't think I am nice to know. So I delivered Alma to Wallace's loving arms and came back here. Anyhow, I have a hunch that if I went to the Penrose party in Mrs. Caldwell's wake she'd make me feel like the Outcast of Poker Flat."

As Brad drove toward the Penrose house Jenny turned to Richard in the back seat. "You really stirred up something! The crew from *See* have practically taken over the town today."

"Sheer luck. The story they were working on broke down so they were able to get men on the job in twelve hours. There will be more in a few days, researchers who are going through their files for stuff on spas in general and the Mojave Desert in particular."

"What do you bet this publicity starts bringing people in here even before there are any proper accommodations for them? And even people wanting to invest. Oh, Rick, it's good, isn't it?"

"What difference does it make to you?" Brad said. "You won't be here to see it."

"I — won't?"

"You know you won't," he said roughly. "The boy is safe now that Richard has come. There's nothing to keep you here."

With the help of the Penrose houseman they parked and walked toward the brilliantly lighted house. A group of men had clustered outside. One of them turned toward them, the chubby man called Chatty Charlie, red lips smiling, small eyes malicious. Brad took Jenny's arm and he steered her rapidly past the columnist before he could speak, with Richard close beside her on the other side.

Silas Penrose and his son stood in the wide corridor to welcome their guests. A number of them had already arrived and they were inspecting the patio, the large living room, the library, and the room which housed Wallace's collection of snuffboxes. Near the door, Alma Deming, in a dress like a flame that set off her dark beauty, was sitting with her foot propped on a pillow and beside her, again in the black and silver that stressed her distinction, was Helen Gates.

Jenny looked from Brad to Richard and laughed. "I feel as though I had two bodyguards." Over her head the men exchanged glances.

"Jennifer," Penrose exclaimed, "you were magnificent. You exceeded anything I had been led to expect." He kissed both her hands lightly. "You have given us all a great experience. And here is someone with a debt of gratitude."

Jenny shook hands with the minister.

"We are indeed in your debt, Mrs. Maxwell, not only for a great performance but for what you have done for the community as a whole and the church in particular. You have made possible a great many projects that were only dreams."

"You are too kind. This was a community project. Everyone who appeared in the play and those who handled the scenery and sold tickets or provided stage props or — oh, so many who contributed. And it has been great fun for all of us."

After a laughing greeting with Wallace, who looked from Brad to Richard as though asking a mute question, Jenny went to speak to Alma. "I'm so sorry you couldn't do your part. Perhaps you'll be able to play at least the last two performances."

"Not after what I saw tonight. I thought you were wonderful. I wouldn't dare compete and I'd probably be lynched if I tried."

Mrs. Gates seemed curiously withdrawn. She smiled vaguely at Jenny and said, "You were wonderful but I knew you would be," as though she were not thinking of what she was saying. After a quick look from Brad to Rick she sat with her eyes roving around the room, watching the guests. *Watching.* As though she thought something was going to happen.

The guests had all arrived now. Half the townspeople were on hand, many of whom had never been inside the Penrose house before. An elaborate buffet had been set out in the dining room. Jenny recognized most of the faces of the townspeople and she had met the crew from *See.* Mayley Prince had arrived like royalty and been accepted because Jenny had warned Silas Penrose of his plan to crash the party.

There was something disturbing in the atmosphere. People were forming small tight groups, murmuring together. Only a handful had come forward to congratulate Jenny on her performance, though they had been exuberant in their praise of the rest of the cast. And people looked at her curiously. She was uneasy. In New York she would have been surrounded after an opening night. Of course, this was only an amateur performance but just the same she was almost isolated. If it hadn't been for Brad and Rick, who stayed so tenaciously beside her, she would have been alone.

The Caldwells were the last to arrive, with that intolerable Chatty Charlie drifting along in their wake. Mrs. Caldwell ought to be warned, Jenny thought, that the malicious columnist would write something devastating about the curtain call she had shared. But Mrs. Caldwell did not seem aware of her danger. In fact, she looked extraordinarily pleased with herself.

She held out both hands to Silas Penrose. "How wonderful of you, dear Mr. Penrose, to provide this delightful party for us poor players."

Her voice rang out and Penrose caught his lip between his teeth and stared rigidly at the floor while, beside him, Wallace choked, and somewhere in the room there was a titter.

When he had his voice under control Penrose said, "The pleasure is mine."

"How like you! I've been thinking so much today about what you said at the dress rehearsal, wondering — sometimes I believe we really think along the same channels."

At this point Wallace proved himself unworthy of his more stalwart father, and he removed himself abruptly. He came to stand beside Alma, the fingers of one hand touching her shoulder.

"You nearly disgraced yourself," she scolded him.

"Us poor players! And our thinking in the same channels. That was too much for me. Dad is a better man than I am, standing like a scholar and a gentleman and not an expression to give away the channels his thinking is really —"

"But I can't help hoping," Mrs. Caldwell went on, disregarding Sarah's attempt to draw her away from her host, "that when we've all done our little all for the church, we can go back to our quiet old ways. Broadway and all its glitter is hardly for us simple people, is it?"

The rumors had reached the young engineer, who had not only proved to be a natural comedian but who had fallen completely under Jenny's spell in the course of the rehearsals.

"Well, no," he drawled in a room that had become silent almost as though, Jenny thought, they were waiting for a cue. "There's one sure thing. Broadway glitter isn't for people who don't know when the applause isn't for them."

"Oh, no," Jenny whispered, horrified, her hands clutching the arms of her bodyguards. "Oh, no! That was cruel. Stop him."

Neither of the men moved but somewhere there was a snicker that set off a series of muffled explosions of laughter like a string of firecrackers. All of a sudden, for no reason at all that she could understand, Jenny was afraid.

Mrs. Caldwell had turned on the young engineer, red color burning on her cheekbones, her body vibrating like a tight wire. "People can laugh," she began.

"Mama!" Sarah was tugging at her arm. "Mama, come on. Come and talk to Alma. Come."

Mrs. Caldwell shook off her daughter's hand. "Don't paw me, Sarah!" She turned to Silas Penrose. "I think you understand. There have been some rumors in this town, very unpleasant rumors, and I think it is time that they stopped."

"That what stopped?" It was Richard Colfax who had spoken.

This is what people were waiting for, Jenny thought, her heart jolting. But what is wrong?

"This is embarrassing. Before so many people. Well, if I must. Mrs. Fulmer and I hoped, once she was warned, it would not be necessary for any public —"

"Just what are you talking about?" Rick demanded.

"About you and Mrs. Maxwell and — your son."

"Oh, Brad, no!" Jenny clutched at his arm. "Brad, you can't —"

"But I can, Jenny," Richard said. "And I'm glad to have the chance. I owe a great debt to Jennifer Maxwell, so great a debt I can't imagine how it can ever be paid. My name is Richard Colfax. I married Jennifer Haydon's sister. She — it was one of those perfect marriages . . . I went into the service and was sent to Vietnam and later reported missing."

He sketched briefly his own experiences, dismissed Louise's death in a few quiet words, touched on his return home and the discovery that his half-brother had attempted to get hold of his son, who stood between him and the Colfax money.

"My wife had entrusted our son to her sister Jennifer. My boy has asthma and shouldn't live in a cold, damp climate. So, to save little Ricky from the two dangers of his health and my half-brother, Jennifer sacrificed her career — and anyone who saw her tonight knows how much she gave up — and she and her husband brought my boy out here. He has had superb care and blossomed under the treatment he has received, all the love and the care.

"As I say, I owe Jennifer an enormous debt. Today I discovered the undercurrent of scandal that is being brewed up by a few malicious women and a notorious columnist, a kind of keyhole peeper, who lives by smearing other people's lives. If there is any more of this disgusting calumny against one of the finest women I ever knew I am going to clap suits for slander on everyone involved. So far as Chatty Charlie is concerned," he added, turning sharply, "I understand your sponsors have paid off for the last time on a suit against you. I'd suggest that you watch your step."

In the silence that followed this speech Chatty Charlie, who was not a sensitive plant, bustled forward. "I'd like an exclusive story on your war experiences, Captain Colfax."

"You won't get anything out of me."

"Now look here," Chattie Charlie's voice had become a whine, "I was promised a story if I came here. If I can't get it from you I'll get it elsewhere."

"Try. Just try."

"Well, I'm sure," Mrs. Caldwell faltered, clutching at Silas Penrose's sleeve, "I was given to understand — that is, Mrs. Fulmer told me she saw —"

"Oh, that!" Wallace laughed. "Poor Jennifer. I drove her home one night when the doctor was called out and I made a nuisance of myself. She put me in my place. The only other time I've ever seen her alone was when she had a flat tire and I changed it for her. That was the time, by the way, when she suggested the idea of the Desert Winds Spa that is transforming this community. What is hap-

pening here is all due to her. If Colfax owes her some
thing, I'd hate to have to estimate what the people o
Desert Winds owe her. I don't owe any of you any ex
planation, of course. Jennifer has forgiven me and I'v
been forgiven by someone who is much more concerned
Miss Alma Deming, who is going to marry me."

"Well!" Mrs. Caldwell turned to Silas Penrose. "I
this," she swallowed, "the news you were going to an
nounce tonight?"

"No, I thought it was up to Alma and Wallace t
choose their own time for that. What I had to say," h
waited while the buzz of talk dwindled away, "was this
After much discussion with my son I have decided t
endow a combination hospital and sanitarium here a
Desert Winds in connection with the spa. I believe — w
both believe —" He broke off as there was an outbrea
of applause.

"How fine! . . . It will make all the difference . . . I
will bring in more people . . . Permanent settlers . .
Build business . . . Save lives."

"Dear Silas!" Mrs. Caldwell seized his hand and clun
to it in spite of his efforts to free himself, "I hope yo
don't mind the familiarity but I've never felt so close t
you before. What a splendid thing to do. I suppose — bu
of course dear Alma is rather young and inexperienced t
take over here as your hostess with so big a project unde
way."

"I wouldn't expect it," he said, his hand free at last
"Anyhow, Alma and Wallace are going to live their ow
lives, probably away from here."

"Silas," Helen Gates broke in to say, "some of you
guests are leaving. They have baby-sitters to take home.

"Thank you, my dear. Perhaps you'll join me in seeing them out." He smiled blandly at Mrs. Caldwell. "Two engagement announcements in one evening could be rather a muchness. But this way, people will probably get the idea. Coming, Helen?"

Mrs. Caldwell caught sight of the square-cut diamond on the hand Helen Gates tucked under her host's arm. She watched them walk toward the wide corridor. The richest man who had ever come within her orbit. Her spiritual kin. And he was going to marry Helen Gates!

There's no fool like an old fool, she told herself indignantly, forgetting that she was only a couple of years younger.

XXI

THOUGH the events of the evening were to be the main topic of conversation in Desert Winds for a month to come, the party never really picked up momentum after Richard Colfax's attack and Mrs. Caldwell's retreat. The guests invaded the room with its buffet and a few drifted up to Jenny with shy, embarrassed comments about her acting and the debt the whole community owed her and assurance that they had never really believed a word of the scandal about her so carefully circulated by Mrs. Fulmer and Mrs. Caldwell. As Silas Penrose commented later, it was an interesting example of collective guilt and shame.

Mrs. Fulmer had been among the first to leave, followed not long after by the Caldwells. All during the exposure of the gossip about Jenny, Brad and Richard had stood like rocks beside her. Now Rick left her side and got to the door before the Caldwells could leave.

Mrs. Caldwell turned her back on him. Sarah was about to follow her when Richard said urgently, "Sarah, please forgive me."

"You had to do it," she said. "We are the ones to ask forgiveness."

"Not you."

"Sarah," her mother said.

"Yes, mama, I'm coming."

Jenny looked up at Brad. "So that's why you and Richard have been hovering around me so carefully. How did you hear about that disgusting story?"

"Richard picked it up from his friend on *See*. Wallace got it through Chatty Charlie, who is a friend of a friend of Joe Colfax. Apparently Joe wanted to retaliate against Richard for packing off Mildred and the rest of her money, so his lawyer tipped off Chatty Charlie. Sent him to see Mrs. Fulmer who could be relied on to spread the stuff all over town. I got it from a reporter who heard it from his boss on *See* and who happened to be one of your devoted admirers."

"I could feel something was wrong but I didn't know what."

"Mrs. Gates knew, of course, but none of us had any idea how it would break out or when. At least it's over now. Come on home. You must be exhausted."

"Not yet!" Mayley Prince had come up beside them. "This girl doesn't escape me again. I want to talk to her before anyone else gets a chance and I have two rivals right here in this room. You're getting a second chance, lady, at that television deal."

Wallace called, "Bradley, there's a call for you," and Brad excused himself. He returned in a few minutes to say, "That guy on the Crest Road has had a relapse. Can you get home?"

"Richard can take me."

He nodded. "Well, good luck to your second chance." He left without another word.

Jenny stared after him blankly. This was to have been

her night of triumph. The play was a success. The church fund was bigger than anyone had dreamed. The spa was going to be a success. And, instead of any triumph for Jenny, there had been ugly rumors that had been believed by half the town, and Brad had said nothing except to wish her good luck on a second chance. He'd lain awake nights, he had told her, trying to find a way out. He had said the future of Desert Winds did not concern her. She wouldn't be here to see it. When Wallace suggested that she and Mayley Prince could talk without interruption in the room which housed his collection, she went in almost numbly.

Here was her great golden opportunity again, and where once it had seemed to answer all her dreams she knew that now all she wanted was to be wanted by Brad, to be loved by him. She could never be the core of his life as she had always expected to be in the life of the man she married. His work would come first. But she would be happy with what he could give her. And he had sent her away.

"It's a piece of fantastic luck," Prince began. "Fantastic. The package deal we were negotiating to replace you fell apart because the four-man team broke up. So there's still a prime spot for you. And with this Desert Winds deal being your idea the publicity is made to order, especially after *See* comes out with the story. Thing is, we've wasted months on this. Beaver is ready to fly out to Hollywood on twenty-four-hour notice. When can you start talking programs, so we can figure out what kind of show this is going to be?"

"There's really nothing to hold me here now," Jenny said dully.

"How about your husband? Will he raise any difficulties?"

"Oh, no. He's all in favor of this."

"Then everything in the garden is lovely."

"Just lovely." There was no light in her face, but she had recovered enough to think of other people. "What are your plans for the night?"

"I'll have to sit up in the lounge of the motel all night," Prince said in resignation. "Then I'll fly back in the morning."

Jenny explained the dilemma to Mr. Penrose, who agreed to put Prince up for the night. The last of the guests had gone. Wallace said, "Richard came with you and Brad, didn't he? Then I'll take you home."

Jenny went to get little Richard.

"If I had known what was coming I'd have gagged the Caldwell woman," Silas Penrose told Jenny. "Wallace and Helen both knew but they wouldn't tell me."

"Better to get it out in the open and air it," Wallace said.

"But tough on this girl. She's the heroine and this should have been her night of triumph."

"That's all right," Jenny said. "Good night. Good night, Mayley."

"Good night, Jennifer. See you in Hollywood. And no slip-up this time. Give me a ring when you know the date and I'll make reservations for you at the Beverly Hills Hotel, unless there's somewhere else you'd prefer."

"It doesn't make any difference."

Richard put her in the car, handed the boy to her, and climbed in back. Wallace took the wheel. "Tired?"

"I passed that stage hours ago."

No one spoke until Wallace had left Rick and Jenny at the door. She put Ricky in his crib and came back.

"Something is wrong," Richard said abruptly. "I've known that ever since you and Brad took me in. I thought then I was breaking in on a honeymoon couple. You've done an awful lot for me. Can't I help at all?"

Jenny struggled with a temptation to put her head on his shoulder and cry out all her pain and loneliness and desolation and disappointment.

"Everything is fine," she said lightly.

"But this marriage that is no marriage —"

"That was the agreement, you know. I couldn't keep Ricky unless I had a husband, and Brad couldn't get this practice unless he had a wife. It was a — a kind of bargain."

"How does Brad feel about you going back to acting?"

"He's all for it. He encouraged it. Of course we'll have to plan something for little Richard.'"

"I suppose, temporarily, Brad would let us stay on in the house."

"I think he'd like that."

"I hate to take my son away. He thrives here."

"So would you, Richard. Here you would have a new life, new surroundings, new people, new objectives. A — a second chance. And if Wallace wants to sell out, you could build something here, something good."

"You always were the girl with ideas, Jenny. Good lord, what hours Brad keeps! I'd hate to be a doctor. Ever since I was discharged from the service I've sworn that I would never miss another night's sleep if I could help it."

Jenny looked at the clock. "You've missed most of this one. It's half-past three. I'm off to bed."

"Good night, Jenny. You were terrific. I have never before known how good."

Before going to bed, Jenny went into the kitchen where she prepared a tray for Brad, with chicken sandwiches, a thermos of hot soup, and another of coffee. Before carrying it into his office she went into her bedroom and fumbled in a drawer. She laid the gold locket and chain on the tray. After a moment's hesitation, she slipped off her wedding ring and put it beside them.

ii

It was nearly five before Brad drove into the carport. The light was burning in his office as Jenny had left it for him lately, a token of welcome. As usual there was a tray awaiting him. At first he was about to push it aside. Then he tasted the soup and realized how hungry he was. He had had only scratch meals for lunch and dinner, the last over twelve hours before, and he had been so on edge, awaiting trouble at the Penrose house, that he had not touched the elaborate buffet.

When he had finished his supper he noticed the little gold glitter. Jenny's wedding ring and his mother's locket, which he had given her on her birthday. She had said then that she would return it when the marriage was over. Well, it was over now. She no longer needed the protection of marriage to look after little Richard. His father could take care of him. And Mayley Prince had given her a second chance.

Everyone should have a second chance. After seeing her performance tonight he was more aware than ever before that Jenny's talent should not be left unused. Being a housewife was fine if that's what one's talent was. But Jenny's talent would wither and die unused.

There was no question of being generous and letting her go. She was not his to release. She had never been his. And yet there had been times — he saw her now, as he had always seen her, in a dozen different guises: a school-girl in shorts and shirt, a nymph in a brief bathing suit, gay and laughing, eager and solemn, her tongue between her lips while she stirred a new dish intently, her mag-netism on the stage. All of that was Jenny but not all of Jenny.

It was not her soft scented hair against his cheek; it was not her courage, fighting back fear and saying, "Talk to me." It was not her gallantry, facing the emptiness of the desert and making no complaint after the first hor-rified exclamation had been wrenched out of her. It was not Jenny abandoning her life and her ambition for the sake of a small boy, being generous to Ricky and her understudy, holding out helping hands to Helen Gates and Wallace Penrose, changing their lives and the life of the community. It was not Jenny championing underdogs like Sarah Caldwell.

And even that wasn't all of Jenny either. She was the woman he loved, loved utterly and completely, as he had done from the beginning. He had come here as he would have gone anywhere to be with Jenny. She was the woman he couldn't give up. And yet he could not ask her to sacrifice her future a second time. There must be some way — he dropped his head on his folded arms on the desk.

Alone Jenny could rebuild her career and have a bril-liant future. As the wife of a struggling young physician she'd have nothing. All along he had been jealous of her prosperity, her success, all the things she could provide for herself and he could not give her.

The sky was growing light when he got up wearily. Wherever he turned he encountered a blank wall. He opened the door from his office to the living room and was startled by a red glow.

"Who's that?"

"Richard. I couldn't sleep. You must be exhausted."

"It's part of the job," Brad told him. He moved around the room restlessly and then groped for a chair. He did not turn on the lights.

"Wallace and I brought Jenny home tonight," Richard said at last.

"Oh? Thanks. Was everything all right after I left?"

"Fine. People couldn't be nice enough."

"This is no place for Jenny. No fun. No excitement."

"Fun and excitement," Rick said thoughtfully. "Personally I don't think that's what Jenny wants. But she tells me she is going into television. Hollywood."

"That's — I'm glad for her. Is she going soon?"

"As soon as I can get someone to look after the boy."

"Oh."

"I'd like to stay on here for a while, Brad, if it's all right with you. Jenny came up with an idea tonight — I'm thinking of buying out Wallace Penrose's share in the spa if he wants to sell. That's one of the things that kept me awake. It could be a new start, a second chance, as Jenny says, and the climate suits my little guy and me."

"Good luck to you. Stay here as long as you like. Nice for me, anyhow. This house is going to be kind of empty when Jenny goes."

Richard hesitated. He got up and knocked out his pipe. "People who interfere —" He began, stopped, tried again. "I've known Jenny for five years. She's had a lot of glamour in her life and a lot of success and excitement, but she hasn't had any real happiness. In spite of all the people who've always surrounded her she has been essentially a lonely person. I think Louise was the only person she truly loved. She — deserves happiness."

Brad broke out suddenly. "Don't you think I know that? Why am I letting her go without a word or a gesture to hold her back? She's so incredibly generous — and I don't want her sympathy. Anyhow, it would be better to have her leave than to go on like this. I can't stand this much longer."

"Those two rooms, you mean. Well, you're a man. Break down the door between them, Brad. I'd have figured you as a man who could make a fight for what you want." Richard hit Brad lightly on the shoulder. "Good luck to you. And good night. You're dead for sleep." As a ray of sun struck his face he laughed. "Good morning."

iii

Hours later, when he had showered and shaved, Richard telephoned the Caldwell house.

"Sarah?" He kept his voice low so as not to disturb the sleeping household. "Would it be possible for you to take over here today? Jenny has to have rest because she's got to act again tonight and she didn't have more than three hours the night before last."

"Of course," she agreed readily. "I'll come as soon as I've had some breakfast and taken Alma her tray."

"I hope I didn't wake you. Honestly, I had no idea it was so early. I haven't been to sleep."

"Neither have I. When I think of the things that happened last night I could die of shame."

"No one blames you. I was afraid you'd blame me."

"Not for a minute. Something had to be done to clear Jenny."

"Well, just remember you had nothing to do with that. The ones who were responsible, if we're going to be honest — and I hope we'll always be honest with each other — were —"

"Careful, Richard! Mrs. Fulmer may be listening in."

"I am not," said an indignant voice, and Sarah began to giggle, a bubble of laughter that rose out of sheer happiness. At length she took a long steadying breath. "I'll be there in half an hour."

It was longer than that. She selected the prettiest of the dresses she had bought under Jenny's critical eye, brushed her hair into a soft shining wave, and worked hard on her makeup. The secret, Jenny had instructed her, was not in artificial eyelashes or heavy eye-shadow but in looking as though there were no makeup at all.

Her mother was still asleep when she slipped out of the house after having taken a tray to Alma.

"Look here," Alma protested, "this has got to stop. With a cane to take the worst of the weight I can get around by myself. In fact, if someone will do the driving I can go to the doctor's this afternoon."

"I'm going there now but I'll come back for you, if you really mean it."

"Wallace will take me."

"How soon do you two plan to be married?"

"As soon as Wallace can find someone to take over at the spa. I suppose when I leave you'll go back to your old job."

"I don't know what mama is going to want. After taking the curtain call with Jenny, and then — you know I think she really believed Mr. Penrose was going to ask her to marry him — well, what with one thing and another and then that ghastly attack on Jenny and the way Richard and Wallace stopped it, I don't know how she is going to react."

"Look here, you take the next chance life gives you and hang on to it. That's the advice of one who knows."

Richard must have been watching because he had the door open almost before she was out of her car. Little Richard in rumpled pajamas, his cheeks flushed from sleep, trailed his father to the door and flung himself on Sarah, almost upsetting her.

She picked him up, laughing. "You little imp!" She kissed the top of his head and set him down. He ran toward the kitchen. "All right, I get the idea. Oatmeal coming up. And orange juice. And a glass of milk."

She poured the orange juice and lifted him into his highchair. "You start on that and don't spill."

Richard followed her into the kitchen, so close behind that he stepped on her heel.

"You are worse than your son," she told him. "Wait until I've fed Ricky and then I'll get your breakfast."

He watched while she set little Richard's breakfast before him and while she prepared his own, bacon and pancakes and coffee.

It wasn't until he had finished his second cup of coffee

that he said abruptly, "Sarah, Jenny is going to Holly-wood. She is going to have her own television show."

"And what about Brad?"

"Any more coffee there?" Brad asked as he came into the room.

"Plenty, and there's enough batter for pancakes and I'll just put on some bacon."

"Old Faithful. You're something special, Sarah. Oh, I meant to ask you, will you come back to the office after Alma gets married?"

Sarah poured batter on the griddle before she spoke. "Then you are going to stay on here?"

"Where else?"

"You're too good for this place, Brad. Jenny has often worried about it. She says you are a racehorse harnessed to a plow. You need a bigger place with more oppor-tunity."

"Oh, you know how long it takes to get all that, and how much it costs?"

Sarah was silenced.

Only when Brad had gone to his office and when little Richard, clad in shorts, was running around the room, did Sarah say, "It's terrible. All that waste. He shouldn't stay here."

"You think it is such a bad idea to stay here?" Richard asked quickly.

"For him I do. Why?"

"I wasn't really thinking of Brad then. I've been turn-ing over in my mind the idea of buying out Wallace Pen-rose's interest in the spa. What do you think?"

She was startled. "I don't know. I don't understand

financing and I certainly don't know how much is involved in this thing, though it must be pretty big. What matters is what you want to do. That is, do you really want to stay here or go somewhere else?"

"That depends —"

"— on Ricky, of course."

"No. On you."

Sarah looked deep into his eyes; then she walked away, staring out into the empty street and the Fulmer house. She did not move at all. Her eyes seemed blind.

He came to stand beside her. "Am I asking too much, Sarah? We haven't known each other long but I think we know each other well. And you love my son."

"Yes, I love your son. But that isn't good enough, Richard."

"But I love you, Sarah. I thought —"

She shook her head. *"Jenny* thought. She told me I looked like Louise. She knew I adore Ricky. She thought it would be a good arrangement to pair us off."

"I think so too, Sarah." When she made no reply he said at last, "I'm not such a good advertising man after all, am I? I don't seem to be selling my product."

"I'm sorry, Richard," Sarah said in a tone of finality she had never used before. "It's no good. Not for me. Not for you either. I am not going to be a substitute wife."

He moved abruptly and caught her arm. "So that's it! Sarah, we aren't children. There has been one tragedy because I was missing in action. There must be no mistake between us. It's true that what first attracted me was your resemblance to Louise. And I loved her. Loved her deeply. But what I feel for you is not simply a shadow of that other love; this is a brand-new love and it's for

you as you are. Yourself. And whatever Jenny's idea may
have been, and I must say I like her ideas, the decision is
mine and only mine. I love you very much and I want you
to be my wife. You and Ricky and I could build a good
life. But if you don't feel as I do I promise not to speak of
it again. You've been hounded all your life so I won't
hound you now."

He turned her to face him, saw the tears on her cheeks,
wiped them away gently. "It's all right. Don't be unhappy. I don't want you to be sorry for me, my darling."

"I'm not sorry. I'm just so happy I can't bear it."

At last she released herself from his tight clasp, from
his kisses. "Rick! Mrs. Fulmer can see us."

"Let her see," he said.

XXII

From the moment when she finally stumbled sleepily out of bed, the morning after the opening of *Heat Wave,* Jenny found herself living in a kind of frenzy. Before leaving for Hollywood that morning, Mayley Prince had cornered the crew of *See* and told them of the projected television program. The telephone rang steadily all day long. People with congratulations and good wishes. People regretting that she was going to leave them. People to assure her that they had never for one moment believed the unpleasant rumors. People asking questions.

Jenny gratefully left most of the calls to Sarah. She herself cornered Richard. "Look here, we have to give a performance tonight. I want you to do everything humanly possible to see that Mrs. Caldwell suffers no embarrassment as a result of her taking that curtain call. Ask people. Beg them. Threaten them if you have to."

He looked at her curiously. "Between them she and the Fulmer woman would have tried to make this town unbearable for you. Why should you care what happens to her?"

"I don't like cruelty, and I don't like revenge. Do your best, will you? They'll turn on her like a pack of wolves, just because they are ashamed of themselves and they have to blame someone else."

He hugged her. "I'll muzzle the whole lot of them with my bare hands, if that's what you want. Anyhow, I might as well learn to live peacefully with the woman. She is going to be my mother-in-law." He asked quickly, "Any reservations?"

Jenny looked out at the patio, where Sarah was playing with little Richard. She had blossomed; she had the confidence of a woman who knows she is loved. This was the right way, the natural way. And Louise could never be totally lost, never quite forgotten.

"No reservations," she said. "I'm happy for all of us. And I'll be happier when you can sell Mrs. Caldwell on the idea of living a more cultural and arty life in San Francisco."

"We're planning to stay on and buy out Wallace. Brad will let us live here for a while. He said the place would be empty without you."

Sarah came into the room after tucking Ricky up for his afternoon nap. "The little fiend is being ruined by all this excitement and determined to take advantage of it. He didn't want to take a nap." She kicked off her shoes and settled on the couch beside the table with the telephone. She looked from Richard to Jenny. "What have you two been plotting?" she asked suspiciously.

"I've been talking about both of you." Jenny said. "I'm terribly glad about it."

"And I was talking about Brad," Rick said, "being lonely here when Jenny has gone."

"But you both know by now this was a temporary arrangement. It has served its purpose."

"Are you pleased with the television setup?" Richard asked idly.

"I — well, of course, it's what I dreamed of." Jenny put all the enthusiasm she could into her voice.

"That's the way Brad sees it. He told me that you had sacrificed that offer once before. Who was he to ask you to make the same sacrifice a second time? And he can't take it much longer, anyhow, having a wife who isn't a wife."

"He never wanted me to be his wife," Jenny flared. "Just Caesar's wife." And to her horror she burst into tears.

"If that's what he wanted," Richard said, "it serves the the guy right to have you walk out on him."

"Though why he should insist on staying here," Sarah said, "I can't understand." She silenced the telephone. "Oh, mama, are you sure? Well, Jenny is right here; I'll tell her." she covered the mouthpiece and said, "Mama says she's too ill to go on tonight."

Jenny squared her slim shoulders and took a long breath. She had what Louise had always called her fighting face, prepared to meet a challenge or disaster or a stumbling block of some sort.

"Tell her I'm on my way." Jenny scooped up her car keys and ran.

Mrs. Caldwell, her eyes swollen from crying, stood in the doorway as though to prevent Jenny from coming in.

"Please let me come in, Mrs. Caldwell. Now you lie on the couch." Jenny went to the kitchen and got a bowl of ice water and found some washcloths. When she came back she said, "I'll put the cold cloths on your eyes and massage the back of your neck. I know just how you feel. An opening night gives everyone that kind of nervous tension."

The bemused woman let Jenny do as she suggested. Jenny's fingers massaged the back of her neck, the cold cloths soothed her hot and swollen eyes. Jenny spoke of the performance of the night before. "Certainly your best; we simply can't do without you tonight. We're committed. It's really true, you know; the show must go on. Of course there were a few slip-ups but we'll smooth them out tonight. The scene shifters will work faster after one performance and the first lines will be heard more clearly because the cast won't be so nervous. And Wallace must be told — the idiot didn't understand that an amateur performance isn't like a Broadway show." If she was aware of the older woman's tension she showed no signs of it. "The way he herded the cast against the back wall. You saved the day by stepping forward like that." She renewed the cold cloth.

From behind its shelter that hid her eyes Mrs. Caldwell said, "Just the same it would be better for you to take that one call alone. Mrs. Maxwell, when I spoke about you as I did last night at the Penrose reception —"

"Oh, I know! That wretched Joe Colfax. Always a troublemaker. At least it's all cleared up now."

"And the things Mr. Colfax said!"

"Richard was just trying to protect me, you know. You'll like him when you know him better. He wants to marry Sarah and I'm so happy about it."

"Wants to marry Sarah!" Mrs. Caldwell took the news more cheerfully than Jenny had dared to hope. "I'm glad to hear it. Sarah needs someone to take care of her and he — I understand there is a lot of Colfax money; at least that's what Charlie — you know the famous columnist —"

"I know," Jenny said grimly.

"That's what he said. I've felt from the beginning a kind of spiritual quality in Richard Colfax. Yes, I think he'll be good for Sarah."

"I am sure he will. And you will be able to go on tonight like a good trouper?"

"You can count on me."

ii

For five nights the Desert Winds production of *Heat Wave* played for standing room only houses. Because there were no midsummer openings in New York other critics flew out to catch the show. Jenny had counted on Saturday as a time for rest before preparing to leave for Hollywood. But she had not counted on the reporters. Up to now they had respected her request to be let alone while she had performances to give. And now — at much too early an hour on Saturday morning — the crew of *See* came for more pictures and an interview. The background material had been collected from their own files and from talks with Richard and the Penrose men. The only notable absentee was Chatty Charlie, who had returned to Los Angeles and an interview with the publisher of his newspaper that left him pale and shaking.

Saturday was Brad's free day — so far as he was ever free from emergency calls — and he had spent the last four days rehearsing what he would say to Jenny, making and discarding various approaches. He would get her away from the house, where they could be alone. Instead, the crew descended on the house like locusts.

Obligingly Jenny posed for them and answered questions about the television program and her future plans, but she barred personal questions.

"Look, Miss Haydon," one of the interviewers said, "you know how it is; we have to get a personal story. Now your marriage —"

"My marriage has nothing to do with all this."

"But you are going to Hollywood and Dr. Maxwell is going to continue to practice here. Correct?"

"No comment."

"How does your husband feel about you taking this job?"

"He approves."

"Have you any other matrimonial plans?"

"Absolutely not."

"Are you planning to come back to the desert?"

"Not for some time. I'll be terribly rushed. There is so much groundwork to be done and people to interview and I'll be consulting almost daily with Mr. Beaver, who is to be the writer for the show."

"We'd like a picture of you with your husband. Okay?"

"My husband doesn't like personal publicity."

"I don't mind in a good cause." Brad had come in so quietly that Jenny had not been aware of his presence. She wondered how much of the interview he had overheard.

"Over here, doctor. Turn toward Miss Haydon. That's it."

Jenny looked up to find Brad's eyes on her face, with an expression in them she had never seen before. There was an odd set to his mouth. Her heart began to pound.

"Thanks a lot, doctor," the photographer said. "I guess that's all. You've been very patient, Miss Haydon."

"In this house," Brad put in, "she is Mrs. Maxwell."

When they had gone Brad said, "Jenny," and the note in his voice was different too.

"I wonder — where's Ricky?"

"His father and Sarah have taken him with them. They have gone to the Penrose place to draw up some tentative agreements about the spa. Jenny —"

"I ought to start packing."

"Jenny, listen to me. What's all this nonsense Richard told me about Caesar's wife?"

"Well, it's what you said, isn't it? A doctor's wife has to be Caesar's wife. And I've stirred up scandal all over the place."

He laughed.

"And don't laugh. It makes me so mad."

"Does it?" His hands were on her arms now, gentle hands but drawing her towards him. "Does it, Jenny? Then why did you cry when you told Rick about it? What's Caesar to you or you to Caesar that you should weep for him?"

"I was — just tired."

"Jenny —" She was so near him now she could feel his heart beating. "I was going to let you go without a word, if that was what you wanted. Only I can't do it. I can't let you go. Not without at least putting up a fight to keep you." As she started to speak he pressed her head against him to muffle her speech. "I don't want you to give up anything, not your career or your television show. Nothing. But I can get an appointment at a teaching hospital with Dr. Ferguson's influence — he and I have been in touch about it — a place near Los Angeles, and we could be together. I couldn't give you — ever, perhaps, what you can provide for yourself. But I want to give you everything you want."

"You don't know what I want. And you don't want a part-time wife or a prima donna in the house."

"I want you any way I can get you. Why do you think I came out here? Because I could be with you, even on your terms. Now I want you on my terms. I'm so in love with you I don't know whether I'm on my head or my heels. Jenny!" He held her back, looking at her. "Jenny!" He shook her a little as though forcing her to speak.

"Do you mean all those things, Brad?"

"About the career? Yes, I do. We can build a richer and fuller life, just because we each have our own jobs, and we will have each other to come home to. Do you love me, Jenny? Can you?"

She reached out her hands and he caught her in his arms, kissed her as though he would never let her go. Her arms went around his shoulders and her mouth was sweet and responsive under his.

A long time later, when Brad was sitting in the big armchair with Jenny on his lap, he lifted her left hand and pulled the wedding ring out of his pocket.

"Remember when I put that on?"

Jenny nodded.

He showed her the inscription he had had engraved: "I love you."

"Even then?" she asked.

"From the first moment when you stood at the top of a flight of stairs. And ever since."

Jenny began to laugh. "I never realized before how crafty Dr. Ferguson is. He knew all the time."

"Knew what?"

"That we had fallen in love with each other right off the bat."

"*We!* Why didn't you — I never guessed."

"Well, you didn't seem to want to do anything about it so —"

"Oh!" Mrs. Fulmer stood in the doorway, looking at the couple locked in each other's arms. "Well, excuse me."

And I might as well not have spoken, she thought, as she crossed the road to her house. They never even noticed me.